Beyond the grave, Beyond the dream . . .

The cathedral darkens. The dying light from hundreds of candles sticking out of sconces. They gutter, one by one, and go out. On the altar, a pine box nestles on crossbeams.

INGEMISCO TAMQUAM REUS

The lid lifts.

CULPA RUBET VUI

Your name is Olivia?

Daddy?

The coffin opens with a crash. A corpse glowing sickly blue drifts out, soars over her head, swivels perpendicularly in the air. A filthy old man, naked. Fingernails at least a foot long, each curving to a sharp point.

Olivia screams . . .

■

"Kaye's finely wrought prose leads deeper and deeper into a labyrinth of human emotions and inhuman terror . . . the monstrous mutilations connected with Aubrey House are balanced by flashes of wit and warmth."

—*Morgan Llywelyn*
author of LION OF IRELAND

"Powerful and troubling."

—*Parke Godwin*

Charter books by Marvin Kaye

A COLD BLUE LIGHT (with Parke Godwin)
GHOSTS OF NIGHT AND MORNING

MARVIN KAYE

Ghosts of Night and Morning

C

CHARTER BOOKS, NEW YORK

GHOSTS OF NIGHT AND MORNING

A Charter Book / published by arrangement with
the author

PRINTING HISTORY
Charter edition / August 1987

ISBN: 0-441-28612-7

Charter Books are published by The Berkley Publishing Group,
200 Madison Avenue, New York, New York 10016.
The name "Charter" and the "C" logo are
trademarks belonging to Charter Communications, Inc.
PRINTED IN THE UNITED STATES OF AMERICA

10 9 8 7 6 5 4 3 2 1

ACKNOWLEDGMENTS

Certain works cited in the front matter of *A Cold Blue Light* again proved useful: Oliver Fox's *Astral Projection* (University Books, 1962); Pennethorne Hughes's *Witchcraft* (Pelican, 1965) and Daniel Schachter's article, "The Hypnagogic State: A Critical Review of the Literature" (*Psychological Bulletin*, Vol. 83, #3, 1976). Two other books were also helpful: Robert Holzman's *Stormy Ben Butler* (Macmillan, 1954), and Susan Blackmore's *Beyond the Body* (William Heinemann Ltd., 1982).

Special thanks to these friends for various favors: Jeannie Gillis, Ellis Grove, Don Maass, Chris Miller and Helen Trautman. I am grateful to Ellen Kushner for loaning me William Long's paper on the architectural oddities of allegedly haunted houses, and to Sondra Moyer for furnishing fascinating details on the many spectres of Bucks County.

Two difficult sections of text benefited from exemplary passages furnished by two writer friends: C. H. Sherman and Jay Sheckley.

My admiration and thanks to Dawn Wilson, whose painting, "Winter's King," inspired Alan Hunter's sonnet of that title.

Above all, I must thank my friend, partner, gadfly, sounding board, fellow rioter/thespian/writer Parke Godwin, who bequeathed me Charlie and Sam as well as useful plot ideas and then bowed out with the absolute minimum of gentlemanly usuriousness.

To
the memory of my dear friend
ILA JEROM

CONTENTS

■

AUBREY FAMILY TREE

ADDISON AUBREY
"Chicago tycoon"

POLLY CRAMER — HENRY   DEREK — CHARLOTTE DANEFIELD

? — KATE LYMAN — BEN   Daughter (Died at age 7)   JASON — ARIELLA ENNIS

OLIVIA   DESDEMONA   MERLYN

Those of us who deliberately teach people to fly from reality through cults, mythologies and dogmas are helping them to be unsane.

—*The Tyranny of Words*
Stuart Chase

MEMOIRS OF BUCKS COUNTY

■

One great lateral slash ripped out Charlotte Aubrey's eyes.

Silence. Fingers of mist trailed up the steep staircase. Giddily, Charles hauled himself up two steps, two more. His face was flushed, his temples throbbed, he needed to rest but forced his legs the final distance in search of Charlotte's kin.

"Charlotte Aubrey's child? Let me help you!"

But the cold blue light thickened and the sad little girl O! with Mama's mottled face slashed/white-hot V angling down her forehead—

"Dear Lord, who hath helped me throughout life's trials, commemo   my dea$^{r}_{d}$ friend's eyes—"

miserate

?

Yes. Eyes . . . Richard's: broodingly aloof; Drew's, twinklecrinkling mask masking pity/contempt; Vita's eyes

no

Vita Vee-Vee Vee V white/hot slashing *no* Vee's Vita's

eyes bulging grotesquely, her poor ravaged face fixed in that moronic grin; and

And?

grin; and

And?

and Merlyn's

No!

eyes

*no*NO*no!*

Dear Lord, let us remember dea$^{d}_{r}$ Merlyn's eyes

cry mercy!

lying there beneath the picture white-hot V slashing slashing slashing out her eyes: Ma—

muh!

Yes! Hurt!

BRRING

hurts

BRRRING

"On the right side, fortunately."

BRRRRINNG

One glowing eye. And

BRRRRRINNNG

One glowing eye. And a question:

BRRRRRRINNNNGG

One glowing eye. And a question: "Mister . . . how does it feel . . ."

BRRRRRRRRIINNNNNNGGG

And Charles Singleton wakes.

His groping hand clutches the clock while one fingertip skitters the round till it finds the button; he strangleprods the jangling BRRRRRRRRIINN–

Blessed silence.

September sun warms closed lids, but beneath the blan- [illegible]harles shivers as he tries for perhaps the thousandth [illegible]nstruct the entire nightmare.

Thousandth?

Well, work it out, boyo.

Very well. Three years to the day that the stretcher-bearers toted the limp Singletonian carcass out of Aubrey House. Therefore, 365 × 3 =

No, you don't dream it every night.

Often enough.

Dear God, let me remember what happened to me.

Dear God, let me forget.

One glowing eye, and a question: that part of the dream, at least, is clear, thanks to several costly sessions on Sam Lichinsky's couch. On the glowing eye of a TV screen, Charles watched himself emerging from Bucks County General Hospital, reporters hemming him in, asking the same insipid but disturbing question over and over, idiot savants word-perfect in a single speech: "Mr. Singleton, how does it feel to be the sole survivor of Aubrey House?"

And Sam Lichinsky gently prodded: "Well, how *does* it feel, Charlie?"

"A little guilt, a little anger, frustration—I couldn't even go to Merlee's memorial service—but mostly, Sam, just emptiness. I mean, all the others went down, but I don't even have any tears left."

And where was God?

The sharp edge of morning slices across the floor. Manhattan traffic mutters, an angry beast penned in some distant draw. Charles traces old phantoms in ceiling cracks as the minutes bleed away. At last, he swings his legs with difficulty over the side of the bed.

"On the right side, fortunately." No mystery there, either. The stroke that probably saved his life, and certainly his reason afflicted the right side of his brain, which was fortunate to the extent that it did not impair his speech. But he suffered massive motor damage. Grueling months of therapy worked him down to one cane, but now his movements resembled Drew's, *the* Drew Beltane and why? Why all the deaths? Four friends succumbed to that godless horror in Pennsylvania.

Godless?

If anywhere in the world is godless, it's Aubrey House.

And how does *it feel to be the sole survivor?*

Charles sniffs suspiciously at the waning morning, decides to tolerate it, sits up. He dons disreputable slippers, fumbles for his green monk's-cowl robe. Cinching the tie, he shambles into the bathroom, averting his gaze from his reflection, but not fast enough.

No deeper wrinkles yet?

A bit grayer, though, not that there's enough hair to notice. But eyes like Giannini's at the end of *Seven Beauties:* still alive, but was it worth the price?

All the votes not yet counted.

Emerging from the bathroom, Singleton cane-stumps into the tiny Manhattan kitchen and makes himself breakfast: an icy Virgin Mary rimmed with white pepper and garnished with a branch-lopped celery stalk; featherweight macadamia nut pancakes, butter-smudged, ginger-dusted, bathed in coconut syrup brought back from Maui; spicy Portuguese linguica sausage purchased in Provincetown; a bitter-chocolate éclair from Burke & Burke washed down by steaming black Kona coffee gently laced with Amaretto.

He downs every last morsel.

But later, seated at his polished mahogany worktable, hands curled lifelessly in his lap, palate haunted by a complexity of aftertastes, Charles reflects upon his recent Hawaiian flight with mingled pleasure and regret.

He had no difficulty in justifying to himself his earlier trip to Martha's Vineyard; that was a doctor-dictated period of recuperation. But he returned from Massachusetts to a silent apartment and the same stark white sheet of paper still rolled in his typewriter. Three days later, he boarded a DC-10 bound for Los Angeles and his connection to the valley isle of Maui.

It was an unpardonable extravagance—he knew it then, he certainly knew it afterward, but while on the island, Charles never reckoned the cost. All painful memories were swept aside in awestruck contemplation of the swan-shaped Kaanapali shoreline. In the tucked-away verdancy of the Iao Valley, Charles found solitude and peace. If he experienced a momentary unease one night standing by the Lahaina seawall and staring down at ill-glimpsed but vaguely dreadful creatures scuttling in and out of patches of shadow on the sands below, his spirits lifted once he quitted the darker places and walked past shop windows glowing with old gold, polished scrimshaw, tinted coral. His days were pungent with the tang of burning sugarcane wafted on the trade winds, his still nights whispered by dreamlessly. Charles loved the mornings above all, lolling seaside in a wicker chair in an open-air restaurant, the nearby surf frothing up salt mist to season the fresh-caught *mahi-mahi* served instead of bacon. He sipped sweet white wine concoctions, dawdled over plates of newly-picked pineapple or papaya. Afternoons, he rode to one or another beach just off the long coastal highway that ribboned between crumpled-lava mountains and the Pacific. His lazy tropical world was tinted pastel; nowhere did he see in sun or shadow that sickly blue that tainted Aubrey House like cancer.

But now, back home again, much of his royalty advance squandered, Charles agonizes over the eggshell-white page sticking up from the roller of his IBM Selectric II. Except for an identifying slugline in the upper left corner—SINGLETON/BUCKS COUNTY/1—the sheet is blank.

My dear fellow, creditors take a dim view of writer's block. Help, angels! Make assay!

But the gaps in memory?

What I can't recall has no bearing on the beginning. For now, shall we restrict our concern to a genuine attempt to fashion something resembling an opening chapter?

So Charles wastes half an hour and more than a quire of paper constructing and then discarding abortive introductory paragraphs. At length, a distant cousin to the Muse inspires him to root desperately through his notes. He extracts a sheaf of typed pages, the formal book proposal which he submitted several months ago to his editor at Porlock Press.

Well, it was good enough for the editorial board . . . as representative a sampling of psychic dilettantes as ever I could hope to poll from my traditional readership. Perhaps I ought to model the first section of the book on the proposal . . . after all, it resulted in a contract . . . let's see . . .

TRAGEDY IN BUCKS COUNTY

A Survivor's Account
of Three Nights
in a Haunted House

If you have ever driven north from Philadelphia on the Pennsylvania Turnpike, you may have noticed some twenty miles above the City of Brotherly Love an exit sign for Doylestown, governmental seat of Bucks County. If you venture off the highway at this point, you will soon find yourself meandering through gentle green countryside dotted with brightly-painted farmhouses and rambling old mansions, a surprisingly large number of which are reputedly haunted.

Ask any inhabitant about the monks who refused to spend a second night at Aldie Manor, that dark tree-shrouded edifice topped with menacing gargoyles and griffins. Or arrange a tour of nearby Fonthill, where the moving candlelight of its late housekeeper often has been seen. Do not neglect to visit the community college complex where the ghost of Stella Tyler still opens and shuts doors in a hall bearing her surname. If you decide to stay overnight in the area, motor a few miles north to the hamlet of Dyerstown, founded six decades before the American Revolution by John Dyer. Stop at the Water Wheel Inn, once Dyer's grist mill, an hostel whose illustrious guest register cannot hold a candle to the ghost said to return once a year to the place: none other than the Marquis and General de Lafayette!

Many are the eerie spots I can recommend along the peaceful byways of the mighty Delaware Valley, but there is one house you had better stay away from. It is situated five miles north of Doylestown off Route 611 . . . a deceptively sunny white frame building with a chilling and bloody history. I know, for I went there three years ago with four friends.

I was the only survivor.

Charles is interrupted by the startling clamor of the telephone. He considers the virtues and drawbacks of an interruption, decides to do without the world while he wrestles with his literary demons. He switches on his answering machine, lowers the volume to avoid the piercing beep and also to keep from learning who the caller is. Finally, Charles disconnects the phone so the bell won't interfere again with his concentration.

Singleton studies the words he has copied from his book proposal. The corners of his mouth draw downward.

Business as usual, boyo.

Yes. Charles let's-have-fun-stalking-spooks Singleton. Chatty little Baedeker and if I tell them, "Don't go there," isn't that precisely where they will decide to flock?

So tell them why they mustn't.

Because.

?

The Aubrey Effect.

Define.

Tentatively, Charles' fingers flutter above the keys.

In 1935, a psychic investigator named Falzer brought a team to Aubrey House. They isolated a unique *psi* phenomenon on the second floor: "A cold blue light that nothing drives away or brings closer. It's just there, a constant."

Rot! We proved it moves.

We?

All right, Drew did. But what does the Aubrey Effect do to people?

Kill them.

Besides that. Dear God, let me remember.

Dear God, let me forget!

The strangest thing about the Aubrey Effect is that it was observed as long ago as 1920, yet the family claimed no one died in the house till 1964, when Charlotte Aubrey passed away at an advanced age. But thanks to the research of me and Drew Beltane we learned of an earlier, secret death—that of Charlotte's nameless daughter, a birth-deficient waif concealed from the world. She spent her brief life hidden in an attic chamber and died in 1911, only seven years old, presumably the victim of disease or an accident.

So Charlotte was the second casualty—and then came Drew and Richard and Merlyn. All met death in the house itself. Though that was a mere technicality—

Soon after Charlotte Aubrey died in 1964, Phyllis and Harold Burton obtained permission to spend a few weeks at the house while the rest of the family were in Europe. The Burtons were mediums and old friends of Charlotte's—though they once antagonized her by writing *Aubrey House, Home of the Spirits*, a small-press booklet which Charlotte did her best to destroy by buying nearly every copy and burning them. She evidently objected to a photo they printed without her permission. It revealed Charlotte pregnant with the daughter whose very existence she later took great pains to deny.

The Burtons returned to Aubrey House to conduct a series of séances. A servant found them one morning sprawled in the salon, their minds shattered. They lived a few weeks at Bucks County General Hospital before death mercifully bore them away.

—and the same thing happened to poor Vita. They took her living body to the hospital, but all the same, she died at Aubrey House. Thank God she did not linger—and that her will specified cremation. Better the purifying flame than to be seen in that last obscene metamorphosis. Rather the four winds that liberated her remnant of ash and bone, her mortal dust drifting down to earth, her immortal soul soaring on high to reunite with Our Savior—

Who let her end in horror.

A childish blasphemy, and ultimately irrelevant. Write your worthless little book, Mr. Singleton.

The five of us arrived late one Thursday afternoon in September. On Saturday, our hostess, Merlyn Aubrey, suffered a fall which injured her face and ankle, so we rushed her to the hospital. On returning at one a.m., I noticed that Vita Henry's bedroom door was open and her light still on, so I called to her but got no answer. I stepped inside and found her lying naked on her bed, her body maimed with livid lacerations, her hair stark white and frizzed like a fright wig, her eyes bulging hideously, her lips widened into a vacuous grin. They ran an EEG on her, but the lines barely moved. Vita passed away in the hospital on Sunday afternoon.

At almost the same time that she succumbed, Drew Beltane died in the house. He, at least, seems to have left this life peacefully in his sleep (or to be more precise, during a mediumistic trance), but not so Dr. Richard Creighton, who bled to death Sunday night on the servants' staircase at the back of Aubrey House. They found him not far from Merlyn's naked body. Her neck was broken, her eyes torn from their sockets. The police claim she ripped them out herself.

Well, that covers all the pertinent guignol details. Now what?

God only knows.

Indeed?

Perhaps not. It's quite conceivable, if not manifest, that the myriad minutiae of the creation do not add up neatly, either.

Tch, Charlie. Such a bleak, sterile notion.

Oh, yes, Drew, I remember how once I accused you of agnostic flippancy. And yet you ignored your own cautionary advice to me and ultimately went to Aubrey as if it were Dunkirk. They didn't award you the bloody V. C. for tilting at things that go bump in the night, did they?

No. Nor for writing books about them . . . especially

books that never get started.

Touché. But this morning has been wasted, nevertheless. Absurd to continue. The parts won't connect, nothing jells. No center, no focal point . . . so how can it possibly evolve into a cohesive whole?

It won't. Not while the memories stay buried.

He impulsively yanks the page from the roller and wads it and the rest of the morning's output into one wastebasket-bound packet.

After lunch, I shall try again.

Rubbish. After lunch, you will merely dispose of more paper.

In quest of some justifiable distraction from self-doubt, Charles reconnects the phone and remembers he has a message waiting. He switches the answering machine to Playback and rewinds the tape to 000.

beep

"Charles, this is Alan Hunter at Porlock. Please call me right away, it's important."

chkbzzzzz

A prickle of swiftly stifled, groundless guilt. Too soon for the publisher to worry him about manuscript delivery, it would not be due for another eight months . . . though at the present rate of productivity, he might need every available moment.

Alan Hunter, senior editor at Porlock Press, was a long-time friend. His enthusiasm for *Tragedy in Bucks County* resulted in a generous royalty advance—

—a substantial portion of which I've squandered when it should have been husbanded for living expenses. But Alan could be no help in that quarter, nor would he be overly concerned about the book's birthing pains—he'd think it a case of necessary authorial angst.

Then what does he want? He sounded uncharacteristically somber.

Dialing the number from memory, Charles waits patiently while an editorial assistant puts him on hold. Then he hears his editor's mellow baritone voice.

"Charles, by any chance did you catch this morning's newscast on Channel Eleven?"

"You know I loathe morning news, ditto mornings. Why?"

"Well . . . my phone's been ringing with reporters asking me for your private number."

"Why on earth?"

A pause.

"Aubrey House."

"But that's three years old. Why the sudden renewed interest?"

A longer pause.

"Because of what just happened there."

Charles does not reply. He feels an upsurge of blood pressure. Recognizing the stress signal, he breathes deeply, deeply, willing his pulse to decelerate.

"Charles, are you all right? Shall I continue?"

"Quite frankly? But go ahead."

"Two brothers were about to lease Aubrey House and convert it to an inn. One of them was just found hacked up on the rear staircase. They claim it happened on the identical spot where—"

"Alan, I know precisely where you mean." *Three years to the day.* "Have you further atrocities to brighten my otherwise dreary morning?"

"No more horror stories, but both brothers were seen entering the house. Neither came out again."

"So what happened to the second sibling?"

"Nobody knows. He vanished."

"Oh, come now, Alan, you're far too intelligent to monger this kind of *National Enquirer* twaddle."

"I'm only repeating what I heard on the news. The police said all the doors and windows were locked from the inside."

"All the trappings of a John Dickson Carr impossible-crime novel, eh?" Charles chuckles grimly, his composure returning. "Look, Alan, I don't recall everything that happened to me at Aubrey House, but there's one thing I'm positive about. The Effect—the cold blue light, if you'd rather call it that—the thing attacks the mind, not the body. It does not dismember its victims."

"Then what you're saying—"

"Is that you've described a murder to me. A nasty one, but mundane, for all that. And I would hazard that the missing brother is the prime suspect."

"Then where is he? How did he escape from the house?"

"I've no idea, Alan, nor do I care."

"Well, considering the timing . . . three years to the day . . . I think I'd better mail out a press release on your book. Are you game for a few interviews?"

"Not really, but since it's you who asks, I'll consider it. But not right now. At the moment, I'm wrestling with words."

"Oh. Sorry. Well, give me a call when you make up your mind."

Polite goodbyes. They both hang up.

Three years to the day.

Poor Alan. He hates to play vulture, yet it would be foolish to pass up this opportunity to—

?

Never mind.

Oh, no, get back on the hook. The opportunity to—

—profit from the death of others.

The phone shrills. Charles gratefully picks it up.

"Hello, Charles Singleton here."

"Mr. Singleton, this is Wallace Burke of the *Post*. I wonder whether you've heard about—"

"Yes, I have heard. May I ask you how you managed to obtain my number? It's unlisted."

"The unscrupulousness of the Fourth Estate, I'm afraid. But as long as I *have* reached you, do you mind answering a few questions?"

Charles sighs. "I suppose not." He immediately regrets his compliance. An icy precognition seizes him. For one hideous instant, he thinks he is still asleep and tangled in the coils of nightmare.

"Mr. Singleton," the reporter asks, "how does it feel to be the sole survivor of Aubrey House?"

A DAY IN THE LIFE OF THE DAMNED

■

Struggling up from nightmare, Alan Hunter woke to the bitter pang of an empty bed and the unseasonal chill that sometimes nips the nether end of April. He felt cut off from the world, isolated from meaning. In a distant continent of his 6½-room brownstone co-op in Chelsea, he heard Miranda, his wife, fussing at their nine-year-old daughter Bess, late as usual for school. He reached for the nightstand and the portable tape recorder on it.

chk

"Dream record, night of April twenty-eighth, morning of the twenty-ninth. It came again. The beginning was different, but the rest exactly the same, as much as I can recall of it. It started in summertime. Sun-spangled cornfields. Tingling anticipation, but then I heard my mother calling and I descended out of morning and over the railing . . . endless falling. Something important happens next, I can never remember what, but afterwards I'm climbing interminable steep stairs, up and up, a constructivist Hell. It's coming after me, I don't know what it is, but it's horrible and I'm sure that sooner or later it'll catch up, so I keep climbing till I reach a door I don't want to open, it's too small, I can't push through. Then the thing finds me, so I start up another flight. Up. Up."

Alan paused. As he tried to reconstruct the dream-mosaic from shards of memory, elsewhere—a hallway and three rooms off, or was it ten thousand miles?—his daughter Bess slammed the front door and left for the day. *Hope she isn't still upset from last night's argument . . .*

Clearing his throat of morning huskiness, he continued. "Eventually, I come to another door that leads outside, but it's inside, too. Like a stage set of the Atlantic City Boardwalk—without the ocean air. Everyone's dressed like the 1890's. A chubby policeman smiles at me and I feel safe, but then I see the thing still crawling after me. It's so small, no one else notices it. Maybe it's an insect, a spider? I dash through another door and I'm right back where I started, pitching over a railing and falling down and down and . . . and end of dream." Alan's thoughts spooled as silently as the cassette. *Pinpointed. Fixed. Defined to the last curlicue of denotation. Lost, a whole kingdom surrounding me, mocking but dead.*

chk

Alan showered and dressed, then made himself breakfast. While he ate, he stared at his wife. Miranda lay on the sofa watching television, pointedly ignoring him. A blue comforter circled her knees; the pink skin between the blanket edge and the hem of her carelessly hiked-up robe prickled with gooseflesh. *No wonder,* Alan mused bitterly. *Her emotional temperature's sub-zero.* On the screen, Phil Donahue played devil's advocate to a husband-wife team of sex therapists and four of their patients.

Alan checked his watch: twenty past nine. *Rush hour*

waning. He swallowed another mouthful of coffee and went to his office to pack Charles Singleton's manuscript, which the two of them had a lunch meeting to discuss. *Disappointing*. Alan snapped his briefcase shut and left the apartment, waving at Miranda on the way out. She did not respond.

So what else is new?

Typically, the token booth attendant didn't mention the delay up the line, but when Alan saw the crowded subway station, he knew he hadn't missed rush hour after all.

Standing near him was a familiar-looking woman in open denim jacket and designer jeans. She had fair skin, auburn hair and pale lips that twitched at the corners as if she couldn't repress humorous thoughts. Alan recalled he'd seen her a few nights earlier at R. J. Scotty's. She was at the next table drinking white wine and reading a thick textbook. Every so often she smiled at him and he endured the harangue of a fellow editor expounding on traditionally metered verse as a moribund art form.

Now she waited near the platform edge, her lively brown eyes occasionally darting glances at him. Newcomers streaming through the turnstiles threatened to spill them onto the tracks. When the overdue train finally shrilled into the station, a tide of commuters surged into the nearest car, sweeping her and Alan with them. They both snatched at the centerpole and made it their mooring-post. They were pressed together by the flood of people.

Pinpointed. Fixed.

The train rocked and joggled them into happenstance intimacy. Alan succumbed to the warmth and texture of her flesh, but even as he did, part of him felt ashamed for yielding yet again to his unslakable need. When some of the mob departed at Thirty-fourth Street, he tried to move away from her, but the car lurched forward and she deliberately closed the gap between their bodies. Alan's breath caught. He struggled to disguise the quickening tempo of his passion.

At the corners of her mouth, subtle creases promised to turn into a smile. She shifted her weight against the center-pole and let the rise of her left breast caress the cup of his palm. Now there was no pretense. They nestled each to each like old lovers sharing a practised intimacy that was almost casual. A ghost of remembered emotion stirred in Alan, partly sweet, mostly bitter, yet to feel it at all, even in dilute form, was a consolation. He felt a gratitude that practically bordered on love.

One stop later, she left the train. As she prepared to depart, she gave his fingertips a hasty squeeze and he almost cried out, *Wait, who are you?* but he was pinpointed, fixed by the awareness that anonymity was the charm that brought them together and must also spin them apart. It was one of life's little deaths, as preposterous as it was poignant, but it soon faded and he was numb again with a coldness that was more than April.

Olivia Aubrey believed she was too thin and tall, that her bustline was inadequate and her hips overly generous, but in truth, though she could not appreciate it, she had that stark angular gracefulness sometimes seen upon an Attic frieze or in the small-breasted, lithe-limbed figures painted on the curving sides of an Etruscan vase.

She did not like her moist everted lips, was embarrassed by one jagged upper incisor, found fault with her high-bridged nose and especially despaired over hair which, once long and sleek, had turned into a mass of split ends that she could only salvage by chopping short. She conceded the handsomeness of her large brown eyes, but did not know that from their lustrous depths the splendor and sorrow of her spirit welled up, refining all her features and rendering her beautiful.

Olivia rose early that day. She slid her feet into a pair of faded blue slippers, stuck her thin arms through the sleeves of a faded pink bathrobe and, turning on the dimmest bulb of a floorlamp with a faded green shade, curled up in an armchair and began to write in a worn leather diary.

APRIL 29 Six A.M. Woke from a bizarre sleep, dreaming about my thirtieth birthday—except it was wintertime, not July—the table set for a children's party, but with 13 candles on a cake straight out of "Dead Souls"—cobwebs and dust, grimy cracks splitting it like a broken mirror, icing the color of yesterday's slush. Ben was there, only younger, and there was another man and Mama, too, naked from the waist down and her skin looked like the cake icing. She cuts a piece, puts it on my plate but I'm too nauseated to taste it. "Olivia, darling"—(Mama speaking)—"please don't wait for us, you know the dead can't eat." And all of them staring at me so I have to take the smallest bit of that horrible cake on my fork and put it in my mouth and it's greasy and sour on my tongue and I feel so sick I think I'm going to spit up . . . and the dream stopped.

Not much point now in trying to go back to bed. Ben will be awake in about an hour ringing his bell. I'd better take a shower and brush my teeth and do my face and see what I can manage with my hair—attempt to make myself halfway presentable for my appointment while I still have a little time undisturbed.

My appointment. Today's the day I've been waiting for, but now that it's here, it feels flat and uninvolving. No. It doesn't feel that way, *I* do. The melancholy beast still lives in my heart, devouring every sprig of hope that tries to take root. And I know—hope, says Elmer Rice, is an intentional delusion designated to shield us from despair. But I wouldn't know about that—the impulse stillborn in me. Yet what right have I to be so cynical? Drab, glib drudge that I am. But every day the same nagging questions. What is there to believe? To trust in and care for? When everything is arbitrary and relative, what can possibly be of worth? No real difference whether I write poetry or wash Ben's dirty underwear. Only my ego yearns for the prestige of some unique accomplishment. But do I have enough faith in myself to make my dreams come true?

An hour later, Olivia stood by her full-length mirror in stocking and slip and high heels trying to make her hair look tolerable. From another room sounded the bright peal of a teacher's desk bell. She did not switch off the hair dryer. Maybe Ben would forget. Twenty hopeful seconds of silence . . . and then a rapid succession of *ting-ting-ting-tings* stuttered on the morning air. Sighing, Olivia switched off the machine and lay down her hairbrush.

Her nose caught the sharp ammonia stench as soon as she entered his room. Benjamin Aubrey sat on the edge of his bed. He was a large, portly man in his seventies. His sparse white hair bushed over a high forehead and blue eyes squinting myopically at the nightstand where his false teeth floated in a dusty water glass. His bare arms and legs were disproportionately spindly and brown patches of psoriasis discolored his skin from ankle to knee. He wore a wine-red pajama top and dingy grey shorts sopping with urine.

The old man stared at Olivia, frowning.

"Who are you?"

"Olivia."

"Who?"

"Your daughter. O-liv-i-a."

He shook his head. "I've got a daughter. Desdemona.

You're not at all like her. Who *are* you?"

Oh. God. It's one of those mornings. "Don't play games," she said brusquely, "you know perfectly well who I am." *But does he?*

He regarded her with mild curiosity. "You say your name is Olivia?"

"Yes. Desdemona is your youngest daughter. I'm the eldest."

"Where is she?"

"At school."

He nodded affably. "That's right. What grade is she in?"

"Des is in college, you *know* that."

Ben glared at her. "Now you're lying to me. She isn't old enough."

"Yes, she is. She's nineteen."

The old man's jaw began to tremble. "Why are you saying these horrible things? Get my wife. She'll tell you the truth."

Olivia went cold. This was the worst part of the morning. Ben was usually querulous, sometimes morose, infrequently cheerful, but no matter what mood she found him in, she always had to face this same dreadful moment.

"Well, what are you waiting for? Call my wife in here. She'll settle this once and for all."

"You know I can't."

"Why not?"

She did not reply. *Maybe for once he'll let it alone.*

"Why not?" he persisted. "Where is she?"

A long, empty silence.

"She . . . she's not dead?"

Olivia nodded.

"How long?"

"Ten years."

Ben began to weep . . . not a soft, familiar sort of sorrow, but raw anguish unblunted by usage. Every morning

—as if for the first time—he had to learn his wife was gone. Olivia took a step towards him to offer comfort, but her face pruned at the stench and she stopped. Eventually, after he'd worn himself out, Ben looked up pathetically at her and asked how he possibly could have forgotten his own wife's death.

"I don't know."

"But I used to have a good mind, didn't I, girl?"

"Yes."

"Then what's wrong with me?"

Olivia gestured helplessly. She had no answer for him because she had none for herself.

She had less trouble than usual that morning getting out of the house. Ben liked their next-door neighbor, Mrs. Betty Culloden, a semi-retired practical nurse who felt sorry for Olivia and frequently volunteered to watch over Ben Aubrey while the young woman went off on personal errands.

Mrs. Culloden was short and round, but could lift her weight in patients. She had a scraggly mustache, a toothy smile, and a laugh like a barking seal, but beneath her raucous exterior was a core of common sense and an expertise in geriatrics that Olivia lacked. On more than one occasion, the nurse tried to persuade her neighbor to put Ben in a rest home, but Olivia adamantly refused.

"He won't get better, kiddo, don't ever think he will," Mrs. Culloden chided. "You think I'm being cruel? Keeping him here's a lot worse."

"I can take care of him."

"Like I can kiss my own backside. You'd have to have eight arms and no need for sleep. The more you give, the more he demands. Keep it up, kiddo, and you'll both be in the hospital. You know what I think's wrong with him, dontcha?"

But Olivia never allowed her to name it.

* * *

The damnably beautiful blonde secretary led Olivia through a network of corridors that resembled a movie set for *The Trial*. They arrived at an end office overlooking the East River and she was asked to wait. She stood there, feeling awkward and stranded, unable even to sit down because the only empty chair was the one behind the editor's desk; two others were piled high with manuscripts.

The walls were covered with floor-to-ceiling bookcases crammed with Porlock Press volumes of general fiction, popular occult experiences of the first-person, eye-witness variety and—yes, *there!*—a number of slender chapbooks of poetry, the Persons from Porlock series. Their sudden truth shamed her.

Panic. Olivia clutched her purse as if it were a life preserver. She considered leaving, but could not bring herself to inconvenience a man who'd specifically set aside time to meet her—*and I couldn't find my way out of this maze, anyway. I should've scattered breadcrumbs.*

She waited and waited, her shoulders and the toes of her polished pumps angled inward as if she were a butterfly pinioned by a collector. But after five minutes, boredom dulled the edge of self-consciousness and she glanced with idle curiosity at the clutter spread over the editor's desk: overstuffed vertically-stacked in-and-out boxes, a separate pile of correspondence weighted down with a conch shell, a walnut pipe rack filled with pens and pencils, loose paper clips, a sharpener, a stapler, desk calendar, blotter, postal scale with out-of-date rates on its gauge, a pica rule tangled in the phone cord, a metal trivet that bore a plastic mug of long-cold coffee.

Olivia also saw a cardboard ream-sized box of white bond paper with a 4″ × 6″ label pasted on its lid. She read it.

TRAGEDY IN BUCKS COUNTY

A Survivor's Account
of Three Nights
in a Haunted House
by
Charles P. Singleton III

What a strange coincidence, Olivia thought. Just then, Alan Hunter entered the office.

Dipping a jumbo shrimp into a silver tub of crimson cocktail sauce, Singleton lifts the curlicued morsel to his lips and worries it with tiny bites while he wonders why on earth his editor just entered the restaurant in the company of a young woman whom Charles has never set eyes on before.

Presumably, Alan and I were supposed to have a one-on-one discussion (dissection?) of *Tragedy in Bucks County* the manuscript of which I submitted to him a month ago to a positively polar silence. Until the phone call: "Charles, let's have lunch soon." In the solemn tones of a surgeon about to pronounce the need for an amputation. Dear God, is my book all that bad?

Not bad, boyo, just incomplete.

But every other book I've done for Alan involved rewrite. That never used to prevent him from issuing my much much needed check for the second half of the royalty advance *to be paid upon submission of a satisfactorily* completed *manuscript*.

Why would Alan bring a stranger to a private business meeting? How can we discuss textual changes?

Not changes. Additions.

I have nothing further to add.

Aye, there's the rub.

Charles impatiently churns the partially-consumed chunk of seafood in the saucepot while Alan Hunter lingers at the bar buying cocktails for himself and his companion. A singularly unpleasant thought occurs to Singleton: what if Porlock has decided to renege on the contract? Maybe Alan brought her along as a buffer, a rococo way of staving off that embarrassing moment when he must tell me they are dropping my book. Except they did all that advance publicity. Doubtful they'd want to lose the edge.

The editor approaches the table. "Olivia, I'd like you to meet Charles Singleton."

Depositing the tail-remnant of shrimp on his butter plate, Charles apologizes for not rising. "I'm afraid that with me, it's a bit of a production number."

"Charles, this is Olivia Aubrey."

Absolute silence.

Singleton stares up at her and knows at once that her surname is not a coincidence.

Merciful Heavens, she has eyes like Merlyn's!

With an uncertain smile, Olivia offers her hand, but Charles, transfixed, makes no move to take it. She withdraws at the seeming rebuff, but then he recollects himself and seizes her fingers in his.

"*Do* forgive a dotard his infirmities, Ms. Aubrey. For a moment you reminded me of . . . someone I haven't seen in a long time."

"So," Alan explains between sips of Southern Comfort manhattan, "when I learned that Olivia belongs to the same family, Charles, I imagined you'd be perking with questions you'd want to ask her. That's why I invited her to join us."

"I see," Singleton says. He watches Olivia nervously muddle her Jack Daniels with a plastic swizzle-straw. "Merlyn was one of my dearest friends. I don't recall her mentioning you, Ms. Aubrey, but she rarely discussed her family. Were the two of you at all close?"

"Not as much as we would have liked. We lived in different cities. We only got together a few times, although—"

Charles' thoughts wander back to those last days when Merlyn said more about her family than ever before. *And what a splendid brood!* Her father, Jason, was a dipsomaniac. Her mother, Ariella, abandoned husband and daughter. And then there was Grandma Charlotte.

Especially Granny Charlotte! That hateful, heartless—

Hst! Faîtes attention!

"—on the few occasions we spent a couple of days together, Merlyn and I got along well. We occasionally exchanged letters. I always felt sorry for her, she looked so sad even when she was laughing. Or . . . no, not sadness so much . . . something else."

"Perhaps what you saw was desperation," Charles suggests. "The two of you were cousins?"

"Yes. My grandfather Henry was Merlyn's greatuncle."

"On which side?"

"The Aubrey side. Henry was brother to Derek Aubrey, Merlyn's grandfather."*

Derek, Charles mused, poor Derek Aubrey. That ill-fated attorney who married the lovely but vacuous Charlotte Danefield. Charlotte bore two of Derek's children: Jason, Merlee's inebriated poppa, the sole acknowledged Aubrey offspring, but there was also that nameless little girl hidden away in the attic. An anonymous weekly food

* For clarification, see AUBREY FAMILY TREE, page xi.

bill that ran seven short years before she died. No one even knew where they buried her. And her grief-struck father Derek—like his son Jason a generation later—drank himself to death.

A waiter approaches. Alan circles his fingertip to indicate the glasses ought to be refilled. Charles requests a Dubonnet with a twist. The waiter departs.

"Charles," Alan says, "I thought you're under doctor's interdict."

"The exception proves the rule. An occasional glass of wine is preferable to cold sober stress."

"Stress? I thought we were having a pleasant luncheon."

Charles smiles at Alan, but elects to address Olivia. "I take it you are a prospective Porlock author?"

"I . . . I'd like to be. I submitted some of my poetry to Mister . . . to Alan. We haven't talked about it yet."

Charles waggles an admonitory finger. "For shame, Mr. H. Never keep artists in unnecessary suspense." He winks at Olivia. "Corragio. Editors rarely buy lunch for those they intend to reject."

The operant word is "rarely."

Alan sips his cocktail and nods at Olivia. "I'm sorry, I should have said something, it's just that I got sidetracked when I found out who you are."

"It's perfectly all right," she says, staring down at her own hands tearing bits from a paper napkin.

"Aubrey House naturally was on my mind today," Alan explains. "I gather that you're in charge of managing it, Olivia. What I've been wondering—"

"Alan," Singleton interrupts, playfully slapping the editor's wrist, "if you don't instantly tell Ms. Aubrey what you thought of her writing, she may run out of napkin and be compelled to tatter the tablecloth." Olivia's hands drop to her lap, but Charles forestalls the apology she is about to utter. "No, no, you have every right to be nervous. Alan has you on tenterhooks, and I'm sure my presence exacerbates your discomfort. I would leave the two of you alone, but once I'm settled, it's a wearisome business for me to get up again."

"Please, Mr. Singleton," Olivia says, checking an impulse to put her hand on his, "I want you to stay."

"Then stay I shall . . . provided that henceforth you call me Charles. Mr. Hunter, I believe it's your cue."

Alan nods. "Olivia, I like some of your work. Has any of it appeared in the little magazines?"

She removes a folded sheet of notepaper from her purse. "I thought you'd want to know that. Here are my credits, such as they are."

Skimming the page, Alan murmurs, "This is all? I'm surprised."

"It just takes so long sending out manuscripts, you know? And there's all the retyping and postage. I just don't have enough time and the things I do mail . . . well, it takes ages for editors to reply." Her hand touches her lips. "Oh! I didn't mean—"

"No offense taken. I know how grueling it is. Compared with poetry, becoming a shepherd seems eminently more practical."

"Alan," Singleton remarks, "avuncular bon mots are all well and good, but what *are* your intentions?" His lips purse. "Oh, dear—you must pardon me, Olivia, for casting myself *in loco parentis*."

Her smile is like sudden sunlight. This time she manages the distance and squeezes his hand. "I don't mind. It's sweet of you, Charles."

A distant echo of Merlee.

"The bottom line," Alan says, "is that I want to publish you, Olivia, but it'd help if you had more placements. Now don't go all glum, I've got an idea I'll tell you about later. But there's a bigger problem. The Porlock series is themed, haven't you noticed?"

"Themed?"

"Like Rebecca Scott's *Press Kit for Judgment Day.*"

"Oh. Oh, I didn't realize . . . and I should have. Just that I never gave it much thought. There's always a governing idea, isn't there? Like Jonathan Brant's *Love Sonnets.*"

Alan is startled. "You know that book?"

"It's my favorite."

He chuckles ruefully. "So you're the one who bought it. It never sold a damn. For what it's worth, it's my favorite, too." He waves it away. "Anyway, Porlocks either feature a single long poem or a related cycle. Not that we can't flesh out a volume with a few miscellaneous pieces. In your case, I'd certainly want to include the one you wrote on the Kennedy assassination."

Olivia is pleased. "Really? I'm rather proud of that one."

"You should be. To evoke Whitman without imitating him is no minor accomplishment."

Singleton's eyes narrow. *What's Alan up to? Why is he playing her?*

"You might make a cycle out of the monologues you sent me," the editor says. "'The Army General', 'The Faith Healer.' Have you done any more like those?"

"Two or three others," Olivia replies. "Actually, I did plan them as a series of related poems."

"Do you have a title in mind?"

She nods. "I'm afraid it'll sound . . . I don't know . . . pretentious."

"Let me be the judge."

"All right. *Dreams of Power and Loss.*"

Alan savors it. "I like it. Do you think you can do enough to carry a Porlock chapbook?"

"I don't know. I never tried writing on deadline. Just when I'm in the mood."

"Could you put yourself in the mood to do thirty or forty more 'dreams'?"

The quantity staggers her. "I have no idea. By when?"

"That is not the important consideration," Singleton interposes. "The question is whether Porlock Press is prepared to make something approaching a genuine commitment. Alan?"

"Charles, you're sounding less like a parent and more like an agent. All I can say is that if Olivia writes them and they're good, and if I can help her place more of her work in poetry periodicals, and if my committee is still disposed to support the Persons from Porlock line when she's got the right material to submit, then maybe I'll be able to offer Olivia a contract."

Singleton sighs. "My dear Mr. Hunter, if airlines and bus companies and railroads reassured their prospective passengers the way publishers entice authors to write 'on spec', most of us would elect to travel cross-country on Pogo Sticks."

Olivia and Charles dawdle over coffee and dessert. Alan sips espresso and Rémy Martin and shifts the conversation back to Aubrey House. "Olivia, I was going to ask you earlier, if you and Merlyn were only distantly related, how come the property is now your responsibility?"

"Because I'm the end of the line. Or nearly. My . . . my father is incapacitated, and the only other living descendant of Addison Aubrey—you know who he was?"

Charles quotes Scripture: "The Chicago tycoon who bought the original tract of land from Ezekiel Lambert in 1870."

Olivia is impressed. "You know more family history than I do. Anyway, other than me, there's just my younger sister, Des. Desdemona. She's a student at Hunter College. So the doubtful honor of managing the white elephant in Pennsylvania went to me."

"Is it much of a headache?"

"No, Alan, the lawyers do most of the work. They send

me papers to sign and occasionally they telephone, but that's all. I've never even set foot in the house."

"Count your blessings," Singleton mumbles through a mouthful of Mississippi Mud Cake à la mode. "And what do you eventually plan to do with that white-frame horror? Merlee, you know, wanted to burn it down."

"Yes. The last time she wrote me, she swore she was going to."

"But she never would have. The house defined Merlyn. 'I own the cold blue light.'" A memory tugs at Singleton. "There she was, down to her last paltry fortune, yet she hired a Rolls to drive us to Pennsylvania. We pulled up in front of the house and Merlee began warning us about asthmatic plumbing and all the other discomforts we'd endure staying there. So Dick Creighton asked her point-blank why she didn't sell the place. One might have sliced the silence with a stiletto." Charles shakes his head. "Merlee never would have harmed the house. If for no other reason, she counted on the income from vacation rentals."

"Now that," says Alan between brandy sips, "is something I've wondered about."

"Namely?"

"How come, Charles, if Aubrey House was rented out fairly regularly, nothing bad happened to any of those people? Excluding Matthew Lambert, of course."

Olivia shudders. "Let's not talk about him."

Singleton pats his lips with his napkin. "Alan, the reason Merlee's tenants suffered no misfortunes, I would hazard, is that they only came for a few weeks of harmless estivation. Look how the Aubreys themselves lived there so many years without incident. For decades, the Effect was considered nothing more than a harmless psychic anomaly, a constant that never moved from its station beneath Charlotte's photograph. Nearly every death caused directly or indirectly by the house was that of an occult investigator—Drew and Vita and me, almost. The Burtons. In his own distinctive fashion, even Richard, I suppose, was somehow probing. And Merlee thought she already knew the answer, that Charlotte was the only operant ghost."

Olivia ponders a spoonful of rainbow sherbet. "Aubrey House has always fascinated me. The stuff of Hawthorne and the Brontës. Who were the Burtons?"

Her strain of romanticism disturbs Charles. "The Burtons were elderly mediums of doubtful competency. They're described in my book, along with all the other pertinent historical data on the house. Perhaps you'd like to read it?"

She nods emphatically. "Very much. When will it be coming out?"

Bravo, Ms. Aubrey! Precisely what I hoped you'd ask.

Singleton turns to his editor. "That, Alan, is what one calls a loaded question, don't you agree?"

Midnight.

Cradled in a near-horizontal position in his black leatherette recliner lounge, Charles listens to FM.

"—allegretto moderato in B-flat minor. So here is the Purgatorio movement from Gustav Mahler's unfinished Tenth Symphony. The Cleveland Orchestra, George Szell conducting, here on WNCN."

A few seconds of silence, then the forlorn little ostinato begins.

Purgatory. How very appropriate. But instead of a mountain to climb, I have a house to revisit. If I dare. Not that there's much choice, Alan made that pellucidly clear. No check until I write a decent ending. Which I can't do unless I remember what happened that Sunday.

Dear God, let me forget.

Perhaps I needn't stay. Just face Aubrey once. Get back

on the bicycle long enough to prove I still know how to ride.

A wave of anger washes over Charles. *How dare Alan put me in this position? Hasn't he any notion what might happen?*

Yes. That's why he said I have to talk it over with Sam Lichinsky. As if that would be enough to protect me. But Alan has no real idea what Aubrey is like. Probably carries a Wuthering Heights scenario in his head, just like that poor locked-in young woman. Olivia. So different from Merlyn. So similar. Quieter. Perhaps less self-damning. Certainly more mature . . . and yet her vulnerability is like an open wound. I hope Alan isn't using her to make the house available to me.

Ridiculous. He wouldn't do that, would he?

Who knows? He's a business friend, but I've rarely glimpsed the inner man. Perhaps he's a tool.

?

Of Sam Lichinsky, doctor to the damned.

Conceivable?

More than once, Sam has stated that if I went back to Aubrey, I'd probably regain the things I've repressed. But I'm not going.

Despite Alan's ultimatum?

He wants a better ending. If I can provide it without returning to Aubrey, he won't care.

Yes, but—

Have done! There are only three options.

Enumerate them.

I can refuse further rewrite, repay the advance, shop around for another publisher.

Some choice. Most of the money's already been spent. Marketing it elsewhere takes time. Next option?

Do what Alan suggests. Phone Olivia, make arrangements to revisit the scene. Find out what happened to me

Sunday night. The why of it.

Painful, but probably inevitable.

Perhaps not. I can live perfectly well with that gap in my memory. How did Richard put it? "Not dragging around chains. Cutting away childhood, old graves, last week." And even if I did go back and open myself like an actor awaiting the inpouring of inspiration, what guarantee is there that I'd break through? Remember enough to complete my book?

None. But what else is there to try?

Turn detective.

?

Maybe Van Helsing is a better name for it. Sift the evidence at second hand.

What evidence?

Drew's handwritten notes to Dick Creighton. Aubrey family documents. And the tapes some of us recorded while we were there.

The police probably have them.

Very likely. But why would they object to my inspecting the files? It's been more than three years since it happened.

It would entail a trip to Doylestown.

That much I can handle.

In nightmare, Vita and Merlyn visited Charles, each of them wearing a face that was both Charlotte Aubrey and Vita's mother and yet it melted and changed to something else and he almost recognized the features as he struggled with the bloated hag whose forehead bore a white-hot V angling *down all?* gouging out her bulging sightless eyes with Merlyn's

one great lateral

dea$^{r}_{d}$ friends

gone

The dream changed. Now it was New Year's Eve. He

was a lonely young man wandering down silent, snow-shrouded streets. Pale blue stars twinkled above as he trudged wearily along, seeking something he could neither recognize nor name but the need for it tore at his heart and drove him on on on into darkness

Waiting impatiently for her sister to return her call, Olivia perched cross-legged on the faded blue bedspread in her faded pink bathrobe, a yellow legal pad balanced on one knee. She lifted her pencil and regarded the unfinished stanza dubiously.

> I hate the clock that binds me to the bed,
> That wakes me to a need I cannot heed.
> My God, forgive my faults and let me go—

Jingle, jingle, Little Miss Laureate. Say what you mean. ("And mean what you say, Alice.")

She scribbled a transposition symbol over the first line, scratched words out, carated in new ones, tried to write a fourth line, failed.

Well, copy it out fresh, maybe something'll come to mind.

I toss upon the bed that chains me to the clock
And batter at a wall of words I can't recall.
My God, condemn my faults, but let me go—

Obscuriouser and obscuriouser. And still no tag. Lady, you're just playing with words. ("And what would you rather play with?") *And he expects you to write thirty more?*

Olivia flung away the pad, rose and walked to the bookshelf. She withdrew a thin volume. Jonathan Brant's *Love Sonnets*. Switching on the floorlamp with the faded green shade, she sat in her armchair and began thumbing through the book, pausing occasionally to admire an arresting image or an especially poignant couplet. She came to her favorite sonnet.

A PERFECT SHELL

I searched the beach to seek a perfect shell,
But only found those chips and bits that fell
Where hungry seagulls hurled them high to land
At morning tide upon the salt-smacked sand.
My mind that perfect shell could clearly see;
In vain, my eyes did seek its symmetry.
So, since I cannot bring that gift to you,
I hope this crafted shell of words might do.

Like shells, our souls at birth are whole and free,
But all too soon are stolen from the sea,
And though the heart a noble start has planned,
Too often it lies broken on the sand.
Then let us lie, who love each other well,
And say we see in each a perfect shell.

And that, my dear, is how you ought to write—simple and direct and I'll bet Alan likes this sonnet, too.

Whoa . . . why should it matter one way or the other what he likes? This would be scann'd. ("My tables—meet it is I set it down.")

Laying aside the book, Olivia fetched her diary and began to write in it.

APRIL 30 Midnight plus. Too keyed up to sleep. Besides, left message for Des to call me no matter when she gets in, and I don't want the phone to wake Ben. It'd be nice if for once Des was in a cooperative frame of mind, but I don't believe in Santa Claus any more, either.

Alan Hunter said I should call him Alan, which in one respect I feel funny about, though at the same time it seems right and natural and God, my syntax is suffering tonight. Slow down, girl. Alan Hunter. A lovely man. The exquisite good taste to like my poetry. Reserved, but there's warmth there, no question. Nameless sadness in his eyes. Behave, dear heart. He's probably married. No ring, no telltale circle to show he'd just removed it, but still . . . but still, do I appeal to him? His eyes said so—I think.

I actually have a chance to be a published Porlock Person. (Droll phrase!) Two conditions. First, that I write a lot more "Dreams of Power and Loss." Tonight's attempt less than auspicious. Beset with fear that I won't be as good as I want to be, an arrogance, not humility. But must the Muse punch a timeclock? Apparently, yes. Second requirement . . . more of my work must appear in print. The way "little magazine" editors take their time answering, I could be a li'l ol' lady before that day comes, except that Alan wants me to submit to "Incisions," a new periodical to be edited by Jonathan Brant! Alan is sure Brant will love anything I send him, but I'm less sanguine at the prospect. J. Brant is so good. I love him, sight unseen. A kindred spirit. (Except that he's published. His dreams became fact. Mine are still dreams.) (Of power or loss?)

A strange coincidence . . . Alan took me to lunch with a Porlock author who turned out to be Charles Singleton, the only one of the four who went with Merlyn to the house and lived. He suffered a stroke, its after-effects evident in the painful way he moves. He's quite epicene. Still, a sweet man. But the question is, was our meeting really a coincidence? Alan asked oh-so-casually whether Mr. Singleton might be able to visit Aubrey House in connection with the book he's writing. A precondition to my being published? I took no chances, said it could be arranged, but the look on Mr. Singleton's face—

The telephone jangled. It rang twice before Olivia could pick it up. Her sister said hello.

"Des, where in God's name have you been?"

"Out."

"This late? On a week night?"

"Ease off, Liv. The weather's great. A bunch of us drove over to the Palisades to see the river."

ting-ting-ting-ting-ting-ting-ting-ting-ting-ting-ting-ti—

"Oh, Jesus," Olivia swore, "I knew this'd happen. Hold the line, I have to see what Ben wants. Don't hang up on me."

—*ng-ting-ting-ting-ting-ting-ting-ting-ting-ting-ting-t*—

Putting down the receiver, Olivia cinched her robe and crossed the hall to the old man's room. Ben was sitting on the edge of the bed ringing his bell, not stopping till she switched on the overhead light.

—*ing-ting-ting-ting*—

"All right, I'm here. What do you want?"

"What's wrong?" His voice quavered. His face was white. "Who died?"

"Nobody died. What do you mean?"

"The phone rang. People don't call in the middle of the night unless something bad happened."

"Don't be upset." She rested reassuring hands on his shoulders. "It was a wrong number."

"A wrong number? That's all?" He looked up hopefully. "You're telling me the truth?"

"I never lie to you, Ben, that's all it was. Go back to bed and try to sleep."

With a sob of relief, he put his arms round her waist like a lost child reunited with his mother. Olivia endured it awkwardly, caught between pity and embarrassment, but then his hands moved down and clutched her buttocks. He pulled her tight against his face.

"Let me go!"

His grip was strong. Her struggles only increased the intimacy, and even as Olivia writhed in anger and disgust, Ben's hot repeated breath stirred irrelevant fires. When he released her bottom to stroke her breasts, she wrenched free and staggered across the room out of reach. Ben tried to rise, but the effort made him short of breath. He flopped back on a heap of pillows, gasping. When he could speak again, he addressed her in a tone of syrupy wheedling that turned her stomach. "Don't go away, I won't hurt you, honey. I'm a prisoner, you have to help me. Be a good girl and help me. Please help me."

"For God's sake, stop it, Ben!" She thought she might throw up. "I'm your daughter."

"Liar!" he bellowed, suddenly vicious. "Daughters don't call their fathers by their first names."

"All right, fine, have it your own way. I'm not your daughter. Who am I, then?"

"Someone else."

"Very clever!" Her voice jittered up the scale. "Who? Can you say? Do you remember?"

"I remember."

"Oh, sure you do. So tell me. Who am I?"

His mouth drew into a wreath of contempt. "You're my dead wife's bastard, that's who you are."

When Olivia returned to her room, Desdemona was no longer on the line. *Naturally.* Cursing her sister, she dialed the dormitory and had to wait the better part of ten minutes before Des deigned to come back to the phone.

"Jee-*zus*, Liv," her sister complained, "do you know how fucking late it is? I was sound asleep."

"I told you not to hang up on me."

"You're always telling me what to do and not to do."

"Would it have hurt to wait a few more minutes?"

"A *few* more minutes? I'm freezing my ass off out here. What do you want from me, anyway?"

She was in the wrong mood to broach the subject. Olivia expected an argument. She was not disappointed.

"No way," Desdemona said. "I already made plans for the summer."

"Can't you change them? I don't ask you for a favor very often." *Because I know there's no point.* "This one is really important to me."

"I can't do it."

"It's not as if I were asking you to take care of him the whole summer. Just a few weeks."

A pause. "This really means a lot to you, huh?"

She's hooked. "Yes."

A longer pause.

"Well?"

Desdemona played hard to get. "I'd like to help, Liv, but I really have made plans, and if I change them, it's going to inconvenience a lot of my friends."

"Whereas you don't mind inconveniencing your own sister. Damn it, he's your father, too!" *He's* your *father*.

"Don't give me guilt trips. I can't handle him the way you can."

"So you'll learn. I'll teach you. And Mrs. Culloden's always willing to help. *Please,* Des?" The note of desperation was a tactic; she could practically hear the calculator clicking away in her sister's mind.

"Well," Des said, "suppose I could shift my plans around, not that it'd be easy. What do I get in return?"

So, uncle, there you are.

> 1:45 A.M. Des agreed. Of course there was a price tag: half June's executor fee for managing Aubrey House, but it's worth it. When her term ends, she'll take care of Ben while I go away and write enough new poems to satisfy Alan. The big question is, where shall I go? No point picking anywhere that I'll be tempted to take in the local sights. It's not a vacation, I have to work. The seashore is out of the question.
>
> There *is* one obvious place, of course. Isolated. Reasonably remote. No rent. Only—

Only it was late and Olivia was too tired to make a major decision. Her mind was filled with the long day's events and impressions: Ben's perennial early morning grief; Alan's enigmatic smile; Charles Singleton's slightly pompous jocularity that masked physical and psychological distress; Desdemona's predictable selfishness. And threading through it all, a dark skein of sexual desire that stirred at the thought of Alan Hunter, that burned in spite of herself when the old man held her. A need that shame could not quell.

Seizing her legal pad, Olivia tore off and threw away

the top sheet. Her pencil-point scribbled swiftly over the fresh page beneath.

AN OLD MAN

Prisoned in the prism of corrosion,
Lustful dreams cascade in palisades.
Fling the shriveled blossoms in the snow—
    My deadly lover caroled long ago!

Willis Parker & Associates, Inc.
invites you to a networking party on
APRIL 29 *at 6:30 p.m.*
at

TYDINGS
948 West 53rd Street, Manhattan

Party is the telltale word, Alan mused sourly, touching tongue-tip to the lime wedge on the rim of his tumbler of club soda ("For four dollars, you could at least use a Collins glass!"). Other Willis Parker networking sessions were held in places accommodating no more than a hundred persons, but the blonde receptionist who greeted Alan at the door said this one night they were dispensing with name badges [ALAN HUNTER/PORLOCK PRESS/PUBLISHER].

"But if we're not wearing name tags, how are we supposed to network?"

She gave him a manufactured smile. "You just go on over to whoever looks interesting and introduce yourself."

"I know *how* it's done," he said testily, "but how is anyone in this crowd supposed to know who's who? I'm in publishing. I'm not interested in meeting petroleum executives."

The artificial smile widened. "I guess you'll have to talk to lots of girls to make sure you find the right one." Pointedly dismissing him, she turned to the next in line.

Alan walked away, annoyed at her assumption that he only came to meet "girls." *That's not why I'm here.*

Of course not.

Alan sipped club soda and reflected on the aptness of Tydings' location. The huge building half a block east of the Hudson River once housed an auto parts warehouse. In 1967, it became a film studio large enough for a dozen seedy camera crews at a time to grind out silent "loops" for coin machines in the nation's pornography shops. It took a new mayor and a team of canny entrepreneurs to convert 948 West Fifty-third Street to a different sort of carnal enterprise: Cupid's Cavern, where members could engage in or just watch the many variations of collaborative sex. It lasted till the post-Lindsay regime began to crack down on Times Square flesh merchants. The Cavern's owners prudently elected to close the doors and reopen four months later as Tydings, a soft-core discothèque designed for discreet assignations. The management might wink at mild foreplay in the dim seclusion of the mezzanine, but overt amorous activity was discouraged, and the use of any mood adjuster other than tobacco or alcohol resulted in immediate expulsion.

The decor—off-white stucco walls, hushed gray carpetry, chrome fixturing, black plastic banquette seating, clear lucite tables—was dubbed by one dour critic, "moderno-nebbish," a label which Alan privately extended to include the knots of chic nonentities crowding the hundred-foot monster bar. *Listen to them: deep-revolving discussions over the noo Woody Allen flick. Isn't it splendid to be thirty and saved by est?* Along the walls, behind the banquettes, sat wistful people *like me,* some smiling with wan encouragement at passersby, others pretending aloofness to mask their desperate need for companionship.

A waitress stopped at Alan's table. She wore a lace-frilled black silk uniform, a cliché out of *Playboy:* the greatest décolletage short of total toplessness; a skirt hem as high as her bodice was low.

"Hi! Can I brang y'all a refill?"

Alan winced at her twangy insouciance and said he did not need another drink. She dimpled at him and departed, jigging and ambling to another table where she leaned over to clear away empty glasses. A napkin skittered to the floor and she bent down to retrieve it. As she did, Alan saw the declivity of her breasts deepen, the twinned curving of her buttocks mold against pale blue panties that were an integral, meant-to-be-seen part of her costume.

Perfect example of the American attitude toward sex: "Here's what you can't have." Fie on't! It hath made me mad.

From the corner of his eye, Alan sensed someone staring at him. He turned and saw four thirtyish women standing huddled in a dismal attempt to lend one another courage. He wondered why they didn't realize the self-defeating result of their camaraderie: *a closed shop. No men need apply.* But the slender brunette on the right met his gaze for a moment before losing her nerve and looking away. She had prominent shoulder-blades and collarbone, small breasts, well-rounded hips, full thighs. *Looks a little like Ava.*

Alan fancied he knew "her type": probably twenty-eight or -nine, on the cusp of a career change. Overqualified in her work, passed over in favor of younger married men with families. Nervous that she's coming up on thirty and is still single . . . though she isn't quite ready to give up her independence. Definitely *not* cut out to be a mother—but suppose she changes her mind after it's too late? The companionship of a daughter (first preference) might be wonderful, but not if it entails the encumbrance of a husband. Has probably thought about getting herself pregnant and not telling the father, but knows that would be unfair to the child. Wishes she could conceive by parthenogenesis, like the women in Charlotte Perkins Gilman's novels. In short (Alan thought), the brunette was probably a typical New York career woman—vulnerable but tough, full of tenderness and rage. Afraid of surrendering her freedom to Mr. Right, terrified she won't ever get the chance to turn him down.

Just like Ava.

He stared moodily into his glass. The last person he wanted to think about was Ava *who got married today* but the brunette reminded him of her. Slim almost to the point of anorexia. Short auburn hair. Brown eyes glowing with laughter and pain. Straight nose, sensual lips bracketed by the most engaging smile lines, white teeth *marred or made special by?* one jagged incisor . . . and Alan suddenly realized he was not thinking of Ava, after all, but Olivia Aubrey. *But why?* Olivia was just a convenience, a would-be poet whose desires dovetailed with Alan's needs.

Poor Charles. A good book hamstrung by a weak ending. Which he can't write because he's afraid to remember.

Alan was worried because he'd pressured Singleton into going back to Pennsylvania. *But it's not just the book, it's for his own good.* Ideally, Alan knew he ought to have discussed it with Charles' doctor, but Sam Lichinsky would not violate patient confidentiality, no point in even asking, so instead Alan described the situation, naming no names, to Bruno Thelwell, a psychologist under contract to Porlock Press to write a book, *Cheating Without Guilt.*

"Your friend," Thelwell said, "must face the thing that frightened him. Until he conquers it, he will never get on with his life. But the showdown must be strictly supervised."

That's all right. I insisted that Charles talk it over with Lichinsky.

At the far end of the club, a deep thrum like an electronic heart substituted its own rhythm for the pace of Alan's pulse. *So ends any pretense at networking.* He hated dancing, especially the modern arm's-length variety. *Kinesthetic triumph of the beast within.* Just then, the brunette brushed past him; she clung to the arm of a portly fiftyish man with silver-gray hair stranded over a balding dome of skin. An absurd pang of jealousy: *How could she look at me and then go with him?*

The polished wood rectangle of the dance floor was lit by a battery of special instruments that bathed the area in carnival colors: turquoise and lavender, scarlet and amber, sea-green, midnight blue, black. *The Masque of the Red Death recorded at 45rpm, played back at 78.* Overhead, a revolving mirror ball scattered diamonds. Crackling yellow ropes of electricity arced up great metal poles that might have been stolen from the laboratory of some gargantuan mad scientist. White light blinked intermittently, transforming the swirling couples into shadow-figures in a magic lantern show.

The storm of music and light dazzled and depressed Alan. In the fevered animism of the twisting bodies, he detected the desperate need to cry out *We are still alive!* to a universe haunted by the spectre of meaningless death. Instead of dancers, his mind's eye imagined row on row of headstones and grass that bent beneath the terrible wind of Tomorrow.

Snatching up his briefcase, Alan fled Tydings as if escaping from a branch office of Hell.

Outside, the night air was river-cool. He stripped off his tie, stuffed it in a jacket pocket and began walking east towards Broadway. Too-familiar thoughts spooled through his mind.

Camus exaggerated. His "terrible dark wind of the future" is less dreadful than life without options. Like mine. Once upon a time, he'd tried to leave Miranda, but only by fleeing to Ava, *too young to know how wrong a choice that was, trying to build a new relationship on the ashes of a marriage.* Ava couldn't bear the guilt and ultimately he couldn't, either. What began as love declined through gradations of uneasiness, distrust, irritation, anger, recrimination, till nothing remained but hostility and pain. Time of their affair: a statistically typical 2.5 months. He could have elected to continue to live alone, but instead accepted Miranda's offer to come back "for the time being." He slept in the guest bedroom; seven years later, he still occupied it. The only things he shared with his wife were memories, expenses and their child, Bess.

Bess.

Outwardly, his daughter was a cheery nine-year-old, but he couldn't forget when Miranda learned about Ava and the battle sent Bess into hysterics. Later, *after Daddy went away,* the two-year-old picked up on Mama's anger and treated Alan coldly when he visited. Even after he came back home for good, Bess had bad dreams for months. Her first years at school were troubled, *not academically, socially.* "She seems more the product of a split home than the child of a happy marriage," one of her teachers told Alan. That was when he resolved never again to hurt his baby.

But he also felt a guilty responsibility towards Miranda who, after all (and never mind the terms) had allowed him to come home again—*and damn it! It still feels like home.* How could he walk out on her again, seven long years later? A shy woman without a vocation, her family far away—and going back to them was out of the question—she'd regard it as an admission of failure. It simply didn't add up: three people suffering instead of just one. And yet Alan toyed with alternatives. In the absence of physical and emotional intimacy within his marriage, he played a masochistic flirting game he could neither win nor walk away from. Like the networking sessions where he sometimes met women with wide, trusting eyes and a desperate need to prove to themselves they had what it takes to become published authors. *Nothing to say, but an all-consuming need to say it.* Alan agreed to read their narcissistic poetry or their first abortive stabs at public confessional, which they dubbed "fiction." He often saw a genuine natural talent for verbal expression. *Some of them potentially better writers than I,* but their chances predictably encumbered by the dead weight of rigid middle-class upbringing. Families who did not understand artistic longings felt threatened by them and consequently treated all such ambitions with ridicule. Amazing how widespread the same sermon was: settle down and get married or do something sensible like teaching English to seventh graders. Dutiful daughters whose dreams could not flourish unless and until they broke the loving stranglehold of the past. Alan fondled their psyches, caressing and stimulating their hopes. Perhaps one in fifty acted on his advice and succeeded. *Like Ava.* But except for her, his nurturing won him nothing more intimate than irrelevant friendships, an occasional and surprisingly painful wedding invitation and

—*the point of the whole business?*—new faces and forms, fantasy fodder. *Olivia, for instance?*

"Hey, lovah, how'd you like some ree-al deep throat?"

Her husky whisper startled Alan. He was waiting for a light at the corner of Fifty-third and Eighth Avenue when a hooker in red leather slacks eased up to him. The steamy stare she gave him, phony though it was, still stirred his libido. He mumbled he did not have the time or the money. She walked away. He cursed himself for feeling flattered *(no, worse, grateful)* that she'd even noticed him. The voice of any woman, even a prostitute, echoed in the empty chambers of his heart.

Sometimes Alan hated going out of doors. Everywhere he saw nipples poking against blouses, buttocks defined by tight jeans. Now he noticed a couple walking arm in arm in front of him. The youth's hand familiarly circled her waist, dipped into the back pocket of her Calvin Kleins. The casual intimacy tormented Alan. He was a starving man, nose pressed to the glass of a restaurant window, trying to imagine the taste of the food being swallowed. He yearned to kneel and worship before this irrelevant young woman.

Crucifixion can't be much worse. At least it kills faster.

Alan entered Kitty City, Mecca of masculine plumbing problems, and handed the cashier five dollars. He got twenty tokens in exchange, clattered down a grimy flight of metal stairs to a garishly-lit basement with cement floor and walls tiled in glossy ceramic brick. Men streamed back and forth from private viewing booths to an on-floor cashier. A straggle-bearded janitor puffed a cigarette and sponged just-vacated cubicles with a wet-mop. Along one wall, half-clad women of mixed races beckoned prospective clients into their "one-on-one" booths. The man who entered paid eight tokens to watch her disrobe. Though model and customer were separated by a glass partition, they could converse by telephone. ("Rap With Your Own

Beautiful Harem Slave!") Such communication mainly consisted of monosyllables. ("Yo, babe, spread 'em.")

Alan avoided the one-on-one stalls. *Too expensive, not enough time*. Instead, he went to the central show arena, a continuous circle of two dozen booths facing an inner chamber. He entered an unoccupied compartment, locked the door, dropped a token in the slot. An ascending window revealed a chunky naked redhead lying with legs apart on a round black plastic poüffe that revolved and afforded onlookers several intimate glimpses before a screen fell over the aperture and another token had to be deposited.

Kitty City was an addiction Alan loathed, yet could not manage to give up, although this evening he felt oddly detached from the spectacle he'd paid to see. He thought it was because the redhead was drearily unappealing, but the attractive Oriental who followed did not rouse his passion, either, not even when she parted the lips of her vagina for his unhindered view.

He remembered this brunette all too well. The preceding winter, his wife Miranda took Bess out of town to visit her grandparents. By Christmas Eve Alan felt so bitterly alone that he rode the 104 bus to 47th, slogged across a Broadway sooty with three-day-old slush, and entered Kitty City hoping to see someone, *any*one, who might at least pretend she was interested in him as a man. The basement peep show was chilly and almost empty. The raven-haired Oriental on the poüffe displayed herself with the enthusiasm of a civil servant processing an actor for unemployment checks. The few remaining customers trickled off; soon Alan was the only one left watching her. He deposited another token in the slot. When his window opened again, the brunette rose and approached his cubicle. Alan's pulse quickened. He thought she was going to give him a better look at her body, but then her lips curved into a disgusted scowl.

"Whyn't you get the fuck outta here and let me go home?"

Alan crumpled as if he'd been slapped. For once, he wished his screen would close quickly and hide him from her angry eyes.

But the memory of that bleak night didn't totally account for Alan's present detachment. *It's still Olivia.* He could not banish her from his thoughts. Because of her, he felt more than usually ashamed of patronizing a place as squalid as a public toilet. *Imagine her disgust,* he thought, *if she ever found out that her favorite romantic poet, "Jonathan Brant," haunted Kitty City to gawk at strange women's private parts.*

His window closed. Alan stuck the remaining tokens in his pocket, opened the booth door and headed for the exit stairs, angry at himself for wasting time and money on *a profoundly anticlimactic experience.* He winced at his own masochistic pun.

Bess and Miranda were both asleep. He tiptoed to his daughter's room and gently kissed her forehead. With eyes still shut, she grasped his hand and rested her right cheek on it. Alan remembered how as an infant she liked to sleep with a fistful of blanket crumpled against that same cheek. For fear of disturbing her again, he waited a long time before withdrawing his hand from her grip. He adjusted her blanket and went into the den.

He leafed through the cable TV program guide, but none of the films he was interested in seeing were on HBO. He'd hoped for one of those mindless naked-starlet romps that Hollywood churns out for the southern drive-in circuit, but tonight violence was rampant: *Death Wish 3, Sudden Impact, Ninja Wars* and the colorized version of *Night of the Living Dead.* Alan gave up and went to his bedroom. He emptied his briefcase, undressed, showered and lay down on top of clean sheets. He switched off the bedside lamp and the room went dark. A patch of ceiling rippled in moonlight like a woodland stream in summer. It made Alan feel as comfortably cool as an ice sculpture.

He used to lie to himself that one night he would steal into his wife's bedroom and rape her, but it was just an angry fantasy. *Hurt a woman?* When he was a child, he was coddled by mother, sisters and aunts. He had no use for his father, a coarse, truculent man absent from home for merciful long stretches of time. Everything tender and loving, all graces, all beauty soon became associated in his mind with femininity. Women were goddesses who tolerated men *who knows why?* but were far superior to them. He could not, therefore, totally blame his wife for rejecting his fumbling advances. He loved Ava for catering to his physical needs, but when she gradually became passive, distant, it did not surprise him, though he asked her why and when she answered, "I just don't want to do things for you any more, Alan, I don't know the reason, I wish I knew how love can disappear so fast," he understood he was not worthy of her. A few weeks later, he was back home sleeping in the guest bedroom. On only one dismal occasion did he and Miranda attempt to reestablish physical intimacy, but it was a pathetic failure. Alan felt as if he were being unfaithful to Ava, even though she was gone.

How *dare* love vanish so quickly?

"A-a-a-laaaannnnn . . ."

His mother's voice. Across the Boardwalk. He looks over the rail. Plunges down and down falling past descending flights of stairs downdowndown *dead if I land* but it doesn't hurt, he springs to his feet and enters the dark, moist cavern where somewhere she lurks to fight screaming *now she's dead* but the thing chasing him is still alive, so he runs fast and it crawls slowly, slowly *but I can't get away* another stair now up up up past the *dead* thing still comingcoming push *push through* door too small head almost through *too tight* out and up up up past the

Boardwalk

crawling round the *spider?* corner

comingRUN

another door

a landing

railing

"A-a-a-laaaannnnn . . ."

He awoke in a sweat—

a

—tried to describe his nightmare into the bedside cassette machine—

ia

—failed as usual—

via

—turned it off.

ivia

Alan lay back, stared at a spot directly overhead, wished he could fling himself straight "up up up past the Russell Hotel"—

livia

—out of body like Charles described in *Tragedy in Bucks County,* light and cool and free from hope and care and pain and would Charles really return to Aubrey House? *Will she?* Then Jonathan Brant could go there, too, and make up the first issue of "Incisions" with

Olivia

to be near her

livia

naked

ivia

kissing her lips

via

her secret lips

ia

her cinnamon smile

a

opening

va

to me

Ava

But what right did she have to stop loving me?

Ava

stop loving me

no

Bess says love never goes away.

go away alan

No

irandAva

Bess says love never stops.

stop alan you're hurting me

I could never hurt a woman.

you're hurting me stop hurting me stop

NO

stophurtingmehurtingmestop

MirandAvia

could never hurt a woman

stophurtingmestop

irandia

never hurt a woman

stophurtingstop

iaviavia

hurt a woman

stopstop

liavia

hurt a woman hurtwoman hurtwomanhurt

stop

hurthurthurthurthurthurthurthurthurt—

OliviAvaaaaaaaaaaaaaaaaaaaaaaaaaaaaaaaaaaaaaa—

Ragged breathing in the dark.

Pulse slowing slowing slowing slow.

Passion spent.

Silence.

Endless night.

Alan pressed his head into his pillow so his wife would not hear his racking sobs.

DREAMS OF POWER AND LOSS

■

In the golden blood of the dying sun, Aubrey House appeared deceptively innocent. Olivia was more or less expecting to see a spacious white-frame mansion, but she was quite unprepared for the sprawling enormity of the fact. The place was built with total disregard for the great distances its servants once trekked on their daily rounds. A wide veranda that ran half the length of the ground level was bracketed by a pair of towerlike structures that rose just short of the third floor and formed the outer ends of a railed, weatherworn widow's walk. Olivia watched the burnished final shafts of day turn all the windows into amber eyes that winked shut, one by one.

Off to the northeast of the main building, the old stable waited openmouthed to swallow her, car and all. Olivia nosed the '73 Buick she'd rented/borrowed from Mrs. Culloden into the furthest of four empty auto bays that the stable had been modified to contain. Braking to a halt, she shifted the gearstick into parking mode and cut off the engine. Outside, the evening sky glimmered with sunset's afterglare, but in the garage sound stopped and the world went black. The transition was as sudden as if some giant hand suddenly smothered car and driver in cotton wool. Olivia often paid lip service to the vaunted peace of the country, but she was really a child of the city's neon companionship. The darkness and silence unsettled her. Her first impulse was to restart the motor and spend the night in Doylestown, but she willed away her nervousness. She switched on the headlights, got out and groped to the wall, feeling along its grimy surface till she touched an electric toggle-plate.

Please work.

Several weeks earlier, she'd written to Waxman, Sand & Barton, the Philadelphia lawyers who handled the estate, to request that the power and the telephone be turned on. At the same time, Olivia asked them to hire a cleaning woman to scrub and dust and air out the house. In this latter instance, the attorneys could be of no assistance. Apologetically, the junior partner, Mr. Barton, explained to her that no one they'd employed in the past would again set foot in Aubrey House.

Then why am I so eager?

For the past month, Olivia could think of nothing but the great convenience of having a rent-free rural retreat where she could write. But now, standing in the silent, pitch-black outbuilding of an allegedly haunted house, she recalled the grim things she'd read in the manuscript Charles Singleton loaned her. She wasn't particularly superstitious, but at the moment pragmatism was no help.

She flicked the switch. A long strip of fluorescent bulbs sputtered on. In the stark yellow glare, Olivia noticed the grimy stripe across her palm where she'd fumbled along the wall. She returned to the car, took a wad of tissues from the glove compartment and wiped away the smudge, then shut off the headlights. Now that she could see, she felt curiously proprietary. No longer was Aubrey House merely a term in legal documents, it was a great sprawling mansion that was entirely at her disposal. Technically the house and grounds were Ben's, which meant that someday it would all be willed to Desdemona, no illusions on that score, but for now at least, it was hers to manage, and she was content with that.

Olivia strolled down the long vista of the garage, a building once partitioned with horse-stalls. Her heels clicked echoes. Halfway down the aisle, she saw a door in the back wall. She tried to open it, but it was locked. She remembered that it led to an overhead set of chambers that once housed eight members of the Aubrey staff, including grooms, stable boys and a groundskeeper. In her handbag was a ring of keys to the locked rooms and cabinets and closets of the house, but she wasn't sufficiently interested to fish around for the one that would open this door.

She continued her inspection. At the far end of the garage, she was surprised to find one remaining horse-stall. To its left was the building's northern wall with one recessed, boarded-up window in it. Olivia walked over to it and saw an all-white plastic flashlight on the ledge. She was glad to find it, hoped there might be batteries in the house to fit it. She hadn't thought to bring her own flashlight, but then it hadn't been her plan to arrive so late in the day. She had Ben to thank for that. When she tried to leave the house to start on her trip, the old man threw a tantrum.

"Don't you dare walk out that door," he warned her.

"I'm not leaving you alone."

"I don't care, you're staying right here!"

"I'm leaving."

"If you do, I won't be here when you come back."

"Where do you think you'll be?"

"Dead. And it'll be all your fault."

No use arguing. Nothing Des said helped, either. Olivia had to pretend to change her mind about going away. Not until Des tracked down and brought back Mrs. Culloden did Ben grow docile enough to be cajoled into taking a nap. Olivia seized the opportunity. Ignoring her sister's accusing look, she took off for Pennsylvania.

Here at the far end of the stable, the air was heavy with a sweetish tang. Olivia held her breath as she stretched out her arm and removed the flashlight from the window. She tried the button, was amazed that it worked. She aimed its strong, steady beam into the stall and instantly recoiled. The bin was stuffed with old hay filigreed with cobweb and crawling with vermin. *Sickening*. She made a mental note to have it hosed out.

Now that she'd seen all there was to see in the garage, it was time to get her valises and carry them up to the house, but Olivia hesitated. The place was surely a mess, and it was too late to start cleaning that night, she was too tired, anyway, so why not go to a motel and get a fresh start the following morning?

Come on, Liv, you're rationalizing. You just don't want to stay here tonight. She felt sheepish about her timorousness, told herself she at least owed herself a look inside the mansion. Going in after dark did not at all appeal to her, but she accepted it as a minimal necessary compromise with her self-respect. *You'll see. It'll be so dusty and close there'll be no question about driving into town*.

She left the garage and stepped along the flagging that led to the main house, picking her way carefully, inspecting the path in front of her with slow, wide-curving sweeps of the flashbeam.

crrkkk

The noise was halfway between a snap and a crunch. Olivia spun round. She darted the flashlight right and left, but only succeeded in rearranging the darkness. The bright rectangle of the stablehouse was a dozen yards away. She saw nothing, but the long shadows were deep enough to hide an army of hobgoblins. Far off, a lone cricket shrilled. To the left of the garage, the last faint blush of twilight still prickled the rolling crests of a lake whose near shore lay within the Aubrey property line. There was a green islet in the middle of the lake; it was a factor that helped decide Olivia to come to Aubrey House. She imagined herself spending lazy summer afternoons there, her back against the bole of a tree, clipboard in her lap as she composed verse that captured the water's murmur in song. A rueful smile tugged her lips. The image of herself trying to emulate Robert Louis Stevenson on a dinky hummock of land in the middle of a Pennsylvania pond was faintly ridiculous. *A far cry from Samoa, Li'l Miss Tusitala.* As for the sound that scared her, it was probably a small night-creature skittering across the flagstones. The sounds of nature unnatural to the neurotic city-dweller. *Irrelevant jitters. Impact of sudden isolation on a herd animal.* Her fears somewhat abated, Olivia completed her journey to the massive front door of Aubrey House. She'd already separated the large key from the others on the ring. She inserted it in the lock. It grated noisily. She knew that it would.

> Merlyn entrusted me with the house keys. Drew and I got out of the car and went to the front door. The lock had not been used in some time and it resisted my efforts. The noise it made might have been the opening of a coffin in some neglected crypt. I remarked to Drew, "Well, whatever is waiting within certainly knows we're here now."

Damned déjà vu. Maybe I shouldn't've read his manuscript.

The huge unlighted entrance foyer was hot, close and forbidding. The stifling heat was caused by the unseasonably early sultry weather, and Olivia realized the closeness was attributable to the fact that the place had been shut up for nearly a year. *No air. Mildew and dust.* But she could not explain away the house's aura of brooding aloofness. She did not feel welcome. *Tolerated, perhaps, but maybe not for long.*

She pried at the darkness. The flashbeam brushed over dark plank floors and paneled walls, past closed oak doors, down the long central hall, up a wide staircase. Several yards to the left she found the broad arch that opened on the living room/salon. She walked through it, groped and found a light switch, turned it on and got her first good look at Aubrey House. *Or what's left of it.* The Lamberts—the ill-fated brothers who had been leasing the house from Olivia—were in the process of converting it to an inn. The salon, she supposed, was intended as the restaurant. The partitioning sliding doors to the adjacent library had been removed. The only furniture remaining in the salon was a liquor sideboard, still stocked, and a dusty nine-foot Chickering grand piano that jutted from the bay window alcove at the far side of the chamber.

The living room had a high ceiling, wainscoted walls and, next to the bay alcove, a marble mantelpiece that erupted in sinister potbellied cherubs. *Gilded Age grotesqueries.* Above the fireplace hung a portrait of a sad-eyed patriarch whom Olivia identified as Merlyn's paternal grandfather, Derek Aubrey, *husband of the Immortal Charlotte.* Derek died of a heart attack in his Philadelphia law office in 1920, but according to Singleton's manuscript, he committed slow suicide by drinking.

A black cradle telephone rested on the top of the piano. Olivia walked over to it. *Okay, Des, I promised I'd call first thing, guess I'd better.* She held it to her ear, waited for the dial tone. Nothing. She jiggled the hook. Still no response. *Damn. Supposed to be working. Well, now I have to go in town or Des'll be furious. And I'd better talk to the phone company first thing in the morning.*

As she hung up, Olivia idly glanced at a folder of sheet music propped on the piano rack. "When April Comes Again." She began to pick out the melody with one finger, but the instrument was out of tune. She winced and stopped.

The telephone rang.

Flinching at the unexpected noise, she snatched up the receiver.

"Hello?"

A tree branch rapped dry fingers against the side of the house.

"Hello?"

An auto driving by on Route 611 spilled headlight glare on the bay windows.

"Hello?"

She stammered her finger on the hook as if it were a telegraph key. No reply. No dial tone. She hung up, trembling.

Her sense of déjà vu was still active. Bad enough when a disconnected phone rang, but what made it worse was that Olivia half expected it. Like her anticipation of the noisy door key, this premonition was also traceable to the Singleton manuscript. *This is how it all began for Merlyn and her friends*—with the sexually frustrated Vita Henry claiming the telephone woke her at midnight, though no one else heard it *and no wonder, it wasn't hooked up yet, either*. Olivia's knees buckled. She clutched the piano to steady herself. *Alone at night in a spooky house miles out of town and the phone doesn't work. Where's my thunderstorm? And the weird housekeeper?* Humor didn't help. Through her mind ran the names of all the people who lost their lives and/or reason at Aubrey House. Richard

Creighton. *Bled to death.* Drew Beltane. *Heart failure.* Phyllis and Harold Burton. *Minds destroyed.* Vita Henry. *Likewise.* Cousin Merlyn. *A broken neck.* Charlotte and Derek Aubrey's anonymous child. *Cause unknown.* Charlotte herself, the only natural death. And less than a year ago, Matthew Lambert. *Cut to pieces.* The weapon never found, and where was his missing brother Cameron?

Okay, L'il Miss Gothic, get hold of yourself. This is a childish case of nerves, that's all.

Granted. But I'm not staying here tonight.

Agreed. But shall we preserve a modicum of dignity in our departure?

Dignity be damned.

Snatching up the flashlight, Olivia quick-stepped across the room, turned off the lights, cleared the front foyer in five strides, slammed the door behind her but did not bother locking it. She trotted up the flagstone path, wished she could go faster. The flashbeam flickered. *How come it's suddenly so dim?*

> Friday morning, I checked the infrared camera that Merlyn permitted me to set up in the second floor hall. I did not get any pictures of the Aubrey Effect because the batteries went dead during the night. The same was true of those in my portable tape recorder. This is not an uncommon occurrence in haunted houses. Ghosts are always thirsty for energy. They need it to materialize.

The night was hot and humid, but Olivia shivered. In the garage, she put the flashlight back where she found it, why she couldn't say. She did not turn off the overhead fluorescents until the motor was running and the headlights were burning. As she shifted into gear and began backing out, Olivia fretted over some minor detail out of kilter, a thing she could not quite pin down. Or refused to. Only after she'd steered onto Route 611 and headed south for Doylestown did she realize what was troubling her.

The window ledge of the horse-stall where she'd replaced the flashlight was thick with grime and mould. Her hand still felt gritty from brushing against it.

Then why wasn't an all-white flashlight filthy, too?

Sam Lichinsky saw right away that Singleton was upset. Usually when the portly little man entered the analyst's office, he approached the desk and shook hands before stretching out comfortably, but not today. Barely acknowledging the other's presence with a preoccupied nod of his head, Charles crossed straight to the sofa, laid his cane on the floor and perched on the edge of the couch cracking his knuckles and avoiding eye contact. The psychiatrist waited patiently for his patient to speak.

"Sam," he said at last, "Sunday is starting to come back to me."

Well, well. "You knew it would, sooner or later."

"Yes. I put in a bid for later."

"Why?"

"Oh, Sam, you know why. I've said it before."

"Say it again."

"The past frightens me. I mean, the things that happened Sunday afternoon and evening at Aubrey."

"Go on."

"My fear makes me repress those memories. There needs no ghost to come and tell us that."

"What is it that you're beginning to recall?"

"Just bits and pieces. A few minor details. Snatches of conversation, odd moments leaching into my mind. Nothing too dramatic. Not yet."

Telling phrase. Lichinsky tasted it. "Not yet, Charles? What makes you say that?"

A mirthless chuckle. "Oh, dear! It sounds as if I were expecting more news at six. *Après ceci, le déluge*, eh?"

"What do you think?"

"I think, Sam, that I am caught up in a process."

"How does it make you feel?"

"Like Alice." An attempt at a nonchalant shrug. "Curiouser and curiouser."

Charles was trying to affect unconcern, but the doctor too easily detected the suppressed stress in his patient's voice, knew he must somehow dull the cutting edge of these recent upwellings from the Singletonian subconscious. *Backtrack. Integrate present with past*. "Charles, we'd better proceed slowly. For the time being, put Sunday out of your mind. Concentrate on the rest of that week. You've never had any trouble remembering the earlier days, have you?"

"No, not once I began writing my book for Porlock."

"Very well. Then tell me what happened to you from Thursday through Saturday."

"Yet again?" Singleton sighed wearily. "Precious little occurred, Sam, so far as I was concerned. Drew and Vita and Merlee all experienced significant and highly individualized things—startlingly individualized, I might say—but not me. Not Dick Creighton, either, but he was our resident skeptic, he didn't really expect to see or hear anything out of the ordinary. I, on the other hand, desperately wished to attune myself to the house's frequency—"

"Desperately, Charles?" Lichinsky scrawled a note to himself. "Why desperately?"

"Because I needed to prove myself. There I was, an established medium, confronted with a whole new equation in haunted houses and I could do nothing. Every time I tried, there was Drew mocking me, holding me up as an object of ridicule." His hands clenched. "I was so determined to solve the Aubrey mystery that even after Drew almost broke his neck on the back stairs battling the presence—and even though he warned me not to probe—I positively insisted on conducting a séance in the dining room. And it was a total flop, Sam. I could sense a spirit, but it wouldn't come to me. Afterwards, Merlyn taunted me about it, said her grandmother would hardly condescend to communicate with an old fruit like me—you recognize Merlee's style?—but it wasn't Charlotte's spirit who avoided me. It was a child who—" A gasp. A sudden pause. Charles' eyes widened.

"What is it? Have you remembered something?"

"Great God in Heaven, Sam, I have! I've recalled why my séance failed!"

"Recalled? Don't you mean that you've realized why?"

"No, no," Charles said, vigorously shaking his head, "this didn't just come to me. I figured it out at Aubrey, but up to now, Sam, it had totally slipped my mind."

"Well, tell me about it."

"That I will. When I held my séance Friday evening, I was sure I would make contact with the spirit of the bastard offspring of Emily Shipperton, Charlotte's nurse and companion. But no such child existed. We found that out next day. Up in Shipperton's original attic room, there are boxes and boxes of family albums, letters and other ephemera. As soon as I set foot in that chamber, I knew an unhappy child lived there once . . . it's an atmosphere I am all too familiar with, Sam."

Lichinsky made a note to himself. "Yes, go on, Charles."

"The day before, Drew rooted around amongst the stored pictures in there and found a stereoscope photo of Charlotte Aubrey circa 1904—the same year Shipperton came to the house. The photograph showed Charlotte on the front lawn in an Empire gown. That was preposterous. Much too hot for the time of year. Merlyn figured out that Granny was pregnant when the picture was taken. She was too vain to let her figure show . . . thus the inappropriate gown. We suddenly realized that 1904 was too early for Charlotte to be carrying Merlee's Papa Jason. All the pieces fell in place then. A child of Derek's and Charlotte's that no one knew about. Shipperton was probably a nurse expert in handling birth-deficient children. Obviously the Aubreys originally hired her as a baby nurse."

"How does this connect with your abortive séance, Charles?"

"I'm coming to that. Charlotte was so ashamed of producing ugliness—y clept—from that loveliness that was her whole raison d'être that she forced her husband Derek to hide the fact from the world. The infant was confined to the attic and Shipperton was as much its jailer as nursemaid. So don't you see, Sam? *That* is why I was unable to communicate with the poor thing's spirit Friday night. My séance was held in the first floor dining room, but when she was alive—"

"She?"

"Intuition. I believe it was a girl. She was not allowed downstairs in life, so her spirit would hardly venture into terra incognita. Ghosts are quite conservative in such things, you know."

Vintage Singleton, Sam thought, suppressing a smile. His patient's faith had been severely tested in Pennsylvania, yet Charles still occasionally fell into the old habit of proclaiming his beliefs as if they were Ordained Truth. "Sometimes," Vita Henry once remarked, "Charles sounds like he'd just breakfasted with God." *If that wretched house really has a measurable frequency, it needn't be anything more than an as-yet undefined kind of energy. Why can't Charles see that?*

"A penny for your thoughts, doctor."

A wry grin contorted Sam's wizened features. "That's not how the system works, Charles, and you know it. Tell me . . . how long did it take you to construct this theory about the failure of your séance?"

"You mean at Aubrey House? Let's see . . . we found out the truth about Charlotte's child late Saturday afternoon, but then Merlyn had an accident and Dick and I took her to the hospital. It was the middle of a storm, there were highway crashes galore and we had to wait hours in the emergency room. And when we got back to the house—well, that's when I found Vita. Or what was left of her. I had so much on my mind, I doubt I thought about my séance again till sometime Sunday."

"When you finally did, Charles, isn't it possible you might have considered holding another séance on the third floor where you claim your child-ghost lurks?"

"Oh, my!" Singleton pursed his lips. "What a provocative thought. It's likely I would have done just that. But in that case, why did I suffer a stroke on the *second* floor?"

"Just what I was wondering. Any ideas, Charles?"

He shook his head. "A total blank, Dr. L."

In other words, the barriers are still firmly in place. "Well, it's evidently premature to deal with Sunday night. Let's go back to your review of the earlier events of that week."

"All right. As I was saying, the house virtually ignored me, but Vita succumbed without a struggle and Drew—"

Sam's attention wandered. He'd heard Charles tell over his beads so often that he could have chanted the litany in unison. Like his patient, the doctor would have preferred to forget the whole miserable business. Two patients dead. Senseless tragedies, *and I ought to have been able to do something for Merlyn, at least.* When Singleton phoned Sam long distance with the news of Vita's death and told him how Merlyn became so hysterical at the hospital that she had to be sedated, Lichinsky instantly made arrangements to drive to Bucks County. There he worked Merlyn through her immediate crisis *and at long last tapped the secret that haunted her all her life . . .*

It happened when Merlyn was twelve. Charlotte was dying. She summoned her granddaughter to her deathbed and told her she would grow up and become "as beautiful as me." *This from a hideous old hag. Virtually turning puberty into a witch's curse.* Charlotte clutched Merlyn's wrist so tight that the child could not pull away. The death-rattle sounded, and in the summer heat, rigor mortis set in swiftly. The dead fist jerked Merlyn down till her lips touched the corpse's in a dreadful parody of a kiss. The little girl struggled to free herself, broke her wrist in the attempt. She screamed and passed out. Her parents rushed in, found Merlyn in a coma from which she did not emerge for months. In order to release her from the dead woman's grasp, the handyman had to snap four of Charlotte's fingers with pliers.

Merlyn's recollection of the horrible afternoon was the vital missing piece in the puzzle of her personality, but Sam realized too late the ominous significance of his patient's characteristic gesture, raking in-curved fingers over her face, *trying to eradicate the beauty she feared would tempt Charlotte's ghost to live again in her flesh.* So Merlyn wavered between maturity and the wish to stay a child forever. Terrified of possession, yet drawn back again and again to Aubrey House, her repulsion offset by morbid fascination because she could not totally deny the woman trying to grow within her. Lichinsky rebuked himself for not comprehending soon enough to save her. When he and Dick Creighton brought a sedated Merlyn Aubrey back from Bucks County General Hospital, where her friend Vita had just died, it was Merlyn who went upstairs and stumbled on Singleton crumpled beneath the photo of Charlotte that he'd torn apart. His act of vandalism catalyzed Merlyn's mingled hatred and envy of her grandmother, *but I was still too thickskulled to remove her from the house stat*. He left her with Creighton and next morning, both were dead. Merlyn's eyes, one of them crushed, lay near Charlotte's mutilated picture. An ironic capitulation: becoming *just like Grandma*. Disfigurement as victory.

"—still don't know why I destroyed her photo," Singleton was saying. Sam's attention returned to his patient. "I still have dreams about ripping out Charlotte's eyes, though not as often. Instead, I've dreamt I'm wandering through Aubrey. I know it's Aubrey, but it's a part of the house I never saw before."

"Can you describe it?"

"A long dark tunnel. Bright lights at the far end."

"That sounds like Perry's book." (William Perry's *Beyond Clinical Death*, which Sam regarded as a naive slop pile of deathbed visions. It sold in the millions).

"Indeed it does suggest Perry," Charles agreed. "Tunnels to the Afterlife . . . though they also figure prominently in out-of-body travel, I hear. Personally, I have always avoided OBEs."

"Why?"

"Because," he said self-importantly, "I am a mental medium. I act as a spiritual conduit, and that is quite sufficient. Drew went OB. Look where it got him. But what does the tunnel image suggest to you, Sam?"

"An obvious vaginal metaphor."

"Yes. Recently it occurred to me that the bright lights

often affiliated with the image might actually be the overhead illumination of a hospital delivery room."

"Hmm. Death as a direct channel into rebirth, eh? Rather a cruel idea, Charles, though it would be an interesting cultural hallucination. Most of us crave new beginnings."

"Except those who long for oblivion."

"What does *that* mean?"

"Nothing dire, Samuel. Merely a solipsistic observation. The organism's tendency towards entropy. You must forgive me. Lately I've entertained the most godless notions."

"The price of being a member of the thinking species."

Charles frowned. "Sometimes I'm not sure I can afford the tariff."

The analyst let it go. The session was nearly over; he wanted to return to the main topic. "You said you've been recalling small things that happened Sunday. Can you be specific?"

"I'll try. Do you remember that egregious ass Armbruster?"

"The sheriff? All too well."

"He actually suspected Drew of raping Vita. As if that poor crippled elf had the stamina, let alone the coordination. Well, Armbruster came to the house Sunday afternoon and demanded to question Drew. I went upstairs to summon him, but found him dead. Drew left a long note for Dick Creighton. I hid it, but eventually the authorities got their hands on it."

"You've told me all this before."

"Bear with me, Sam, I shall be faithful. Until recently, I couldn't remember anything that Drew wrote in that letter."

"But now you do?"

"Partly. He blamed the Aubrey spirit for Vita's demise. Drew went out of body to fight the ghost on its own turf, so to speak. On the deepest level, the level of the id. Drew returned to his body long enough to write down what he'd seen. He said the ghost was definitely Charlotte." Charles pinched the bridge of his nose between thumb and forefinger. "I'm getting a headache."

"All right, Charles, relax. Breathe the way I showed you. Monitor your pulse."

Singleton inhaled over a steady four-count, held it two seconds, exhaled through four beats of his heart. Again. Again. He repeated the process once more, then sat back and released the pressure on his nose. "It's fading." He looked at Lichinsky with a wistful earnestness. "Sam, I don't care what Drew claims he saw, I believe he was wrong, even at the point of death. There was a child's spirit in that attic room, or at least the . . . the *remnant* of one."

When the session was over, Singleton made no move to go.

"Yes, Charles, what is it?"

"I need your opinion, Sam. I promise it'll only take a minute."

Lichinsky glanced at his watch. "I can spare three."

"I shall be round with you. I've mentioned Alan Hunter."

"Your editor at Porlock? Yes."

"He thinks I should go back to Aubrey House."

Lichinsky sat up straight. "What? Why?"

"To jog my memory so I can write a better ending to my book."

"Isn't he aware of the danger to your health?"

"Oh, yes. That's why he urged me to discuss it with you first."

"What's there to discuss? You could have another stroke. The odds of survival would be less favorable than last time. I hope you didn't tell him you would go."

"In a way, I did."

"In a way? I haven't time for puckishness, Charles. Please explain."

"Alan agreed to release half of the second portion of my royalty advance if I said I'd return to Aubrey. I need the money." Singleton smiled. "I confess I entertained a vague notion that you might be behind Alan's suggestion, but obviously you aren't."

"Certainly not. You're beginning to regain your memory right here in New York. Why would I send you to a place that might subject you to profound systemic shock? The risk far outweighs the possible advantages. But what did you mean when you said you'd agreed 'in a way'?"

"I thought I might return to the vicinity, but not the house itself."

"What good would that do?"

"It might help me get my life back on the rails, Sam. The police still have Drew's notes and the tapes that some of us recorded while we were there. Reviewing the evidence may enable me to finish my book. And if not, I might at least venture a drive-by."

"I question the wisdom."

"Well, perhaps we should talk about it next session?"

"Yes, absolutely." Lichinsky was relieved. "So you aren't planning an imminent departure?"

"No, I'm still toying with the idea. Though I did promise Alan, more or less. And I *have* set an inquiry into motion regarding the impounded documents. Before the end of summer, I suspect I shall indeed undertake the pilgrimage."

After Charles left, Lichinsky swiveled round and switched on the Dictaphone. "Charles Singleton. Approaching crisis. Memory is returning, much to patient's distress. And yet he is coming to regard a return to Aubrey House as the key to personal salvation. Patient has shown progress in dealing with once-stultifying aspects of childhood—mother's cruelty, father's brutality to mother. Patient now less apt to blame parents for latter-day failures, though problem still very much with him . . . witness his conviction that an unhappy child once lived in the Aubrey attic. But certain dogmatic stances *are* eroding. Spiritualism beginning to give way to a burgeoning rationalism. Suspect patient is on the brink of significant personal achievement, Aubrey trauma notwithstanding. As per that trauma, note that before Aubrey House, patient maintained uneasy equilibrium as resident genius of First Universalist ESP Workshop. But four days in Pennsylvania with the late Dick Creighton and Drew Beltane undermined patient's shaky self-respect. I think he wants to regain same by going back to the house and becoming the final interpreter of the so-called cold blue light. Charles pretends otherwise, but slowly and surely, I am convinced he is giving in to this need."

Lichinsky shut off the machine. He was worried that he would lose Charles the way he did Merlyn. He glanced down at the note he scribbled during the session.

CS on all wave-lengths. All and none.

Basically a dependent man, Charles tried to cover his tendency to identify with authority figures, but he was pathetically mutable. Sam wondered how Singleton could delude himself into thinking that he, of all people, possessed the necessary psychological strength to attune himself to the house's "frequency," whatever it was.

The last time he tried, he had a stroke. The next time, he's liable to end up like Vita. A drooling vegetable.

JUNE 19 Wednesday, 4:17 p.m. Too tired last night to write usual journal entry, so here's a double helping of Ye Trials & Tribulations of Ms. Olivia Aubrey, poetess manquée. I'm sitting in the kitchen of the house, now the cleanest room downstairs. The sun is spending the afternoon in the living room. I'm scribbling by the light of a 150-watt bulb that I risked my neck installing. I found a rickety ladder in the adjoining laundry room. Latter is where Merlyn slipped and hurt her ankle and cut her face on broken glass from a jar that exploded. Half the room is still taken up with shelves stacked with bottles of putrefying preserved foods: a mausoleum of green and white parasitic life forms. Hideous!

Arrived yesterday at twilight. Not according to plan, but my early start was predictably screwed up by Ben, who balked at being left alone with Des. (Hard to blame him). He uttered dire predictions of his imminent demise if I left. Sometimes I feel like I'm in the middle of a maze designed by Strindberg. Give us this day our daily suffering.

I first saw Aubrey House in the failing light of day. Instantly seized by an extreme case of jitters. The naive city slicker who thinks the most scary thing imaginable is a deserted IRT station at 1 a.m. Compared with Aubrey House at night, a mugger in a ski-mask seems downright friendly.

Said jitters not wholly a product of my imagination. Out in the garage on a grungy windowsill I found a working flashlight without a speck of dust on it. How possible?

Spent the night in a dreary Doylestown motel. Soft "R" movies on TV. Purely out of boredom, I tried watching one. Its mindlessness made me laugh at first, but then the smarmy meanness got to me and I turned it off. Left room for an on-premises cocktail lounge, tried to unwind with Courvoisier. Covert glances from a good-looking guy who, though sitting with a strikingly handsome blonde, kept staring in my direction as if trying to place where he'd seen me before. He's probably myopic, never saw past the end of his table, but I choose to think he preferred gawking at me to the incredible woman he was with. Attitude compounded of vanity, brandy and an unsatisfied horniness.

Didn't get to bed till after 2. Troubled sleep. Aubrey House got into my dreams. Details confused, but Mama was there, so was my anonymous father and, of course, Ben. And off in the shadows, someone else, couldn't see too clearly, but I think it was a child. She kept whispering my name.

I was plenty busy this morning. First stop, telephone office, asked when they would put line in service. They said it was operant as of last night.

Relieved to hear that. It rang while I was in the living room, but when I picked it up, the line was dead. Guess they were just getting it into service. End of mystery. (And yes, I'm disappointed). I called Des. She had nothing much to say, only that Ben's driving her crazy. What did she expect? Anyhow, the Aubrey phone works. No longer cut off from the world.

Bought groceries, cleaning stuff, left note at supermarket that I'm looking for a cleaning person. Results doubtful. Lawyers said everyone Merlyn used to hire said no. I pitched in on the kitchen, the least daunting downstairs task. A big room, as modern and well-equipped as a restaurant's. The Lambert brothers certainly could have turned Aubrey House into a splendid inn.

Gave the upstairs a cursory glance: more chambers than I've ever seen outside a hotel. I picked out a bedroom, the one opposite the second-floor landing. Immense bathroom connected to it: a tub Tiberius might've staged elaborate debaucheries in. (I do seem to have my mind on salacious matters.)

After I'm done in the kitchen, I'll dust the library, set up my typewriter, lay out pencils and foolscap and the terrible fifteen-foot thesaurus and try to woo the Muse in earnest. The library opens off the salon, a showcase of a room (the lib.) with a cosiness designed for the composition of metered effusions. There's a cherrywood desk—

Olivia paused in her writing. She raised her head and listened, not sure she'd heard anything. She rose and entered the downstairs hallway, stopped. Yes. The low rap at the front door came a second time. She walked to the portal, looked for but did not find the peephole that is de rigueur in every New York City apartment.

"Who is it?" Olivia called.

An indistinct murmur. Olivia asked again, but still could not hear the reply. Shunting aside prudence, she unlatched the door and let it swing open.

A chunky grey-haired woman in her sixties waited on the porch, her wrinkled hands clenching one another below her midriff. Gravity and the world's weight seemed to defeat her: her shoulders slumped, her fleshy chin drooped on her chest; her watery grey eyes were downcast. She did not speak.

"Yes?" Olivia asked.

The woman mumbled something.

"I'm sorry, I can't hear you."

Staring at Olivia's feet, she said, "Saw your ad in th' market. Came right by."

"I see." Olivia regarded her dubiously. *Hardly the cavalry to the rescue. Barely enough strength to stand up.* "Well, I *do* need help here . . . but it involves some pretty major cleaning. There's scrubbing and dusting and a million other chores." *Why am I discouraging her? I won't find anyone else.* "I'm afraid the house has been closed up for the better part of a year."

"I know. Ever since Matt died." The words dropped like stones.

"Then you know about Aubrey House? And you don't mind working here?"

"I need th' work." For the first time, the old woman looked directly at Olivia. In her tired eyes was a plea of such intensity that the young woman took an involuntary step backward.

"You're sure you can handle the heavy work?"

"Never used t' bother me."

"What do you mean?"

"Before. When I worked here."

"You mean you were employed on the Aubrey staff?"

"Yes'm."

"When? Who hired you?"

"Oh, Mr. Jason took me on, years 'n' years back. After he passed on, his daughter kep' me."

Something fishy. "Well, I'm her cousin. Olivia Aubrey."

"Pleased t' meet y', ma'am. I'm Hattie."

"Hattie who?"

Another inaudible answer.

"I can't hear you. What's your last name?"

"Lambert."

"Lambert? The same family—?"

Hattie nodded. "Yes'm. My sons."

A cold breeze from the lake ruffled the long spears of grass.

> Well, somewhat against my better judgment, I've hired a housekeeper. Hattie Lambert, a direct descendant, it appears, of Ezekiel L., the Revolutionary War colonel who owned the tract of land later bought by my putative great-grandpop Addison Aubrey. Hattie claims she used to work for Merlyn, but I'm doubtful. She's the mother of the late Matthew Lambert, ditto his missing brother Cameron. How can she bear even to set foot in the house, let alone clean it? And if she makes me so uneasy, why did I hire her?

Closing her diary, she went to the living room. Hattie, who admittedly worked wonders with the library, was upstairs tidying Merlyn's old bedchamber, the one Olivia had chosen to sleep in. Olivia walked to the grand piano, picked up the telephone and dialed a Philadelphia number.

"Waxman, Sand and Barton," the receptionist answered.

"This is Olivia Aubrey. May I speak to Mr. Barton?"

"I'm sorry, he's away on business and won't be back till Friday. May I take a message?"

Through the archway of the salon, Olivia saw Hattie

coming downstairs. "Uh—just ask Mr. Barton to get in touch at his earliest convenience."

The receptionist took the number and rang off.

Write me down as overly suspicious, but I called Lawyer Barton to find out whether Hattie ever really worked for Merlyn. If she's telling the truth, why didn't she accept the job when Barton tried to get me help weeks ago?

It's now shortly past 6 P.M. Still daylight, but I'm not hungry. I'm going to browse the town's shop windows and eat out. I promise that I will sleep here tonight. Yes. No night terrors. I'll lock up tight and if anyone is disposed to prowl the grounds, I wish them joy of the worm.

Who am I kidding? Sleeping here tonight will take a huge act of courage.

Alan stared at the bedroom wall and tried to remember how the fight started. Miranda was nagging Bess about one thing or another and the nine-year-old answered her mother disrespectfully. "Do you hear the way she talks to me?" his wife demanded.

"Yes."

"She would never talk to you that way."

"I know. What do you want me to do about it?" ("Don't let your wife turn you into the household constable," his psychologist friend Bruno Thelwell once told Alan).

"Why do *I* have to tell you what to do? She's your daughter, too."

"Yes. Can we talk about this later?" *When Bess is out of the room.*

"Excuse *me,* Alan . . . as far as you're concerned, there's never a convenient time to bring up anything unpleasant."

"That is *not* true, and you know it!"

"Don't you yell at me!"

And their tempers soared. Miranda accused Alan of shirking responsibility; he blamed her for cataloging his faults in their child's presence. They shouted at one another and Bess ran out, crying. Miranda trembled on the edge of hysteria.

Alan went to his room, slammed the door and threw himself down on the bed. A long time passed. He got up and went to his desk. Beneath a pile of works-in-progress in the righthand bottom drawer he found a single tattered sheet of unlined paper covered on both sides with handwriting. For perhaps the thousandth time since Ava left him, Alan reread her final letter.

> Dearest, you are ruining me. I don't want to wake up in the middle of the night without you at my side. How dare you become so important to me? You have made me wonder whether any achievement will really matter if you are not there to appraise the years with and laugh at the disasters and shout about the triumphs. Is it sham, after all, this vaunted "independency" I have grappled to me like a warrior's shield? Perhaps being an independent woman nowadays is just a fancy contemporary term for being afraid to trust in anyone's enduring interest in what or who I try to be. You have filled me with tenderness and reassurance, and yet you had no right. Don't you see how central you have become to me, Alan? I look for you, I wait for you, I want you when it is dark inside and out, and I am seized by nightmare. But part-time is not enough. I must have something solid and warm and real—not one of your comforting theories, not a poem. It is the pulsing flesh and blood man I want, with eyes and arms and body and heart and lips and a voice. It is too lonely without you here. Why do you stay with her? What does she still give you? There must be something, or why aren't you here teaching

me how to laugh? Your tenderness is torture. I wonder how I can possibly go on.

And she didn't. We didn't. The devolution of love, once begun, so swiftly accomplished. Her letter was the ultimate goad that made him leave his wife and daughter, but Ava could not handle the guilt. ("Don't cast me as the other woman. I didn't tell you to walk out on them.")

Oh, but you did. Right here in print.

The vituperation of Ava's attacks inverted the passion she first displayed for Alan. Their first night together he did not understand why he couldn't even penetrate her. When he was limp and ashamed *and not before then* she put her arms around him, comforting both the man and boy, whispering, "Oh, Alan, you are so gentle, incredibly gentle." *Which is when I began to love her.* Then she told him how every man she'd ever slept with tore and humiliated her till her body manufactured its own defenses and closed up so tight that no one could ever again hurt her in the name of love. Alan held her then and they slept and when they woke, Ava's heart and body accepted him and for the first time she felt pleasure and afterwards, they both wept with joy.

But it ended.

Alan returned Ava's letter to the desk drawer.

Well, worse things can happen to the human heart.

Such as?

When it turns to cinderblock.

He removed the dust cover from his typewriter, sat down and began writing to Olivia Aubrey.

Almost bedtime.

Olivia dawdled over brandy in the Aubrey library. She'd stayed out much too late, it was nearly midnight. When she got in her car, the impulse to keep on driving took her past Doylestown and southward on Route 611 till at last she found herself caught up in the inner city traffic along North Broad Street in Philadelphia. She followed the thoroughfare till the black bulk of City Hall loomed up, then turned west and parked in the lot just off Market Street. She had a leisurely dinner in a seafood restaurant a few doors from the corner of Thirteenth and Chestnut. Between courses Olivia scribbled away on her omnipresent notepad. Sum total: three meager lines of poetry to add to the cycle.

A SIREN

Where coral splits the rosy sea
I cupped my hands and drank cold water.
All the long line his fingers fall.

She wondered where it came from, why it was. *Well, maybe I wrote about a Siren because I was in a seafood restaurant. ("Mermaid cutlets, Madame?").*

Olivia stuck the poem into a folder containing the seven other "dreams" she'd written so far. She squared the sheaf with one edge of the cherrywood desk, fussily tugged a wrinkle from the typewriter dust cover and felt satisfied that the battlefield had been readied for the morrow. Finishing her brandy, she picked up the empty snifter, shut off the lights, stepped out of the library into the main hall and carried the glass to the kitchen, where she rinsed and put it on the drainboard. Half-circling the butcher block island, Olivia entered the mud room to make sure the back door was locked.

Midnight. *No mysterious phone calls tonight, at least.* The house was almost palpably quiet. Olivia had already grown accustomed to frequent breezes rustling under the eaves, rattling doorknobs and whispering against windowsills, but now the dying summer held its breath.

She heard a soft scraping sound in the basement.

Oh, no, Li'l Miss Nervousness, no flutters this time. Old houses settle and shift and make meaningless noises. Check it out.

Olivia walked to the far corner of the mud room where a flight of wooden steps led downward. She felt for, but did not find a light switch. She went over the layout of the house in her mind and remembered that the stairs led to the wine cellar, a cul-de-sac lit by one bulb hung from the ceiling. It could only be turned on by pulling its cord, so, to descend, one needed a flashlight but she'd forgotten to buy one and wasn't about to go out to the garage to get the one she'd left there.

The only thing I'd find in the wine cellar, anyhow, would be water bugs and mice scraping their teensy rodent feet, so forget about it.

Forget about what?

That's the spirit.

Reassuring herself that the back door was secure, Olivia returned to the kitchen and shut off the light. She might have taken a short cut to the second floor via the servants' staircase off the laundry, but that was the spot where Merlyn died and Matthew Lambert's body was found, so she walked down the main hall, instead, pausing before the dining room where a portrait of Charlotte Aubrey was supposed to hang. Except for the photo albums in the attic, it was the last picture of Merlyn's grandmother in the house. The large photograph that Charles Singleton destroyed had since been taken down. Olivia almost turned on the lights to look at the dining room portrait, but decided it was a sight she could do without *for tonight, at least.*

The front door was already locked. She darkened the entry foyer and climbed the main staircase with just the moon's pale beams to guide her. A fey mood took her. She was mistress of the mansion, wearing its secrets like a dark cloak. How else should she glide through the silent house except in shadow?

On the second floor, she turned left and walked to the master bedroom once slept in by Charles Singleton. Polished walnut armoire, escritoire, an immense canopied four-poster. Returning the way she came, Olivia stopped at the octagonal sitting room once occupied by the late Vita Henry. She traced her fingers over glass mosaics set in seven windows, entered the adjacent bedroom, opened the closet. Yes, they were still there: neatly-stacked cardboard boxes containing costly fashion dolls purchased in 1904 by Derek Aubrey before he learned his deficient child could only play with soft, harmless toys like rag dolls. Olivia reentered the hallway, traversed its length, stopped under the discolored patch where Charlotte's photo used to hang.

This is it. The cold blue light. The spot where the pool of *psi* energy supposedly stayed put for decades. The

Falzer team probed and tested and measured it with laboratory techniques and instruments and defined it as a pale blue mist that neither responded to or withdrew from psychic stimulation. They said it was something new in occult research: a constant.

> Drew Beltane rejected the Falzer theory as vehemently as he did God and the Afterlife. "Charlie," he argued, "our species is in space, yet we still cling to outmoded beliefs."
>
> Admittedly, it is hard to rethink attitudes of faith. Dick Creighton wrote off tradition as "ancient error hallowed by rote repetition." Yet one might question the tenets of Church (man-made, after all) and not compromise the essential truth of God's existence. But when one encounters the Aubrey Effect, one admits that His ways are even more mysterious than generally credited . . .

Olivia did not feel especially apprehensive as she stood under the infamous spot. *Maybe I'm not attuned to the so-called invisible world.*

In that case, why don't I like that door?

The portal in question was a few feet farther down the corridor. Singleton once mistook it for a linen closet, but Olivia knew what it was.

It led to the servants' staircase.

Her tour done, she stretched out in bed and pulled the cool sheet up to her chin. Merlyn's old room was spacious, soft and luxurious from the deep-pile carpeting to the contour mattress and downy pillows, but the night was still and oppressive. Olivia had cracked the windows, but the scent of lavender heavied the air—a holdover from the time when the chamber belonged to Charlotte. The perfume clung to the furniture and the wallpaper and never faded.

Olivia's muscles ached. She flexed and released them, one group at a time. Little by little, a gentle lassitude stole over her limbs. The distant drone of an automobile neared the driveway, stopped. The world was silent. A moonbeam slashed the top of a dresser where a rag doll with a faded, lopsided grin lay crumpled.

Though her body succumbed to slumber, her mind ran on unchecked. Birthing lines of verse teased at her. Characters she might build dream soliloquies upon—a woman, no longer young. A city priest. A country cleric. An editor. A lonely child. A man trapped in a limestone cave.

I cupped my hands and drank cold water.

Her back to me.

How do I describe him? Square-cut jaw. Wide, inquisitive brown eyes. Trim mustache.

Who?

". . . prisoner . . ."

All the long line his fingers fall.

Olivia gets out of bed. She crosses the hall to the nurses station where her mother sits.

"Mama, I have to check him in. He's very sick."

Her mother smiles at her but says nothing.

"Mama, don't you hear me?"

Mrs. Culloden nods. She has blonde hair.

"Patient's name?"

"Benjamin Aubrey."

"Next of kin?"

"No."

Go down that hall, child.

A long empty passageway. Olivia struggles against air so thick with lavender she can hardly walk. The cold cement floor slopes downward. Above her head, harsh fluorescent lights buzz and flicker.

The doors of all the rooms she passes are open. She looks in and sees on every bed a body covered from head to toe with a bloody sheet.

The same body in every room.

Let me look upon thy face, O Lord.

No, my child.

ting-ting-ting-ting-ting-ting-ting-ting-ting-ting

Treading on a wilderness of fingers.

Their tips bleed pus.

The slope angles sharply down. Slippery. The ceiling recedes. Insect buzz of overhead lighting fades.

Calling.

"O-liv-i-aaaaaaaaaaaaaa—"

Mm-muh?

Hello, little girl. What's your name?

"O-liv-i-aaaaaaaaaaaaaa—"

No. I'm Olivia. Who are you?

Charlotte?

A sudden rush of sensation. Olivia reeled, found a wall, slumped against it. Her shoulder brushed a light switch. The hall went bright, dazzling her eyes. She put out a hand to steady herself. Clad only in her night-gown, she stood barefoot in the second-floor corridor. Her hand touched the door to the servants' staircase.

Christ Almighty, what am I doing out here? I never sleepwalk.

What, never? Looks like you just learned.

I never did before.

Well, dummy, maybe you were asleep at the time.

Her attempt at humor did nothing to settle her nerves.

Olivia cracked open the door and stared into the darkness on the other side. The skin of her forearms prickled; she held her breath and listened.

This time, it ain't mice.

Footsteps.

The stairwell acted as a wind tunnel, carrying the stealthy shuffling shuffling shuffling up the shaft to her ears. Too substantial for a spectre. *How much* does *a ghost weigh?* More likely, Cameron Lambert on the prowl for a new victim. Olivia stifled a whimper as the shuffling shuffling shuffling drew closer to the foot of the servants' staircase.

She eased the door shut, ran on tiptoes to her bedroom, snatched up her purse—*God help me if the car keys aren't inside!*—dashed back across the hall to the main stairs, paused to listen. *Nothing*. The silence frightened her. One cautious step at a time, Olivia descended, testing each tread to make sure it did not creak. In the foyer, she slid bare feet along the cold hardwood floor, fumbled at the front latch, turned the knob, slipped through the door, off the porch, onto the flagging.

Clouds hid the face of the moon, but the mica in the flat stones sparkled with starlight. She kept her head down to find the pinpoints of light that revealed where to place her feet—and so did not see the stranger till he reached out and grabbed her.

Olivia screamed.

We were so wrong. It's lower. Deeper.

"Those are the last words Phyllis Burton wrote in her diary before she and her husband held their last séance at Aubrey," Singleton said. "Of course, you understand what she meant, Richard?"

Creighton tilted his angular New England jaw up so he could look directly at Charles. "I haven't the slightest idea what it's all about. Please enlighten me." Said without the least trace of sarcasm.

Singleton touched his fingertips together, forming a steeple. "Lower. Deeper. Mrs. Burton was referring to the mind, Richard. The Falzer team dismissed out-of-body travel as a valid investigative tool, but Drew didn't. He knew the only way to approach the Aubrey ghost is by going down deep in the mind to the level of the id. That's where the spirit surely dwells."

And that's just where I went, Charlie.

Ah, yes, Drew, you certainly went out of body. But what did you find there?

The remnant of Charlotte Aubrey.

"Sure about that?" Creighton asked. "Maybe you saw her daughter. There may have been a family resemblance."

Gentlemen, gentlemen, Singleton chuckled, *haven't the years taught you wisdom? There is only one way to investigate a psychic phenomenon. One must gather and collate data. One synthesizes, forms hypotheses, but always stays open to new interpretations. Whatever you read at Aubrey, Drew, doesn't have to be Charlotte or anyone else. Remember the blind men and the elephant?*

I will arise and go now.

"Where are you headed, Charlie?"

"To the attic, Drew. It's where I should have held my séance in the first place."

Better not go, boyo. It gets loud and messy in the id.

You should know, Drew. You didn't make it back. But I will.

Sure about that?

"Frankly, Dick, I hope I fail. Had Drew proposed such a bleak, agnostic theory to me, I surely would have rejected it . . ."

Silence.

Fingers of mist trailing up the staircase. Charles entered the third-floor chamber where the sad little girl lived forgotten by her own mother who had a white-hot V slashing down her forehead whenever she was angry, *and she was always angry at me but when Papa comes home, he hurts her yes*

Downstairs. Charles found the picture and punished Mama, slashing—

white-hot V

—out her eyes

Charles Singleton wakes. He recognizes the danger signals: racing pulse, shortness of breath.

Breathe. One two three four.

Hold. One two three four.

Exhale. One two three four.

Again and again till his life-rhythms stabilize. Threat gone.

Charles switches on the bedside lamp, picks up the pencil and pad he always keeps at ready on his nightstand.

So now I know.

He scribbles a memo to himself, puts away the writing implements, turns off the light and goes back to sleep. For once he is not afraid to dream.

Removing the kettle from the top of the stove, Olivia let hot water trickle down the Melitta cone. When the liquid reached the four-cup line, she put the filter in the sink and poured coffee for herself and a tall man who just then came into the kitchen from the front hall. She looked at him apprehensively, but he shook his head.

"There's no one upstairs," he said. "The house is sealed tight."

"Why doesn't that make me feel better?" She handed him a cup and saucer, sat on one of the kitchen stools and motioned for him to do the same. "I'm afraid I don't know the proper protocol. Should I call you Officer Pelham, Inspector Pelham . . . or what?"

"Or what." He smiled at her. "My official title is sheriff, but I'd prefer if you'd call me just Josh."

"All right, just Josh. Sit down and answer me two questions."

He took the stool next to her. "Okay. Shoot."

"Last night I was having dinner in the Conleigh lounge. You were at one of the other tables."

"Guilty as charged. So?"

"So you were staring at me. Why?"

"Whoops . . . sorry and all that, ma'am. I didn't mean to be rude." A boyish grin, there and swiftly gone. "Why does any man gawp at a good-looking woman?"

"My ego would flutter, but you were with a gorgeous girl."

"Hm. If I called Barbara a girl, she'd slice off my ears." Josh shrugged. "She's okay, but we weren't on a date."

"Just okay?" Olivia cocked an eyebrow. "I presume you hold a degree in Advanced Understatement?"

"She's not my type."

"Methinks the gentleman doth protest too much. Aren't you supposed to prefer blondes?"

"Gentlemen do. No one ever accused me of being one."

"Touché." Olivia was amused. "Nevertheless, the way you looked at me last night had nothing to do with physical attraction."

"I wouldn't say that. But you did pick up on a certain puzzlement. You reminded me of someone and I couldn't think who. Now I know."

"Now you know what?"

"That you look a little like Merlyn Aubrey. Around the eyes."

Be nice if that were true. "You knew my cousin?"

"No. I only met her once."

"When?"

"The . . . the day before she died."

"Oh." A brief, awkward silence. "Do you mind telling me about it?"

Josh frowned into his coffeecup. "Well, Harry Armbruster was still sheriff, I was his deputy. They brought in what was left of Vita Henry to Bucks County General Hospital. When she died, your cousin became hysterical and had to be sedated. They called her psychiatrist in from New York. Harry wanted to question Merlyn about Mrs. Henry's death, but the shrink wouldn't permit it. The next morning, it was too late."

"You . . . you didn't find her, did you?"

"I sure did." A long silence. "The case finished Harry."

"How?"

"It broke him. He demanded answers. There weren't any. He couldn't accept it. He must've reread the Aubrey file forty or fifty times. The upshot of it was he decided to spend a couple of nights here. That's what finally did it for him."

Olivia set down her cup and saucer. "He stayed in the house alone?"

Josh nodded.

"Wh-what happened to him?"

"Nothing grisly. After the first night, he looked troubled, but I couldn't get him to talk about it. He stayed over a second time and the next day, I got worried when Harry didn't show up at the office in the morning. I telephoned his house, but he answered, all right. He sounded lousy . . . washed out. I asked him what was wrong. He claimed it was just that Aubrey House was drafty and he'd caught a bad cold, so he was going to spend a few days in bed. I didn't like how he sounded. Not the usual sour Harry Armbruster. Attempted to question him, but he hung up."

"Did he sound frightened?"

"No. Empty. Like he'd lost something and wasn't sure what. Couple of days later, he came back to work, but he looked like hell. Didn't seem to give a damn about anything. He dragged around like that for a while, then said he'd decided to take an early retirement. I tried to shake him out of it, but nothing doing. Inside of two months, Harry was living with an older brother in Atlanta and I was sheriff. End of story." Josh held out his cup and Olivia refilled it. He took a sip, then said, "All right, you mentioned two questions. What's the next one?"

"I want to know what you were doing outside in the middle of the night. You scared me half to death when you grabbed me."

"I thought you were trespassing."

"But this isn't public property."

He held up a forestalling hand. "Look, I was driving by and thought I saw a light upstairs. As far as I knew, no one's lived here in quite a while, so I decided to check it out."

"You saw a light? Where?"

"I'm not one hundred percent positive I did. Just a glint from the corner of my eye. By the time I turned my head, it was gone. Could've been the beam of a flashlight."

"What part of the house, could you tell? Upstairs? Down?"

"The attic."

A breeze buffeted the house. Olivia started.

"Take it easy. It's just the wind."

She smiled sheepishly. "I'm on edge. The house has been—well, disquietingly quiet."

Josh clucked appreciatively. "Disquietingly quiet? Milady talks like a poet."

"That's what I am. Or trying to be." She sounded apologetic. "Don't tell me it's a profession only slightly less lucrative than becoming a shepherd, I already know that."

"Last thought in my mind. I've dabbled myself on occasion."

Unexpected levels. "You have?"

"Got the gift from my daddy. Just limericks, stuff like that." Another of his sudden grins. "You show me yours, I'll show you mine."

Olivia laughed. "It's a date."

The moment passed. Josh looked pensive. "Aubrey House has been on my mind a lot lately."

"Yes? Why?"

"Instinct. Or maybe a sense of timing. I just got a letter from Charles Singleton. You know who he is?"

"We've met."

"He wants permission to root through police files."

"Any reason why he can't?"

"Any reason why he should?"

"It's important to him, Josh. To his health. What's your problem with it?"

His fingers drummed. "The Lambert murder is still under investigation. But Singleton says he isn't at all interested in that. He just wants to review the materials connected with the deaths of your cousin and Creighton and the others."

"Then you'll allow him to?"

"I suppose." His fingertips continued their tattoo. "But I'm concerned about the periodicity."

"How about a translation of that remark?"

"I mean, three years to the day after your cousin died, we found Matt Lambert's body on the same spot."

"What's that have to do with Charles Singleton?"

"Not just him, Olivia . . . you, too. The fact that you've showed up now . . . so close to the anniversary . . . I'm worried someone might want to turn it into an annual event."

JUNE 20 Getting on towards morning. Can't sleep. Josh Pelham is downstairs watching out for me. He's the sheriff, ma'am, in these here parts, and let me capture him succinctly: A HUNK. The poet in me cringes, but the animal side of Yrs. Truly concurs with the inescapable nomenclature. A catalog, then, of said hunkdom: very tall, possibly 6′5″ (!), startlingly blue eyes, I could impale myself on their shafts; aquiline nose, sculpted Byronically with a hint of cruelty, though latter belied by mobile lips quick to grin like a teenager. Light brown hair, a somewhat darker mustache. Wiry. Large hands with powerful musculature. Combination of strength, gentleness. One hopes. Inasmuch as I've allowed him (begged him) to stay downstairs rest of night. Says would've suggested it, anyhow, but considering footsteps I heard and light he claims he saw ("Claims," Li'l Miss Suspicious?), why am I so nervous with him in the house? Can't sleep.

Perhaps it's the stories he told. Particularly the one about Cameron Lambert. Josh thinks said CL might still be lurking about house and/or grounds. (O, my prophetic soul!) Josh is convinced CL hacked up his brother Matt. Why? One theory: possible sibling rivalry over Barbara Lincoln, head of local library. She's the blonde I saw Josh with. Easy to imagine blood feud for the likes of her. Though that doesn't explain why CL would still be hanging around Aubrey House.

Tonight is not first time Josh thought he saw mysterious lights here. He's inclined to be less pragmatic than one's mental image of a policeman (maybe it's the poet in him?) but still he asked me to obtain a copy, if possible, of the original architectural plans of the house. I asked him why he hadn't gotten them from Waxman, Sand & Barton. Said he tried, failed. Didn't elaborate. I promised I'd follow up on it.

The fact that the light Josh saw might've been a flashbeam worries me muchly. I told him about the too-clean flashlight in the garage. He looked, claims (that word again!) there's none there now. Which is another Class A Unsettler. (And so is Josh.) (Yes.)

All right, truth time. The reason I'm nervous about the man is—after all!—he's 6′5″ and comes equipped with handcuffs and gun. How do I know he's not into manacling poor damsels? More to the point: how do I know this poor damsel wouldn't like it?

Methinks Yrs. Truly is just a wee bit horny. (A wee bit?) Trust the lawman and go to sleep.

Twilight. A bird begins to sing just outside Olivia's window. Rising, she walks into the hall and heads for the servants' staircase. Before she reaches it, the door swings open and standing in the shaft, half in shadow, half in pale blue mist, is a pretty little girl who beckons for Olivia to follow. *Yes, show me the way.* The child falls backward, her mouth opening to scream, but all sound is frozen up in the first chill of morning.

And now it's your turn, bastard.

Daddy?

Olivia falls *dead if I land,* but when she strikes bottom she feels no pain as her body shatters on impact.

"Step right up and see the Amazing Broken Woman!"

Ben?

"Watch her eyes roll out of their sockets. See the small bones of her wrists splinter. You'll find the rest of her in the tent, but only if you're eighteen . . ."

daddy, i lost my hands

With a convulsive shudder, Olivia opens her eyes and finds herself back in bed.

No, stupid, you were never out of bed. More Aubrey House nightmares.

Olivia decides she'd rather mope about the house all day, tired, than subject herself to another bad dream. She gets out of bed, dons slippers, cinches her robe, walks into the hall and calls downstairs to Josh.

No reply.

"Josh?"

The house is silent.

All right, don't panic. He probably just fell asleep.

Probably.

Olivia hurries to the first floor, traverses the hall, enters the kitchen. The morning sun dazzles her eyes. "Josh?"

Unintelligible gibbering from the laundry room. She rushes in, sees him and goes rigid with shock. Josh is sitting stark naked on the floor grinning mindlessly. Livid bruises and deep, running cuts cover his chest and limbs. His hair is completely white, his eyes bulge horribly. Spittle dribbles out of his gaping mouth and down his chin.

Olivia slumps against the portal in helpless horror as the thing that was Josh lurches erect and shambles toward her *oh no no please keep away keep away keep* but the words stick in her throat and she can only shudder as the hulking beast falls on her, one knee shoving her legs apart. His flesh rakes into her as the old man clutches her buttocks and pushes his mouth *breathing hot* against her clitoris while Mama and the man whose face she cannot see hold hands and smile fondly at one another while their daughter screams and screams and—

"Olivia, wake up!"

She opened her eyes. Josh stood half-in-half-out of her bedroom doorway. *A gentleman, after all.*

"Are you all right?"

"Yes." She sat up in bed. "I was having a bad dream."

"I presume you hold a degree in Advanced Understatement?"

Josh went back down to start a fresh pot of coffee. Olivia lay back on her pillow. Her throat felt raw.

Jesus God, how can I tell when the nightmares stop?

click

"Dream record, night of June nineteenth, morning of the twentieth. It finally came clear—*the* dream. Let me describe it while it's still fresh in my mind."

As the twin spools of the cassette tape recorder revolved with an almost inaudible hiss, Alan Hunter collected his thoughts.

"The beginning's not important, it never starts off the same way twice. The real opening is the railing. Black iron bars . . . five or six uprights topped by a horizontal crosspiece. It's strange . . . when I reach the railing, I realize I'm dreaming because that's the only time I ever see it. Not that the knowledge helps much later, when things get scary. Once I mentioned it to Charles Singleton. He said there's a term for a dream you know you're in the middle of—it's called a lucid dream.

"Well, anyway, as soon as the railing appears, I know what's going to happen, but it's too late to prevent it. I tumble over it and then for a long time, I'm plummeting straight down past an endless flight of stairs that twist and turn every which way. A constructivist set-piece courtesy of Dr. Caligari. Then I see the ground coming up fast and I think I'm about to die. But when I land, I just sort of bounce. Like a slow-motion trampoline. There's no pain at all. Just the opposite, in fact—a wonderful sense of freedom. Euphoria I hope will never end. Only it does.

"The next part of the dream is what I never used to be able to remember. I'm in front of a doorway. I walk in and find myself in a dark basement with cold cement floor and concrete walls. At the far end, another opening. Faint green light flickering from it. I go up to the threshold, step through and I'm in an almost identical chamber. Only variation is that the opposite doorway is set off at a slightly different angle and the light coming out of it is a bit stronger.

"The same pattern repeats over and over again. I go into room after room. A kind of spiderweb leading to a central place I don't want to get to, but I know I have an appointment I can't avoid, so I don't turn around or stop. All the while, the green is glowing brighter and brighter. And hotter.

"Finally, I reach the hub of the maze. A dense, damp, stifling cavern. I can hardly breathe. The floor is a firewalker's pit with smoldering green coals staring up at me. And yet—how can I explain?—the room is totally dark. Contradiction of conditions, but it makes perfect sense at the time.

"An awful sense of foreboding. I know I'm not alone. Silence. I wish I could hear something. *Any*thing. But then comes the voice and I know I was wrong, it was better the other way. The words are harsh breath in my mind: *round about, go round about* but I think, *no, straight through!* and the beast leaps on me, claws tearing at my throat. I have a knife. I stab it until the thing shrieks and dies, falling on the coals. I see it clearly for the first time. It resembles the sphinx . . ."

Alan wiped his forehead with the back of his hand, was surprised how freely he was perspiring.

"The next part of the dream is the worst. I don't know why, but I cut off one of its claws. It's a dreadful mistake because as soon as I do, the fingers begin clutching open and closed and it starts crawling towards me. I run, not the way I came. In the opposite direction. The rooms look identical, except now the green light flickers fainter and fainter and finally fades out. I emerge from the labyrinth and come to a stairway going up so high I can't see the top.

"I think I don't have to hurry now because, after all, I've been running and the thing can only creep . . . but then I hear a scrabbling behind me and there it is only a few feet away. I start up the stairs, terrified. I can't go fast enough, I'm worn out. Hauling myself up one step at a time. Another step. Another. Struggling to catch my breath, but I don't dare stop.

"I reach a landing. Off to one side is a separate set of steps, a short flight leading to a closed door. I hurry over to it, but it's too small to push through. I put my hand on the doorknob, anyway, and a message flashes in my brain like a neon sign in capital letters—IF YOU GO THROUGH, THERE WILL BE A SHOWDOWN. That stops me. I wonder what to do . . . and while I'm standing there, something tugs at my trouser leg. I'm too frightened to look down at it. I frantically shake it off and dash back up the main staircase, two or three steps at a time, tiredness forgotten.

"Eventually, the flight comes to an end, opens out on the Atlantic City Boardwalk . . . except it's indoors and outside at the same time. Sort of a big stage set that's supposed to represent the seashore. Lots of people promenading in Edwardian garb. Parasols and lace caps, walking sticks, velvet stovepipe hats. There's a fat policeman with a handlebar mustache who looks like a fugitive from the Keystone Kops. When he smiles at me, I feel reassured. I think I'm finally safe. But as soon as I think that, the hand appears, clutching the door frame opening off the staircase. It drops to the Boardwalk and scuttles sidewise towards me like a crab or a tarantula. Nobody else sees it. I try to get the policeman to protect me, but he just grins idiotically and won't look down. For a couple of seconds, I'm petrified, and then I find the strength to run . . . there's an open doorway . . . I duck into it—Bingo! I'm right back where I started. At the railing. Momentum carries me over it and down I go, et cetera. Only this time while I'm falling, I wake up. End of dream. Hallelujah."

Silence. The tape machine spooled. Alan sat lost in thought. Then he spoke into it again.

"I almost forgot to mention. The monster I killed . . . it had a woman's voice."

click

Bright summer sun dappled the cool room with diamonds of fire. The scent of lavender was overpowering. Out on 611, a hiss of hydraulic brakes proclaimed the passing of a bus. But in spite of these palpable appeals to her senses, Olivia pinched her forearm to reassure herself that she was really awake. It hurt. She wondered whether it was possible to dream pain.

It was shortly past noon. Olivia got out of bed and went into the adjoining bathroom, but when she saw the size of the tub that must take scads of time to fill, she crossed the hall and used a stall shower in another bedchamber.

Twenty minutes later, she donned a lightweight green frock and descended to the kitchen where she found Hattie Lambert on hands and knees scrubbing the linoleum. The old woman looked up and managed something vaguely like a smile.

"Mornin', ma'am. Fix y' some breakfast?"

"More like brunch. How'd you get in, Hattie?"

She lowered her eyes. "Th' gentleman allowed me through th' door."

Uh-oh. The fertile seeds of gossip. "Sheriff Pelham was here on official business, Hattie."

The old woman rose to her feet faster than Olivia would have thought possible. "Official? He found m' boy Cam?"

"No. I'm sorry. Josh— The sheriff imagined he saw a light in an upstairs window last night, but he must've been mistaken. He looked and didn't find anyone. Still, it made me pretty nervous, so I asked him to stay the night." Olivia paused, then—with more emphasis than she'd intended—added, "Downstairs."

"Ma'am, y' don't owe me no explanations." Hattie clasped one hand in the other and winced.

Olivia asked her what was wrong.

"Touch of arthritis, is all. Now would y' like a few bites o' food?"

"Thanks. I *would* appreciate something light. Juice and coffee and maybe some toast. That'll be plenty. I'll be in the library." She stepped towards the door, then stopped. "Hattie, you're sure you don't mind? I mean, your hands are bothering you and, anyway, you didn't hire on as cook."

"Oh, ma'am, it's my pleasure!" Said so fervently that Olivia accepted it as literal truth.

The next few hours passed with a blissful lack of incident. Olivia ate breakfast in the library. Hattie cleared away the plates and silverware and then disappeared to perform whatever chores she thought deserved priority. It occurred to Olivia that she probably ought to assume a more active supervisory role as Mistress (Pro Tem) of the Household, but she was frankly glad to be left alone to do her work. *And happy there's another human being in the house.*

The poetic muse shed her graces on the young woman

that afternoon. She completed three new "Dreams of Power and Loss," two of which Olivia thought merely serviceable. But she felt rather satisfied with the third.

A DISPLACED DREAMER

Knobs in clans fall off in caravans,
But burnished weave discloses simple skin,
And speckled sheets reveal no Wonder Hats
And questions do not whirl in Vendomats.

The Magus molds me keys; I pry.
A portal gapes, and I, no longer caught,
  Am free beyond the jamb.
A portal shuts, and I, no longer fixed,
  Am trapped behind the jamb.

The telephone rang. Olivia stepped into the living room and picked it up.

"Hello?"

"Olivia Aubrey, please," a woman's voice said.

"This is she."

"Please hold for Mr. Barton."

Olivia was surprised. The junior partner of Waxman, Sand & Barton—executors of both Jason and Merlyn Aubrey's wills—was supposed to be out of town for another day. *Maybe I'm a more important client than I realized.*

"Hello, Ms. Aubrey?" The rich mellowness of a trained speaking voice, one the owner was obviously enamored of.

"Yes, Mr. Barton. Thank you for getting back to me so soon. I was told you'd be unavailable till tomorrow."

"My secretary relayed your message. I'm calling from Miami."

I'm that *important?*

"In that case, I owe you a bigger thank-you."

"Not at all. How are things at Aubrey House? Running smoothly, I hope?"

Olivia did not reply.

The attorney clucked dolefully. "I sense a problem."

"Perhaps. Perhaps not. I won't take up your time discussing imponderables. However, there are two matters you *can* help me with."

"And they are?"

"Number One is that I've hired a woman named Hattie Lambert to help around the house. She says she once worked for my cousin, but I couldn't find her name on the list of approved domestics that you sent to me."

"No, it wasn't, but it used to be."

"Oh? Why was it removed?"

"Your cousin Merlyn told me to take her name off."

"Why?"

"I have no idea. To the best of my knowledge, Mrs. Lambert performed her duties conscientiously. Her employment history dates back to the time of Charlotte Aubrey. But one day—I think it was six or seven years ago—your cousin discharged Mrs. Lambert and told me she was not to be hired again under any circumstances."

"Weren't you curious why?"

"Assuredly. But your cousin did not appreciate anyone questioning her motives, least of all a—" He paused.

"Yes, Mr. Barton?"

"I was going to say 'a mere hireling.' I beg your pardon."

"That's all right. Merlyn, I recall, could be more than a bit imperious when she was in the mood."

"Indeed, yes," the attorney agreed. "When she was in that humor, according to my partner, Mr. Sand, Merlyn's resemblance to her late grandmother was astonishing. Ms. Aubrey, you said there are two matters I might assist you with. The second?"

"I'd like an opportunity to examine the original architectural plans for Aubrey House."

The lawyer said nothing.

"Mr. Barton? Are you still there?"

"I am." A deep sigh. "I have been dreading this."

"Dreading what?"

"Your request."

"Why? What's the problem?"

"The problem is that we no longer have the plans. They've been stolen."

"What?"

"Ms. Aubrey, I really regret this. I wanted to inform you immediately, but my partners persuaded me to hold off in the hope that the plans eventually might turn up again."

"Eventually? How long have they been missing?"

"For more than a year, I'm sorry to say."

I'll bet you are. "How did you lose them in the first place?"

"Well, it was shortly after the Lambert brothers signed our letter of agreement pertinent to their leasing and eventually buying the house. They wanted to study the plans to see what structural modifications might be necessary to turn the salon into a restaurant. They made an appointment to that end, but since both of them still worked full-time, they could only come in at the close of our business day. Therefore, I arranged for my secretary, Mrs. Ramirez, to stay that evening. I personally handed them the plans and permitted them to work in my own office."

"Did Mrs. Ramirez stay in the room with the Lamberts?"

"No, she had her own chores to do. At six-thirty, she asked whether they'd be much longer. They said yes, so she went across the street for supper. When she returned an hour later, the Lamberts were gone and so were the plans."

"Then they took them."

"I didn't say that, Ms. Aubrey."

"It's a reasonable assumption, don't you think?"

The attorney hesitated. "I . . . ah . . . of course I questioned Matthew about it."

That was *good of you*. "And?"

"He claims they left the plans spread out on the top of the desk. For what it's worth, I think that Matt was telling the truth."

"In other words, your office was burglarized?"

"It's possible."

"What else was missing?"

"Nothing else."

"You expect me to believe that someone broke in and only stole a set of blueprints? Why? What good would they be to anyone—including the Lamberts?"

"That very question has occurred to me, I confess."

"Well, what did the police think?"

"We didn't report it to the authorities."

"Why not?"

"We deemed it inadvisable. Such a step, we feared, might cause a deal of embarrassment to the Lamberts. We took into account the fact that the Aubrey Estate had a deal to gain from continued association with Cameron and Matthew—but remember, we had no contract yet, just a letter of agreement. My partners and I questioned the wisdom of antagonizing them."

"Well, I guess you had a point," Olivia said, "but you shouldn't have kept me in the dark all this time."

"Oh, I *do* agree . . . you are totally and inarguably correct!"

First thing we do, let's kill all the lawyers. "Mr. Barton, you say you think Matthew Lambert was telling the truth. Did you deliberately omit his brother?"

"I . . . never questioned him."

"And why not?"

"Ms. Aubrey, if you knew Cameron Lambert, you would understand why I preferred to deal with Matthew..."

Six P.M. A quiet day and not unproductive. Three major events—1. Barton, the genteel shyster, called. Said reason Hattie wasn't on Aubrey recommended list is that Merlyn canned her. Also revealed ONE YEAR AFTER THE EVENT that Waxman, Sand & Barton lost plans to the house. Probably stolen by Cameron Lambert, who knows why? Ought to find new attys. for Estate, but W, S & B are the ones specified in various wills, and why should I care? Eventually, it'll all be sis' headache. At least, Barton suggested talking to old man Waxman. Prior to W's present semi-dotage, he was fairly tight with Charlotte. Probably knows as much about house as anyone extant.

Event # 2. Des phoned. Whine: "I can't cope with Daddy." I MUST come back ASAP. Ben threatening to shuffle off (to Buffalo?) this mortal coil unless I return posthaste. Ironically, conditions here have suggested a retreat, but Des' me-first attitude triggered the Imp of the Perverse: "I'll be home when I'm damn good and ready." So stay-go status decidedly ambivalent. Memo: discuss with Josh.

Event # 3. Confronted Hattie. Found her perched on a kitchen stool, cup of hot tea clasped between her two arthritic hands. Hunched over, staring into steamy depths as if reading destiny in the dregs. When she looked up at me, she must have seen it in my eyes—

"Y' found out, didn't y', ma'am?"

"That my cousin fired you? Yes."

Hattie stood up and set her teacup on the shelf. Her jaw was clenched, but in spite of her determination not to show emotion, she could not keep the tears from welling up. "I'll just go get m' things. I'll be outta here directly."

"I didn't ask you to," Olivia said. "Why don't you sit down and finish your tea and tell me what happened?"

> Hattie lost her job because of the late Drew Beltane. He wrote to Merlyn from Scotland and asked permission to investigate Aubrey House. She turned his letter over to W, S & B. They quoted preposterous rental rates. It infuriated Beltane. (Hattie didn't tell me that. Her story dovetails with things I read in the Singleton manuscript.) When Merlyn's lawyers wrote to Drew, they included a list of domestics he could hire to have the house cleaned and aired.

"So I get this letter from Scotland," Hattie explained. "He offers t'pay for any old letters 'n' diaries 'n' account books I c'n find here. He promises t' copy whatever I send 'n' ship it back by return mail. Well, Cam was in a tight spot 'n' needed bailin' out, so I rooted through th' library desk and sent some stuff off to Scotland. Sure enough, back it comes PDQ along with a check. So now I go up to th' third floor and there's tons o' stuff, boxes 'n' boxes . . . only while I'm wrappin' up some more of it t' mail, in walks Miss Aubrey and she catches me. The fire comes into her eyes, just like the old lady."

"You mean Charlotte?"

Hattie nodded. "So just imagine! She fires me over a bunch o' worthless paper maybe sixty, seventy years old. What real harm did I do? Borrowin' trash nobody had the least use for. Not like I stole nothin'—"

"Maybe my cousin interpreted it differently."

"But I'm tellin' y', ma'am, none o' th' stuff up there

meant diddly to Miss Aubrey. She took th' papers I'd wrapped an' tossed 'em in a corner without even opening them. And she never did."

"You can't know that."

"Beggin' your pardon, ma'am, but it's th' God's honest truth. Last year, m' boy Matt was clearin' space up attic 'n' come on th' very same package."

"How could he know it was the same?"

"Ma'am, I must've told th' story to my boys a hun'erd times if I told it once. He read the address. 'Drew Beltane' so on and so on, 'Scotland.'"

"Is that package still up there?"

"Don't think so. Matt 'n' Cam carted a lot o' truck out to th' stables."

Olivia poured Hattie more tea. The old woman sipped it in sullen silence for a moment, then shook her head. "Ma'am, I worked for your Aubrey family for decades. I still can't believe your cousin threw me out for a bunch of old trash that nobody could possibly care squat for. Me, who's a kin o' Simon Cameron's . . ." She tossed her employer a meaningful glance and waited for a reaction that was not forthcoming.

"I'm sorry, Hattie, the name doesn't ring any bells for me. Simon who?"

"Simon Cameron. You never heard o' him? Used t' run a newspaper here in Doylestown. Later come t' be Secretary o' War under Abe Lincoln. Simon Cameron, ma'am —four times a senator an' a distant relative to th' Lamberts—that's who I named m' boy after."

Olivia heard something more than mere pride in the declaration. What? *Defiance. Throwing the fact in my face . . . but hoping I won't notice.*

Hattie continued. "I own m' boy got into scrapes. Matt was no angel, neither, but Cam's big fault was his temper. He sometimes took a poke at Matt. Sure, an' t' other way 'round, too, but don't tell me Cam'd hurt his own flesh-

'n'-blood the way Matt got hurt. They din't let me see m' poor baby, but I heard what, 'n' I seen th' pictures. Was that right? Lettin' a bunch o' goddamn reporters mess 'round over 'm, but not his natural mother?"

The tears finally came. Olivia rested a hand on Hattie's shoulder. The old woman clutched at it and pressed it against her cheek. Olivia was caught between pity and embarrassment. Perhaps Hattie sensed it; she released her employer's hand and, with an effort, stopped crying.

"Well, Matt's dead and that's that," Hattie said flatly. "Whoever done it, it weren't poor Cam. Y' ask me, he's been hidin' ever since, maybe out there in th' woods, half starved . . ."

How comforting. Olivia thought.

Well, I hope I haven't roused the dead by countermanding Merlyn, but I've asked Hattie to stay on. Literally. With all those rooms upstairs not being used, I thought it might be a good idea (certainly a comforting one) to have round-the-clock company. Hattie was thrilled with the suggestion. Getting to sleep might be just a little easier now. I hope.

At least there is an immediate side benefit: Hattie cooks! And bakes! Even as I write, here in the kitchen, the air is laden with appetizing aroma. It's really very sad. What Hattie desperately needs is someone to mother—

The doorbell rang. Olivia put down her pen and got up, but Hattie bustled past and with an imperious gesture that startled Olivia, motioned for the young woman to sit back down. She did.

"Madame," Hattie said, "you gotta get used to bein' done for. That's why you hired a staff." With that, the old woman left the room with head and nose held high.

The abrupt change in manner amused Olivia. *A long*

overdue return to dignity? She didn't even mumble.

Hattie returned. "It's the sheriff, madame."

"Ask him to come in."

The eyebrows of the staff arched. "In the kitchen?"

"Oh. I guess not," Olivia said sheepishly. "Where is he? In the hall?"

"Certainly not. I showed him to the salon, madame."

"Uh . . . fine." *How come I'm starting to feel like the servant?*

The only functional piece of furniture remaining in the salon besides the piano was the bar. Olivia found Josh leaning against it.

"I apologize for Hattie's sense of protocol," she said. "It's more traditional than practical, I'm afraid. If you'd like a drink, please help yourself. Or are you still on duty?"

"Yes and no." He poured himself a small glass of cream sherry. "Would you like anything?"

"Thanks. Jack Daniels, neat. What do you mean, yes and no?"

"I mean, officially I'm off duty but unofficially, I'm concerned about you." A boyish grin. "Especially if you're accustomed to guzzling raw bourbon." He handed her a brandy snifter half full of whisky.

"Technically, sir, it's sour mash, but I guess I can't expect a cream sherry man to appreciate the finer points of Tennessee firewater. Skoal."

He touched his glass to hers. "Prosit."

"Why are you worried about me, Josh?"

"I didn't say worried, I said concerned. There's a difference. So you've gone and hired Hattie Lambert."

"Uh-huh. I invited her to move in. Why? Is hiring a cleaning woman a police matter?"

"You claim you heard footsteps last night. Maybe it was Hattie."

"No. Not possible. And wouldn't you have found her when you were searching upstairs?"

"A person could hide pretty well up there. All those interconnecting rooms."

"True." Olivia let a sip of Jack Daniels trickle along her throat. *Wish it didn't feel so good going down.* "But I didn't ask Hattie to stay here until this afternoon."

"When did you hire her?"

"Yesterday."

"Then she was on the premises and could have gotten at your keys."

Olivia frowned. "You're suggesting wax impressions?"

"That's how it's done."

"Why would she want to?"

Josh shrugged. "All sorts of reasons."

"Excuse me, madame."

Olivia whirled and saw Hattie in the archway. *How long's she been standing there?* "Yes?"

"Ought I set another place t' supper? It's 'bout ready."

Josh shook his head. "Actually, Olivia, I was hoping you might let me take you out to dinner tonight. Unofficially. I know it's an eleventh-hour invite, but—"

"But I don't mind." *Too eager, Li'l Miss Desperate.* "Only I can't, Josh. Hattie has been working in the kitchen for hours and—"

"It's no bother, ma'am!" Hattie interrupted. "Stew'll keep 'n' taste twice's good reheated. You go on out 'n' enjoy y'self."

"Well, I still have to freshen up and change. Do you mind waiting, Josh?"

"Go right ahead. But casual, okay?"

Olivia hurried upstairs. A quick shower, hair mousse and spray, perfume, lipstick, rouge, eyeshadow. *Hey, lighten up with the makeup, Liv. Too obvious.*

So?

She put on a white cotton dress cinched at the waist with

a wide black leather belt, found a purse, and was ready. She'd been in such a hurry to rejoin Josh that, up till that moment, she hadn't thought about Hattie's alacrity in promoting her date. But now, as she descended the staircase, Olivia wondered.

Maybe Josh is right to be suspicious. Hattie may want us out of the house so she can search for signs of her son Cameron.

Charles Singleton stood in Sam Lichinsky's doorway, rain pouring off him. The doctor waved him to the sofa.

"I'm not here for a session," Charles said. "I happened to be in the neighborhood and hoped you might have just a few minutes to talk."

"The storm cancelled all my afternoon appointments, so I have lots of time."

"Oh, but you could pack up and head home."

"Eventually. I'm in no hurry to get drenched. Sit."

Singleton leaned on his cane with both hands. "Sam, I'm sure I'm imposing. It's not that important, it can wait."

The analyst suspected the opposite. He'd never known Singleton to drop by unannounced. "It's really all right, Charles. I didn't bring rain gear. Rather than brave the elephants, as they say, I'd sooner kill time and hope the monsoon lets up. Now for heaven's sake, take a seat."

Charles wiped his damp scalp and ruefully inspected his wet fingers. "Well, it *is* rather soppy outside. I'd welcome the chance to dry the Singletonian corpus, but not on your couch. I'd ruin it."

Sam offered a box of tissues. "Pull up one of the plastic chairs from the reception area, then, and tell me what's on your mind."

Charles did as suggested and ensconced himself in a salmon-colored concave thing that resembled the cupped palm of a giant's hand. He sponged his neck with a wad of tissues.

"All right," Lichinsky asked, "what's up?"

"My friend, I have at long last succeeded in remembering what happened to me Sunday night at Aubrey House."

The casual manner in which Charles couched his momentous declaration startled the doctor. He hid his surprise with a wry smile that made him look like one of the Three Wise Monkeys. "I think I'm going to make some coffee," Sam said, "just to remind us that this is social and not professional . . ."

Lichinsky filled two Styrofoam cups with hot water. Singleton swirled four packets of artificial sweetener into his, much to Sam's unspoken disapproval. *Instant is bad enough,* he thought, *without turning it into Sweet 'N Vile.*

"Well, Charles," he prompted, "what have you remembered?"

"Almost everything."

"Almost?"

"Almost. I recall that I did indeed go to the third floor to try another séance."

"In Shipperton's attic room?"

"Yes."

"Then why did we find you lying in the second-floor hall?"

"Because I went there to destroy Charlotte's photograph."

"I see. All right, before I ask you why, we'd better

backtrack. The last time I spoke with you, all of this was still a blank. When and how did this great enlightenment occur?"

"Last night," Charles replied, "I dreamed I was at Aubrey House explaining to Drew that the spirit isn't Charlotte, but her unacknowledged daughter. Next thing I know, I'm sitting in the attic chamber."

"And?"

"I can't say precisely, you know how dreams are, Sam. But when I woke this morning, I felt as if I'd suddenly been handed a blueprint of the things that have been lost to memory all these years."

"Hmm. Just like that, eh?"

"Dear, dear, you certainly sound skeptical."

"Do I?" Lichinsky shrugged nonchalantly. "Maybe that's because you're not officially on the couch. I shouldn't indulge in social converse here in the office. It seems as though my professional inscrutability has gone and slipped a notch."

"Oh, come off it, Sam, we both know this is a legitimate session. I hadn't planned it that way, but I fully expect you to bill me for your time. I appreciate the attempt to put me off my guard and draw me out, but I am hardly blind to artifice, not after all these years as your patient."

Lichinsky laughed ruefully. "All right, then, since pretense has been dropped, shall we return to the usual format? Perhaps you'd like your customary seat on the sofa."

"No, no, I'm comfortable as is, Sam. Just tell me what your reservations are."

"I never said I had them. What about you?"

"I have none." Charles waggled a finger chidingly. "None of that answer-a-question-with-a-question business, Samuel. I read quite clearly that you are not as enthusiastic about my breakthrough as I thought you'd be."

"I come from Missouri. I want to be shown."

"Shown what?"

"The reason why you've figured out the answers."

"I'm not sure I know."

"You don't have to, not yet. Let me worry about the wheels within wheels. Tell me what you came to talk about."

"Very well. Do you know what I mean when I refer to the Drew Beltane Theory of Fragmented Survival?"

"I'm not prepared for a pop quiz on the subject."

Singleton wove his fingers together and assumed his best pedagogical manner. "According to the Drew Beltane Theory of Fragmented Survival, ghosts may not be survivals of complete, integrated personalities, but perhaps just pieces of the same."

"Didn't you give me an article on this a long time ago?"

"I did indeed, Sam. An issue of the Falzer Journal that Drew frequently contributed to. At Aubrey House, he explained his idea by asking Vita to play a chord on the salon piano. A chord is made up of individual tones that interact to create a composite musical event . . . a G seventh, an F sharp minor, what have you. As the chord fades, certain tones linger longer than others. Drew thought the same thing might happen to the human spirit. Some personality traits may die with the body, while others could hang on for a time and produce that phenomenon commonly referred to as the ghost."

"Well and good, but how is this relevant to what happened to you Sunday night in Aubrey House?"

"Because, Sam, musical tones interact with their harmonics up and down the scale. If the analogy holds for the psyche, then mightn't there be considerable danger for the medium who happens to possess a personality similar to the 'fragment' he is trying to communicate with?"

Lichinsky nodded. "I see. An ingenious notion. You're suggesting that because of your own difficult childhood, you found yourself peculiarly vulnerable when you matched the wave-length—or to maintain your musical metaphor, the key signature, perhaps—of the remnant or spirit or ghost or whatever you want to call the child alleged to have been confined in the Aubrey attic."

"Precisely, Sam. I believe that's just what happened. My feelings about my mother got mixed up in my head with the way the little girl felt toward Charlotte Aubrey. I mean, the séance began with my opening up to that child, and suddenly I *was* her—yet at the same time I was a frightened little boy hoping his Daddy would come home and punish Mama before she inflicted another undeserved beating."

"How did you feel when you were two personalities? Would you describe the sensation as split-screen?"

"Not exactly, Sam. More like a TV screen displaying two distinct pictures side by side . . . and yet the effect was synergistic."

"Can you explain?"

"I'm trying to. Two images that are separate and yet also swirled together into a third picture with its own logic. Me as a little boy and me as an affection-starved girl-child and my fear and her longing blending into a new hue: rage. And we went downstairs."

"And attacked Mama by destroying her picture."

"Yes. I must have been operating on pure id. I think the only thing that prevented me from losing my mind like Vita was the wire in my brain that shortcircuited. Ironically, my stroke may have saved my life." Charles gulped air, exhaled raggedly. "And that, my friend, is that. The conclusion of the mystery of Mr. Singleton's amnesia."

Maybe. "Quite a load to set down. How do you feel about it?"

"How am I supposed to feel?"

"Now who's answering a question with a question? There are no rules, you know that, Charles. People who try to live up to some mythical code of emotional etiquette burden themselves with needless guilt if and when they fail."

"Do you think that's what I'm doing, Sam?"

"You tell me."

"How I feel? The way Camus puts it . . . like the stones of the river. Neither elated nor upset. Curiously flat."

"It happens. Patients sometimes expect epiphanies of psychological enlightenment. But not infrequently, uncovering an important inner truth can be a thoroughly prosaic experience."

"Well, that, my good Dr. L., is a perfect description of what I feel."

The men finished their tepid coffee. The rain whispered. Lichinsky rested chin in hand and regarded Singleton thoughtfully.

"What is it, Sam?"

"Earlier you said you'd remembered almost everything. Why the qualifier?"

His patient shifted uncomfortably. "I honestly don't know. I have this vague, restless notion that I am still forgetting one final fragment."

"Can you narrow it down? I mean, whether it has something to do with Charlotte or the child or—"

"Or. Or." Charles fidgeted with his empty cup. "I think . . . I'm not at all sure . . . I *think* it concerns Drew. And maybe Richard. But it can't be too important. The major events of that night have all returned to me."

Lichinsky watched his patient turning his coffee cup in his hands. Clockwise, counterclockwise. Charles avoided eye contact.

"At any rate, Sam, I have made up my mind. I am definitely going to revisit the house."

There. I knew it was coming. "I've still got serious doubts about the wisdom of that, Charles. What would you hope to accomplish? You've solved what you need to solve."

"All but that niggling final fragment."

"You claim it's unimportant. Then why risk it?"

"*Is* there a risk?"

"Of course there is. Restimulation of unpleasant experience is never easy. Even here in New York you've had your share of difficult moments. Returning to the scene of so much tragedy might be infinitely worse."

"No, I don't think it will be." Singleton stood up. "Sam, I have been turning this decision over and over in my mind for quite a while. I have an unfinished book manuscript waiting to be cranked through my typewriter, remember? This morning I sat down at the keys. Boldly. Resolutely. And still the damned thing would not come. I cannot put it off any longer, Sam. I simply *must* go back to Aubrey House."

Lichinsky also got to his feet. "All right, if you must, you must. I'm not wholly convinced it's a bad step. There might be benefits—emphasis on 'might'. But you'd better not try it alone."

"Are you suggesting we go there together?"

"That's one way to handle it."

Charles shook his head. "A very expensive way, I fear. I can't afford to reimburse you for all the time that would entail."

The doctor waved away the discussion with a deprecatory flip of a palm. "Let's not worry about things before they happen, Charles. But take my advice. Think about this idea for a day or two."

"My mind is made up, Sam."

"I'm not disputing that. But mull it over some more, anyway, all right? And come see me again before you leave town."

"I shall. You have my word."

Outside, the rain continued to fall.

After Charles left, Sam spoke into his tape recorder.

"Surprise visit from Charles Singleton. His memory has mostly returned. That Sunday night, he went to the top floor to hold a one-man séance. During trance, presumably hypnagogic, patient says he hallucinated simultaneous regression to his own boyhood *and* virtual possession by the girl-ghost he expected to find up there. He—'they'—went downstairs to hurt 'their' mother. Thus the vandalizing of Charlotte Aubrey's picture. This suggests Charles' stroke was caused by more than mere physical stress, although one must not minimize the presence of an unwise quantity of alcohol in his bloodstream that night. But vicarious fulfillment of old fantasy of hurting mother had to be laden with intermingled elation and guilt that surely contributed to systemic overload." The doctor paused and pondered the phrase Charles used: *one final fragment*. Various thoughts ran through Sam's mind, but they were all too speculative to set down.

click

He removed the cassette, labeled and filed it, then crossed into the reception area and peeked through the parted slats of a venetian blind. The rain had slowed to a drizzle. The storm was leaving New York and traveling southwest.

Charles' phrase continued to niggle at him. What if Singleton went back to the house and remembered the last detail . . . and it turned out to be the very thing he'd been trying so hard to repress all these years?

One final fragment.

Oh God, how do I begin? Tabloid headline: Another Aubrey Horror! With subheads: A New Friend. The Sheriff's Betrayal. (Too strong? Well, he certainly used me.)

Barbara is downstairs fixing tea. My tables—meet it is I set it down . . .

Josh and I left for dinner a little before seven. The storm coming from the northeast turned the world dark. While he was concentrating on the road, I studied Josh's face. Cheeks with a trace of baby fat, mustache notwithstanding. Frank, humorous eyes, ditto mouth. Slight pinching that in another man might hint at cruelty, but surely accidental byproduct of Byronic aquilinity. Josh lacks those subtle puckerings and crinkles that age employs to stamp character on a maturer man like Alan Hunter. Sum total? Innocence to the Nth.

And yet . . . (O, how we writers adore ellipses . . .)

What has Josh been doing all the time Cameron Lambert has been missing? Why does he suspect the fugitive is still somewhere close by? (And if he's right, why can't he apprehend him?) But why would a murderer hang around precisely where he'd be likely to be caught?

When we reached the outskirts of Doylestown, Josh slowed the car and parked in the middle of an affluent suburban neighborhood neatly lined with chestnut trees. One great stone cathedral and lots of "old money" mansions hidden behind high shrubbery. Not a restaurant in sight. One clashing modern touch: across the street, a one-story glass-and-brick building with big picture windows through which I saw stacks and shelves and tables where readers and students sat. The county library.

"Why are we stopping here, Josh?"

"There's someone I want you to meet. It'll just take a minute."

"Someone" turned out to be the head librarian. We found her in the Community Room hefting an ancient 16mm Victor projector onto a table. I recognized her immediately: the blonde Josh was sitting with the other night in the cocktail lounge. Her name is Barbara Lincoln and she's magnificent. Thirtyish, six feet tall or close to it, figure like an Olympic swimmer. She had on a pale yellow silk blouse and white cotton slacks that curved over large breasts and trim hips that I'd commit a felony to possess. Corntassel hair coiffed in an upsweep. Smooth forehead, vivid blue eyes crinkled at the corners, but it'll be a good ten years before the latter qualify as crow's-feet. A wide mouth ready to laugh.

Normally I would have figured Josh was clueing me in on a previous involvement, but he'd already gone on record as not being interested in Barbara.

Looking at her (all right: gaping), I found it hard to believe any man could resist.

Josh introduced us. "Aubrey?" Barbara asked, arching a perfect eyebrow. "One of *the* Aubreys?"

"Practically the last," I replied.

Josh excused himself, claiming a call of Nature. (He had a call to make, all right, but of a different sort.) Barbara and I regarded one another awkwardly, then she broke the ice.

"I've got to set up for tonight's movies. It's free. Want to come?"

"I don't think we'll be done with dinner by then, but thank you. Josh said you were just friends, but I *did* notice the two of you together the night before."

"Thought you looked familiar. Fear not, the gent speaks sooth. I dated Josh once or twice. Nothing deep or exclusive."

The largesse of the truly rich.

"What movie are you showing this evening?"

She undid the straps of the reinforced cardboard film container. *"The Innocents."*

"Isn't that 'The Turn of the Screw'?"

"Yes."

"I think I'll pass on that one," I remarked drily.

Barbara laughed. "I suppose I can understand that. Are you staying at the house itself?"

"Mm-hmm."

"True to Aubrey tradition."

"What does that mean?"

"The Aubreys have the local reputation of preferring the company of ghosts to us po' folk." As she spoke, Barbara attached the full reel to the projector's upper arm and threaded the leader through sprockets and slots and claws. I admired the deftness of her fingers. (Never noticed before how ungainly my own hands are.)

"So what brings you to Bucks County, Olivia?"

"Call me Liv. Four syllables are more than the human mouth ought to be made to produce. I'm a writer. Would-be, I mean. I needed a secluded place to work."

"Secluded, huh? You certainly found that. Most people around here don't even like to drive past Aubrey House. Don't you find it eerie, Liv, staying there all by yourself?"

"But I'm not alone. I have a housekeeper."

She paused in the act of inserting the takeup reel on the lower arm. "You do? Who on earth?"

"Her name's Hattie Lambert."

The half-smile on Barbara's lips disappeared. "You can't be serious."

"Why not?"

"Don't you know who she is?"

"Yes."

"And you still hired her?"

"No one else will work for me. What's wrong with Hattie?"

Barbara switched the projector on and ran down more leader. "Nothing."

"Not too convincing, ma'am."

"I should keep my big mouth shut. The Lamberts are a mean, vindictive lot. And they all hate the Aubreys."

I started to ask her how she knew so much about the Lambert family, but just then Josh returned and told me it was time to go. His attitude brooked no delay. I said so long to Barbara and followed Josh out to the car.

Earlier, he told me we might have dinner in North Philly, but the place he chose turned out to be a lot closer. It was not a leisurely meal. Josh scarfed down his food and hardly spoke. The only time he rose to a topic of conversation was when I repeated what Barbara said about the Lamberts.

"Well, I guess she knows what she's talking about," Josh said.

"Why?"

"Reason Number One: Barbara knows a lot about Lambert—and for that matter, Aubrey—lore. She's got clipping files in the library on both clans. Some of the stuff dates all the way back to Revolutionary War times. Pre-Aubrey stuff . . . Colonel Zeke Lambert. His grandson got rooked out of the land by your ancestor, the Chicago tycoon."

I told him he had his history wrong. Addison Aubrey legitimately bought the tract.

"That's the Aubrey version, Olivia. Lambert tradition maintains that the colonel's grandson got taken by old Addison."

"Maybe. You said Reason Number One: Why else is Barbara knowledgeable about the Lamberts?"

"She used to date Cameron."

(Later she denied it. "I only went out once with Cam. That was enough.")

Dinner was quickly done. By eight-thirty, we were on our way back to Aubrey House. Some date. I told myself I shouldn't've let Josh see me standing next to Barbara Lincoln. That may have wised him up.

When we rounded the last curve before the Aubrey driveway, Josh pulled over. I wondered whether he'd decided, after all, to try some grab-and-grope with me—and wasn't sure how I'd respond—but he got out of the car and crossed the highway. Flashlights flared. A ring of Pennsylvania state troopers surrounded Josh and they spoke in low tones. I cursed myself for a naive sap. Yea, verily, Li'l Miss Wallflower, you've been had. (And not.) This, of course, was what our impromptu "date" was all about: a charade to convince Hattie she had the house to herself. The reason Josh detoured to the town library? So he could park me for a few minutes while he got on the phone or maybe the police band radio to marshal/coordinate his troops.

I was hurt and angry. I felt betrayed. I opened the door and started to get out to tell Josh what I thought of his tactics and manners, but a trooper "suggested" I remain in the vehicle. I did. A moment later, Josh approached and asked for my front door keys. I almost said something vile but just then I glanced at Aubrey House and saw a light glowing in one of the attic windows. I decided to cooperate.

A long time passed. It was oppressively hot. The coming storm grumbled. Josh and most of his men disappeared into the darkness, but two troopers stayed with me and the car. Their two-way radio crackled, but the only other sounds were the chirp of crickets and the mournful quaver of an owl in the woods.

Ten minutes. Fifteen. Then there was a new noise, a thin whine that swiftly grew louder, more strident. An ambulance.

Olivia stopped writing when Barbara Lincoln entered the bedroom with an elegant silver tray on which was arranged two Wedgwood china teacups, a matching teapot with teabell dangling inside and a plateful of cookies and brownies baked that afternoon by Hattie Lambert.

"It's already half-past midnight?" Olivia asked, surprised, laying back on her pillow and closing her diary.

"Yes," the librarian said. "Sorry I took so long. I thought I'd better fasten the windows before the storm came." She crossed the room and put the silver tray on a nightstand, moving with a fluidity that Olivia admired and envied. "Well, Liv, how are you feeling now?"

"Marginally better. Still sifting through a tangle of feelings. It's good of you to put up with me."

Barbara perched on the edge of the bed and rested her chin in her palm. She smiled at her new friend. "I'm just glad you thought to phone me from the hospital. I was flattered." She reached over to the teapot and began pouring. "Milk? Sugar?"

"No thanks, neither." Olivia took one of Hattie's brownies and nibbled. *Delicious*. "You're being splendid, but if I were a big girl, I would've gotten a room in town and not inflicted myself on you."

"You're anything but a punishment, lady. Here's your tea."

"Merci, bien. At least Josh didn't argue when I asked him for your phone number."

"The least the louse could do. He treated you like shit." Barbara handed Olivia a napkin and for a time, they sipped tea in silence. Then the librarian asked about Hattie's condition. "Did they let you see her, Liv?"

"Only for a few seconds."

"Did she have anything to say?"

"Not much. She grabbed my hand and tried to talk, but most of her words came out jumbled. The only thing I could make out was, 'But Cam wouldn't hurt me—' "

Barbara's cup halted halfway to her lips. "What? What did she mean?"

"Isn't it obvious? Anyway, after she said it, she went unconscious."

Barbara set the cup down without drinking any tea. "Liv, if you think Cam is hiding out here, shouldn't you leave PDQ?"

"Tomorrow. You're here tonight and Josh stationed a policeman outside."

Neither spoke for a time. Then, with her lips compressed into a thin line, the librarian said, "In case you're wondering . . ."

"What?"

"Whether Cam was capable of hurting his own mother. The answer is yes."

> 2 A.M. Still can't sleep. Rain rattling on the roof like marbles. Barbara managed to close her eyes; she's sleeping beside me. I suggested (halfheartedly) that she take one of the other bedrooms, but she knew I didn't want to be alone. Maybe she doesn't, either. I mean, she gives the impression of strength, but there was a moment when I thought I read panic in her eyes. When we were talking about Cam. Anyway, I'm plenty grateful that she's under the covers of the kingsize bed with me. I feel the warmth of her thigh against my leg as I write in my diary. Creature comfort. She smells good, too.
>
> We talked a while about the Lamberts. Barbara's a storehouse of knowledge. A colorful family. The colonel was quite the dashing hero and one of his sons went west during the gold rush. There was a black sheep, too: Josiah Lambert, the colonel's uncle. Josiah was friends with Benedict Arnold. During the war, Josiah profiteered by selling weapons to both sides. He was finally arrested for stealing a militia payroll. Shot as a traitor, though the loot was never recovered. Fascinating. Barbara promises to let me browse through the library clipping file.
>
> I'm still angry at Josh. I know he was only doing his job, but he might have found some other way. Who is he, really? Obviously not the callow lad I took him for.
>
> Wonder what Mr. Alan Hunter is doing now?

Sleeping, dummy, what else? Why do I think of him so often? I only met him once . . . but I toy with the notion that he matters. Romantic foolishness, of course, though I've been scribbling away at a sonnet to Alan. But I can't quite bring it off. Who said something unfinished is a golem? Isaac Singer?

Eyelids finally growing heavy. Maybe I can actually sleep?

The sound of churning water. Murmuring nearby, a woman's voice that she almost recognizes. Olivia cannot see, but a gentle hand guides her into the whirlpool. Hot water swirls over ankles and calves, over her intimate parts. The soft insistent press of warm lips on her naked breast. Tongue tip lapping her nipple.

The woman's voice again: "Oh, God, Jay, love me!"

Mama?

"Lower, Jay. Deeper."

Words heard long ago. Mama tossing on her sickbed with a dementing fever. Uttering secrets she never wanted Olivia to hear.

. . . pregnant . . . yours, Jay . . . Ben thinks . . .

Ben knows, Mama.

The lights go on. Olivia sees again.

Vortex. Water down the drain, spinning and the wheel slows as the croupier takes chips from her.

"Black. You lose."

The wheel spins.

"Black. You lose."

The wheel spins.

"Black. You lose."

No more money. Des takes it all from the croupier. Her sister sticks her tongue out and sound stops. The crowd disappears. Des turns her back, is suddenly across the room, is gone.

Empty casino. *No*. One wheel starts to spin. Olivia crosses an enormous room strewn with pianos and boxes of old clothes. The turning circle stops. Two crossbeams that end in wide mouths opening and closing.

Kissing.

Vortex.

"Follow me. Collect your winnings." Olivia feels the voice against her thighs. The gaping archway. Down a long sloping hallway past slabs that hold dead men covered with bloody sheets.

The crossbeams spin.

A corpse sits up in one of the rooms.

Alan?

She runs towards him, but Josh slams the door in her face and the floor tilts down like a coal chute, dumping her into the basement *and I am trapped beyond the jamb*.

DIES IRAE, DIES ILLA

SOLVET SAECLUM IN FAVILLA

Bright light splashes down from stained glass groins. A solemn voice intones Latin.

QUANTUS TREMOR EST FUTURUS

QUANDO JUDEX EST VENTURUS

The cathedral darkens. Not the sun. The dying light from hundreds of candles sticking out of sconces. They gutter, one by one, and go out. On the altar, a pine box nestles on crossbeams.

INGEMISCO TAMQUAM REUS

The lid lifts.

CULPA RUBET VULTUS MEUS

Your name is Olivia?

Daddy?

The coffin opens with a crash. A corpse glowing sickly blue drifts out, soars over her head, swivels perpendicularly in the air. A filthy old man, naked. Fingernails at least a foot long, each curving to a sharp point.

Daddy?

ME, BASTARD.

Ben's hands stretch out sidewise like crucified Jesus. His gigantic penis stands erect as he flies at Olivia with hideous speed. She tries to scream, but his rotting mouth stops her. His swollen tongue prods between her teeth. Her throat burns. She shoves him off, but he comes back. Again. His member stabs at the lips of her sex. Olivia twists aside and sees that the long curved daggers at the ends of his hands are not fingernails but sharp metal spikes. She catches at them, jerks them toward his body. The old man thrashes in terror. Fighting for each gained inch, Olivia bends the ten points inward till with one great convulsive thrust, she forces them into his chest.

BITCH!

His scream fades. The old man goes limp. His head lolls over the crook of her elbow. Olivia mourns and curses him and—

No! My *pieta!*

—and then she woke.

Darkness.

The cold breath of storm whispered up her legs. She went stiff, afraid to move.

Oh, God, I know where I am!

Olivia extended her hands to either side. Each touched a wall. She slid one foot forward, guessing that somewhere not far ahead the floor stopped and the servants' staircase descended at a steep angle.

—beware the sensation of well-being. When Drew Beltane followed the presence into the rear stairwell, he experienced such a rush of good feeling that he pitched dizzily down the flight headfirst and nearly fractured his skull. Later, when I held my séance, Drew urged me to be on guard against sudden euphoria because it was a danger signal that the "cold blue light" is about to attack . . . analagous, perhaps, to the way the hairs at the nape of the neck prickle just before lightning strikes.

Well, Olivia thought, *euphoria's one thing I don't have to worry about. Too damned scared.*

She heard the scream again. In her dream, it was Ben, but now she realized it was Barbara. Forgetting her own terror, Olivia turned around, instantly bumped into the door, pushed it open, ran down the hallway to her bedroom. She found Barbara sitting up in bed, pale, trembling.

Downstairs, the policeman on duty pounded at the front door.

"What happened?" Olivia asked, patting the blonde's shoulder.

"I woke up and you were gone and Cameron Lambert was standing in the doorway."

"Where did he go?"

"I . . . I don't know."

"Barb, are you sure you were really awake?"

"Ten seconds ago, I would've said yes—but now that you ask, suddenly I'm not at all sure."

"Believe me, I understand."

"Liv, you'd better go let that cop in before he busts down the door."

Olivia did so. When she returned, Barbara was busy shoving the dresser against the bedroom door.

"But what if there's a fire, Barb?"

"I'll chance it if you will, love."

My God, what did Cam Lambert do to her?

Late morning. Olivia opened her eyes, saw she was alone, panicked and yelled for Barbara. A cheery hail from downstairs. A moment later, the tall librarian came up with a tray laden with breakfast, a newspaper and a large brown envelope.

"I borrowed a robe, Liv, do you mind?"

"Of course not." Olivia felt like she had a new sister. She admired the garment Barbara selected: black silk with lace at collar and cuffs. *Obviously belonged to Merlyn.* It was too short for Barbara, barely ended below her hips. Her muscular legs were tan and lightly covered with a down of golden hairs. Olivia stared at her with something akin to envy.

Olivia picked up the newspaper. It was a local one. She asked Barbara where she'd got it.

"A reporter was at the door. I told him you've gone home to New York. I also took the phone off the hook. You need rest."

"You're an angel, Barb." Olivia opened to the front page and read the lead article.

HAUNTED HOUSE CLAIMS
MOTHER OF LAST VICTIM

DOYLESTOWN—Another casualty occurred last night at the infamous Aubrey House, 4.9 miles north of here on Route 611. Mrs. Hattie Lambert, 64, was stabbed in the forehead, neck and shoulders. She is the mother of the late Matthew Lambert, whose hacked body was found in the same house last September.

Joshua T. Pelham, Bucks County Sheriff, found the victim in an attic storage room. She had been attacked by an unknown assailant wielding what might have been a carving knife. The weapon has not yet been found.

"There were no signs of a struggle," the sheriff revealed. "Mrs. Lambert must have been sitting there for some time. There was a tray of food on the floor beside her but the meat was cold and the ice cream was like soup. Nothing was eaten."

Mr. Pelham scoffed at the notion of supernatural foul play. "Whoever did it is a bona fide flesh-and-blood maniac," the sheriff opined. He also added that the victim must have seen her attacker's face. "If she recovers, I have no doubt she'll be able to identify the culprit."

Mrs. Lambert was rushed to Bucks County General Hospital. Her condition is reported as critical.

Aubrey House has a bloody history. One year ago—

"They don't mention she's in a coma," Olivia observed.

"Probably to give the impression that Hattie will name the guilty party any second now. Discourage the gawkers from snooping for poltergeists. Killer at large. No ghosts need apply."

"Maybe." Olivia noticed the brown envelope. It was addressed to her in Desdemona's handwriting. She opened it, withdrew a loose scrap of folded paper and a sealed business envelope that bore the Porlock Press logo.

"Good news?" the librarian asked. "You could use some."

"From my hypothetical publisher."

"Well, don't keep us in suspense. Open it."

Olivia nervously ticked her fingernail against the envelope. "Maybe I'd better build up to it." She opened the folded message, instead; it was written on cheap lined paper. The scrawl might have been that of a five-year-old.

Dear Olivia,

Why don't you come back and take care of me? I always took care of you. If you don't come home soon you won't find me here any more.

Your Father

The message infuriated Olivia.

Barbara patted Olivia's hand. "Methinks yond brow darkens."

"It's nothing." She crumpled the note, tossed the wad on the breakfast tray and picked up the Porlock Press envelope.

Dear Ms. Aubrey,

You've been on my mind lately. Phrases remembered from your poetry reecho: "How many sorrows shall we strangle in the crib?" "Butterfly, perched upon a palm, sips a shape of gold." The quality of the woman implicit in every line. I've shown your work to Jno. Brant. He's impressed; offers to publish your Kennedy assassination poem in 2nd issue of *Incisions,* his new "little" magazine, to be deliberately issued on Nov. 22nd.

I mentioned to him your Brontean digs in Pa. It appealed to his romantic nature. Jno. needs somewhere to lay out miscellaneous paraphernalia (word processor, manuscripts, etc.) to put the 2nd issue together. Would you consider allowing him to spend a week at Aubrey House for that purpose? I'd like to join him, and so would Chas. Singleton. Perhaps this is a cheeky suggestion, I don't know, but I confess to hoping you'll not only say yes but be on hand as hostess—unless you don't consider it proper. Call me at my office?

Fondly,

Alan

She reread the letter, cheeks flushing. The notion was delicious: a week with Alan *and* Jonathan Brant, *kindred spirit*. Swinging her legs over the bed, Olivia slid into slippers, rose and flung her faded pink bathrobe about her shoulders.

"Something *that* important?" Barbara asked.

"Yep. Got to make a long distance call post-haste."

She rushed downstairs. The phone was off the hook. Picking it up, Olivia depressed the bar to clear the line for a dial tone but as she did, it rang.

Damn! "Yes, hello?"

"Hi, kiddo, it's me."

"Mrs. Culloden?"

"One and the same. Look, hon, are you sitting down?"

The question brought Olivia up short. Her breath caught. "What's wrong?"

"It's Ben."

Olivia was still standing by the piano when Barbara came in. The off-the-hook signal jabbered unheeded. The blonde took the phone out of Olivia's hand and hung it up. She looked into her eyes and saw the pain. Barbara gently stroked Olivia's cheek.

"What's the matter, Liv?"

"My . . . father. He's dead."

A long silence.

"He took his own life."

Barbara rested her hands on Olivia's shoulders. "Come on, love. I'll help you pack."

After phoning the library to make arrangements for it to run without her for a day or two, Barbara carried the luggage to the car and stuck it in the trunk. Then she fetched Olivia, settled her in the right front seat and sat in the driver's seat herself. She backed out of the garage, spun the wheel, headed for 611 North. As she nudged the gas pedal, she asked Olivia whether her father was very old or sick.

"Moderately up in years, but his mind was going."

"I'm sorry. How did he take himself off? Or would you rather not talk about it?"

"He sneaked downstairs while my sister was on the phone talking to a friend. Slashed his throat with a kitchen knife."

"My God, how awful."

"Differentially," Olivia replied. "At least he's no longer hurting." She lapsed into gloomy silence.

I refuse to feel guilty, Ben. No more mornings when you don't know where you are or who I am or why Mama isn't with us any more. Maybe you did the smart thing.

Convince Des of that.

I refuse *to feel guilty.*

(*"I* always took care of *you."*)

The fantasies were done for good. No more Mistress of the Manor, no playing hostess to Alan Hunter or Jonathan Brant or Charles Singleton. *All dreams cancelled on account of suicide.*

The lush Pennsylvania countryside fled, was replaced by the paler green of New Jersey. Minutes and miles bled drop by drop into the past. *Present drab, future bleak.* Aubrey House would go to Desdemona. Olivia would have to find a job and a place to live. There'd be little time or energy remaining to write, but what did that matter? No real difference whether she wrote poetry or washed dishes or collected garbage. Existence arbitrary. No fixed final meanings, nothing to trust in or believe.

Wonder whether Ben mentioned me in his will? What's the going rate nowadays for dead wife's bastard?

A COLD BLUE LIGHT

■

The Colonial Inn is an expensive four-star restaurant on East Sixty-first Street near Park Avenue. The menu changes to reflect the season and the cuisine is "elegantly American," which the chef interprets broadly to include whatever ethnic/regional influence he is in the mood to indulge. The appointments are exquisite: Irish linen, crystal goblets, Tiffany silverware, porcelain blue china. No staff member at the Colonial has ever been known to speak above a polite murmur in the dining room and even the kitchen is relatively quiet. An ancient sommelier presides over the wine cellar; there is a legend that he once had an assistant manager discharged for entering his subterranean domain with too heavy a tread.

The clientele of the Colonial match the décor. Jacket and tie are de rigueur even in hot weather. Luncheon reservations must be made at least one week in advance, while dinners are generally booked a month or more ahead of time during the theatre season.

Alan Hunter eyed the doorman of the Colonial doubtfully. That worthy wore black velvet pantaloons, a lace-frilled long-sleeved shirt, a sparrow's-tail waistcoat worked with gold thread and scrollwork brass buttons. He had a supercilious expression which seemed to convey the thought, *Yes, Yes, of course it's August, but that's your problem*. I *never sweat.*

He opened the restaurant door and Alan entered. He was glad the management was not above furnishing air conditioning. It was all the editor could do not to tear the tie from his throat.

"Alan," someone said. "Over here."

He glanced left and saw Charles Singleton seated at a small marble table in the bar, his cane hooked over the back of a brocaded chair. Alan walked over to him and shook hands.

"Good to see you, Charles. What're you having?"

"Dubonnet. The maitre d' strongly advises against mixed drinks." Singleton held up a small card printed on fine stock. "The menu has already been selected by our hostess, and the chef has provided these libatory guidelines. I wonder whether we'll be required to pass an entrance exam before they permit us to dine."

Alan smiled as he took the opposite chair. "I'll tell you, this sure isn't in my league."

"More than a league," Charles punned. "We're fathoms out of our depth. What on earth made her select the Colonial?"

"Beats me. I was surprised to hear from her at all."

"Indeed. Her situation seemed to admit of no further dialogue. But here's the headwaiter."

The gentleman in question appeared silently and asked Alan if he cared for something from the bar.

"Yes, thank you. A Southern Comfort manhattan."

"If I may be so bold, sir, the chef has listed those liquors best suited for the luncheon he is preparing."

Alan nodded. "The fact is noted, but my order stands."

"Very good, sir." The depth of the waiter's scorn was implicit in the unruffled equanimity with which he accepted the déclassé countermand. "If you would care to follow me, gentlemen, your table has been readied."

Alan helped Charles to his feet and handed him his cane. The waiter guided them to the rear of the restaurant and up a flight of steps. Singleton pulled himself up one step at a time with the aid of the handrail. They were shown to a small, private chamber tastefully decorated with tapestried wall hangings and a great cut-glass chandelier. Pointing to it, Charles whispered, "Reputed to have once hung in the palace of Victor Emmanuel."

Olivia Aubrey sat at the head of the table, her place by right. She greeted them with a smile and a casual wave of her glass of Jack Daniels.

Alan pointed to her drink. "Bet that's not on the chef's card."

"It sure isn't," she grinned mischievously. "Today is pure ostentation, don't y' know? Whatever the chef serves will be too good for the likes of me. Alan, Charles, I'm delighted to see you again."

"Likewise, Ms. Aubrey," Singleton said, lowering himself into a chair. "The more pleasurable for being serendipitous."

"True," she nodded. "Alarums and Gilbertian reversals, gents. Deus ex bourgeoisie. But let's get comfortable and enjoy the posh. Afterwards, I'll reveal my deep, dark secret."

Luncheon began with cream of sorrel soup, proceeded through individual servings of turbot véronique accompanied by a vintage chablis, Château Rothschild 1982; ginger ice; quails with polenta and new peas served with a smoky Pouilly Fumé; mixed greens with devil's rain dressing. The meal ended with gâteau St. Honoré, espresso and benedictine in miniature goblets molded from Belgian chocolate.

Charles Singleton nodded at the waiter to indicate he would like a refill of coffee. "Olivia," he stated, "you have doubtlessly inflicted me with a terminal case of gout, but if I survive, I shall entreat with all my heart to be adopted as your faithful lackey."

She blew him a kiss. "You've got the inside track, dear heart."

During the meal, Alan couldn't take his eyes off Olivia. He wondered how the shy, sad-eyed hopeful of a few months earlier could turn into the smiling, confident young woman sitting at the table's head. It wasn't her chic dress or pearl necklace, nor was it even the carefully-applied makeup or the stylish hairdo. *She's positively glamorous. Why? Because she herself believes it now?*

Charles leaned towards her. "Olivia, this magnificent repast surely will cost you three of your four shapely limbs. To what do we owe this gala occasion?"

She toyed with her liqueur. "I ought to apologize for behaving like a kid in a candy factory. I had a quote unquote milestone birthday recently and self-indulgence is a new experience. This afternoon *is* a shocking splurge, but after the estate is settled, I'm going to be rather well off."

"Your father was wealthy?" Singleton asked. "I didn't get that impression when last we spoke."

"I hope you didn't mind that phone call, Charles. I needed to unburden. I know we hardly know each other, but . . . well, I think of you as a family friend."

"I should hope so. I am that."

"Anyway," she continued, "you didn't hear 'rich' because I didn't know it myself then. Now . . ."

"Now," Singleton said, "you are having second thoughts on disclosing your deep, dark secret?"

"Maybe." She worried her lower lip with her teeth. "I'm not going to chicken out, but the trouble is there's just no subtle way of putting it."

"Putting what?"

"That I'm the illegitimate daughter of Jason Aubrey." Complete silence. A waiter within earshot actually frowned. "Gentlemen, I'm afraid I've shocked you."

"Heavens, no," Charles said, recovering. "The fact is a stunner, but you're hardly culpable." He puffed like a personification of Wind on an old sea-chart. "Then you're not Merlee's cousin, after all."

"No. She was my half-sister."

Alan regarded her speculatively. "Olivia, you didn't spend all this money today just to tell us this."

"No. My little announcement is by way of preface. My big news is that my father—I mean the man I used to think was my uncle Jason—left very careful instructions in his will concerning me. He made two conditions. First, I had to be at least . . . a certain age. Second, my legal father had to be deceased." She took a deep breath. "Gents, you are now looking at the new owner of Aubrey House."

Two weeks later, Alan waited on the curb in front of his apartment building with a tan suitcase, typewriter and a large sealed cardboard box beside him on the sidewalk. He shaded his eyes against the bright September morning sun. He still couldn't believe he was about to go to Pennsylvania with Olivia (and Charles). When Alan told his wife Miranda, she surprised him by raising no serious objections to the trip. *But maybe that's because I tried to make it sound like I don't really want to go.* Bess was sorry her daddy would be away for a week, but he promised to bring her a special present when he returned.

One thing that made the trip go down easier at home was the fact that the time he was away would not be subtracted from his accrued vacation. Porlock regarded the trek as a last-ditch attempt to salvage *Tragedy in Bucks County.* Singleton's manuscript delivery date had been officially extended, but even that term had almost expired and Alan warned his author that he could not buy him any more time. "Either you turn in revised copy by the end of September or we'll be forced to terminate your contract." Which would mean the return of the royalty advance money *which Charles probably doesn't have a red cent of left*.

An enormous black Rolls-Royce turned into his street and slowed at the curb. *My God, it's them!* Though Olivia said she'd rented a car, it never occurred to Alan that she meant a chauffeured limousine. The driver got out, opened the rear door and took Alan's luggage.

Olivia sat in the middle of the back seat. She was smartly dressed in a sleek designer dress, tinted stockings and polished high-heel shoes. *Hardly traveling clothes*. On her far side Singleton looked pale and pinched.

Alan got in and greeted his friends. "Are you awake, Charles? I know you regard mornings as a personal insult."

"I'm awake," the other man replied. "Doing my best to hold up, considering the circumstances."

"What circumstances?"

"He's referring to the Rolls," Olivia explained. She did not seem nearly as perky as last time Alan had seen her. "I'm afraid I've upset Charles. I didn't mean to."

"There, there," Singleton consoled her, patting her hand. "I know it wasn't intentional. But when this battleship drew up at my awning, I experienced decidedly unpleasant déjà vu. Merlyn also hired a Rolls to take us to Aubrey. But let's say no more about it. Coincidences *do* happen." He sat back in his seat and closed his eyes. Olivia exchanged concerned glances with Alan.

For the first time, the weight of the responsibility Alan had elected to assume bore upon him. Going to Aubrey House partly meant salvaging *Tragedy in Bucks County,* as well as laying out the second issue of "Incisions" ("Sorry, Olivia, I don't think Jonathan Brant will be able to join us, after all"), but mainly it promised the chance of a sweet illicit moment out of time with Olivia. (*Dream on, Lothario*). But now, looking closely at Charles, Alan saw deep lines and an unhealthy hue.

"What do we do," Olivia whispered, "if he becomes ill?"

Relishing the nearness of her, Alan took out his wallet and showed her a three by five business card. He gestured for Olivia to lean closer so he could also whisper. As she did, he enjoyed her clean soap-scent, was fascinated by her ear's delicate tracery. *Rein in, kimosabe. Fastest libido in the East.*

"This is Charles' doctor," he said, pointing to Sam Lichinsky's name. "I promised I'd call if anything the least bit stressful happens. Maybe you'd better copy the phone number, too."

Olivia nodded, found a pencil and inscribed the data on the back of an envelope that she took from her purse. Before she could turn it over to write, Alan glimpsed the return address. *The letter I sent her. She kept it.* He felt inordinately flattered.

"Oh, dear," Singleton said suddenly.

"What's the matter?" Alan asked.

"I just realized this is nearly the identical date that I set out for Pennsylvania last time. One day later, actually."

"Yes," the editor nodded. "I was kind of hoping you wouldn't think of it."

"So you knew. Tch, tch. I suspect you are a mere pawn of the insidious Dr. Lichinsky." Charles sat back and smiled feebly. "And they say you can't go home again."

The Lincoln Tunnel led them to the New Jersey Turnpike, which, in turn, connected with the Pennsylvania Turnpike. They did not stop to eat. There were breakfast things in the car: fresh orange juice, croissants and coffee.

Olivia offered chilled Soave. It marginally improved Charles' disposition. "Merlyn," he said, "brought champagne. Naturally."

Olivia murmured to Alan, "Thank God I changed my mind and bought Soave."

The chauffeur took the Doylestown turnpike exit and got onto Route 611. Straightening up, Charles riveted his gaze out the side window. Olivia, who all morning had been comparatively relaxed, closed her eyes and looked tense. Alan still felt the warmth of her leg against his.

The amber fires of autumn dappled the land. Stands of shagbark and chestnut oak broke the long rolling rhythm of pasturage and crop fields.

"New Yorkers," said Alan, "tend to forget how glorious a color green can be. Our eyes are underprivileged citizens."

"Editors!" Charles sniffed. "Scratch one and discover a writer."

"I *beg* your pardon."

"Oh, Alan, stroke your own ego. You court the native tongue like a lover, but you never actually place it between the sheets . . . excuse the atrocious figure of speech. Seriously, though—why don't you have a tilt at writing?"

"Un bel di," the editor promised, suppressing a smile.

Both Charles and Olivia's eyes turned to the road. They said it simultaneously: "The next turn." They looked at each other, startled, then laughed.

"Shall we hire out as a Greek chorus?" Charles asked.

Olivia smiled at Alan, presumably because their companion's mood appeared to be taking an upswing, *but what happens when he actually sees the house?*

The Rolls turned off 611 into the driveway and there, far across dun fields, rolling lawn and sparkling water, Aubrey House shimmered in the September heat.

"Well," Olivia murmured, "I'm home."

Singleton glanced oddly at her but said nothing.

"Well," Alan asked, "how does it feel, Charles?"

He sighed. "Somehow, I've been expecting that question."

"Sorry to take your emotional temperature, but Lichinsky told me it's my job."

"Dear Sam worries unduly. I remember virtually everything that happened to me last time. Aubrey has no surprises left."

"Translated, that means you feel all right?"

"Well, Alan, if 'all right' equates with a total lack of emotion, then I am fine. I have seen the house. Qua house. I know what it is capable of and I shall be on my guard. Period."

Leave it to a shrink to overreact and upset people. Nothing wrong with Charles, he's in perfect control. Alan turned his attention to Aubrey House. Surprising how unforbidding it looked. Actually rather cheery. Expensive, expansive. Its overgrown lawn dipped and rolled forever. A distant sparkle of water. Not too far from the house was a two-story building that Alan assumed to be a stable, but Olivia identified it as the garage. The chauffeur swung the wheel in that direction, but she directed him to pull up to the front door, instead.

"I hope the hostess isn't being rude," she said, "but I've got an errand of mercy that won't take long. Do you mind going on in ahead of me?"

"Not in the least," Singleton replied. "I, for one, will be glad to uncramp my middle."

The car stopped. Olivia handed her keys to Charles. "I'm not freaking you again, am I?"

"No." He smiled. "You *have* studied my manuscript, haven't you?"

"What are you two talking about?" Alan asked.

Singleton explained, "The last time I came to Aubrey, Merlyn appointed me to open the door with her keys."

"Oh." *Déjà vu galore.*

The men got out. The chauffeur toted their luggage and Alan's cardboard box to the front door.

"What on earth do you have in there?" Singleton wondered. "It looks like it weighs a ton."

"It's stuffed with manuscript and galleys. This isn't a vacation for me, I have to work as usual."

As the Rolls started back down the drive, Charles fitted key to lock. The door swung open. Singleton stumped onto the threshold and stopped. "Oh, dear. It's a bit harder than I thought. I feel like Dante having a second go at the Pit." A deep breath, a squaring of shoulders and he reentered Aubrey House.

Alan wrestled the suitcases through the entryway, shoved his cardboard carton into the foyer and closed the door. The smell of old wood newly polished; he looked up and saw the great central staircase and did not like it. It proclaimed, *I am very costly,* to which Alan silently appended, *and ugly.*

Singleton had already entered the living room. Alan followed and saw a largish chamber nearly devoid of furniture. His friend rested on his cane and shook his head.

"Are you okay, Charles?"

"My petals haven't shattered. It's just that the last time I saw this room, it was quite different." He gestured at the leering cherubs over the mantel. "Note how Aubrey taste lagged behind Aubrey affluence." Charles pegged over to the piano. "Take this warhorse, for instance."

"What's wrong with it?"

"Oh, a Chickering grand is a perfectly acceptable instrument, but a serious musician who could afford better would have chosen otherwise. Rather like purchasing ordinary champagne when one could as easily afford vintage. One mightn't fault the former, but a few extra dollars does make a difference to the discerning." Charles struck a C chord and did not stir till it faded.

"You look thoughtful," said Alan.

"A touch of nostalgia. I was remembering an impromptu concert Vita favored me with the day of our arrival. I do miss her."

Alan walked to the bar. "There's no champagne, but otherwise there's plenty of booze. May I fix you something?"

"No, thanks, but I'm sure Olivia would say to help yourself." Singleton clucked dolefully. "The demon rum. An Aubrey tradition more honored in the breach."

Alan measured an ounce of Southern Comfort into a highball glass. "You're alluding to Olivia's real father, Jason?"

"I am. *And* her grandfather Derek." Charles pointed to the portrait of a bearded man clad in turn-of-the-century garb. "That's Derek. Drank himself to death nearly fifty years before his son Jason did the same."

"I wonder why."

"Oh, the reason for Derek's dissolution seems clear enough. He gradually fell apart when Charlotte forced him to confine their child to the attic. But as for Olivia's daddy? Who knows? Perhaps he pined away for his true love."

"Olivia's mother, you mean."

"Yes. I always wondered how Merlee's mama, Ariella Ennis Aubrey, could possibly walk out on her family when she did. She and Jason took Merlyn to Europe for dire medical assistance. I thought Mama Aubrey must be heartless to abandon Merlee at that critical time, but maybe that's when she found out about her husband's affair and his illegitimate daughter. Perhaps she just couldn't hack it. After all, Ariella lived in Aubrey House, too. What is anyone's breaking point?"

"Good question," Alan murmured, swallowing an ounce of liquor. "The same thing's probably occurred to Olivia.

Hope she isn't giving herself needless guilt trips for 'breaking up' sister Merlyn's home."

Singleton shrugged. "She's a poet. I'm sure she has flagellated herself on that score, too. Now, my dear professional gadfly, inasmuch as I have imprudently returned to the scene of the crime, I may as well relive all the unpleasant moments while the fit's upon me. Will you come and hold my hand?"

"Sure." Alan finished his drink and followed Charles through the archway and down the main hall to a door opening on the kitchen. He was pleased to see that the latter was free from Victorian excesses. It was, instead, a modern facility equipped with deep freeze, Westinghouse refrigerator, electric stove, microwave wall oven, breakfast grill and a long butcher-block work island over which dangled a formidable array of sharp knives and cleavers.

Charles stepped through a portal in the kitchen's northern face. Alan walked after him and found himself in a dim rectangular room with two high grimy windows that let in a few straggling rays of sun. A stone floor; pipes; ceiling beams half hidden in the semidarkness; on the left, three clothes washers and a pair of heavy-load dryers. To the right was a space filled with several aisles of tall plank shelves holding clay jugs and widemouth glass jars fitted with sealed caps. Alan strolled down one of the rows and read labels: tomatoes, plums, cherries, pears, apples, pickled melon long since penetrated by mould and fungus. *Decay preserved for the ages.* Somewhere, a thin sibilant seeping hiss.

This was where Merlyn suffered the accident that sent her to the hospital with Creighton and Singleton on the night that Vita Henry lost her mind.

Merlyn ran down the servants' stairs and into the laundry room just as one of the jugs, imperfectly corked, blew apart from fermentation pressure. She slipped in the mess and sprained her ankle and tore open her cheek. Dick and I drove her to Bucks County General Hospital.

When Alan reached the end of the aisle, he found Charles hovering near a plain wooden door set in the east wall. It swung gently in a whisper of air from the upper stories. He joined Singleton and peered up into the darkness. *So this is where it all happened: where Creighton bled to death and Merlyn broke her neck. Where the police discovered Matt Lambert's butchered carcass.* For the first time, Alan stopped thinking of Aubrey House with that suspended disbelief that he exercised when reading a ghost story by E. F. Benson or M. R. James. Now, standing in hushed shadow, he was potently struck by the fact that he'd voluntarily committed himself to spend several nights in what was reputedly an extremely dangerous place.

"What's wrong?" Charles asked; his intent gaze and the rigid lines of his face betrayed his stress. "You feel something?"

"No. Do you?"

"Oh, yes," Singleton nodded. "The Aubrey Effect is stronger than ever. It's odd . . . I can read it like a fluctuating current on the skin of my arms. I never experienced anything like this before. This is the way Drew Beltane read power. I never could."

"You sound worried."

"I am."

"How come? I think it'd be a useful gift."

Charles shook his head. "I'm too inexperienced. I feel, but I can't calibrate. And I remember something Drew once told me."

"What?"

"That reading the power is the first step in going under."

* * *

They went back to the foyer and mounted the main stairs to the second floor where a corridor also ran the length of the house, paralleling the downstairs hall. Over them, a coven of bronze guardian angels and fat cherubim erupted from the wainscoting with sinister asymmetry. By the light of heavy sconces, Alan walked a long vista of doors that reminded him of the endless corridors in MacDonald's *The Princess and the Goblin*. He gave a low whistle. "No wonder the Lamberts wanted to open an inn."

Charles pointed to the front of the house. "The first door on the right is the master suite, which I rather fancy. There's a canopied four-poster that I slept in last time."

"It's yours, as far as I'm concerned."

"Straight down this side is where Vita was, and Drew was next door to her. Right here—" Singleton indicated the door opposite the stair landing "—was Merlyn's bedchamber. I believe Olivia is using it now. It's where Granny Charlotte once slept and to the right is Derek Aubrey's bedroom; Dick Creighton used it. There's a connecting door between the two suites, but one presumes Charlotte kept it locked."

A connecting door? Alan made up his mind which room he would sleep in.

Charles continued toward the rear of the house, stopping at the spot where he'd had his stroke, the place where Charlotte Aubrey's photograph once hung. Lichinsky had warned Alan that Singleton must approach it with extreme caution, but all there was to see was a faded rectangle of wallpaper that the picture frame once hid. Charles regarded it indifferently. Alan ambled a few steps farther down the hall, pausing before a narrow portal. An unpleasant sense of déjà vu. *I've been here before. But that's impossible.*

"That also leads to the rear stairs," Singleton said.

Alan shoved the door open and looked in. Darkness. He shivered.

"Now do you feel something?"

"No, Charles. It's cold, that's all."

"And you're disappointed."

"How did you know?"

"Because," Charles said, smiling grimly. "I recognize a closet romantic when I see one. I pray you beware, lad. Aubrey has a tendency to cure that condition."

Alan let the door swing shut. "You're looking somewhat peakèd. Why don't we postpone the rest of our tour till later?"

"No, no, I'm bearing up better than the good Dr. L. thought I would. I'd just as soon tilt at the last windmill while it's still daylight." He tapped Alan's wrist playfully. "There! 'But a touch of my hand, and ye shall be upheld in more than this.' Come along now—this way. Excelsior!" He did a smart about-face and goosestepped up the hall to the front stairway. Alan smiled at his esprit.

The third floor: still more rooms; dust-sheeted love seats, chairs, footstools, furniture, knickknacks of bygone times when three generations of Aubreys lived beneath the same roof. The corridor was shorter; it ended at a junction with an elbowed passage off which the household servants' quarters opened.

Charles firmly planted his cane, gripped it with both hands and leaned on it to rest. With a touch of the old Singletonian flair, he turned to Alan and said, "The last windmill, boyo—the attic prison where Emily Shipperton was both nursemaid and jailor to Charlotte and Derek's poor urchin."

As Charles spoke, someone emerged from one of the rooms behind him. Alan could not help but gape at the most beautiful woman he'd ever set eyes on. In one swift hungry glance he admired what he saw—her lustrous flaxen hair, her sparkling sapphire eyes, crimson flush of glistening lips that parted when her naked tongue licked the moist corners of her mouth *like a jungle cat savoring its prey*—and what he could not see, he coveted.

Charles misinterpreted Alan's expression. "Well, it seems as if Aubrey is affecting you, after all. What are you feeling now?"

"Charles, turn around."

Singleton did. "Oh! I had no idea there was anyone else in the house."

She smiled and came forward to greet them. "Hi, I'm Olivia's friend Barbara Lincoln. She wrote that you were all coming today. Let me guess . . . you're Mr. Singleton, right?"

"Indeed."

She pursed her lips. "A choice, now. Jonathan Brant?"

"No. He couldn't make it. I'm Alan Hunter."

"Well, I had a fifty-fifty chance." Her smile broadened. Alan dared to imagine it was mainly intended for him. "So you're Olivia's editor?"

Alan told Barbara he was pleased to meet her *to put it mildly.* The two of them shook hands. Alan liked her firm, warm grip. He liked it even better when Barbara gave his fingers an encouraging little squeeze just before releasing them. *Meaning—what?*

A voice called from downstairs: "Alan? Charles?"

"Liv's back!" Barbara hurried down the corridor to a door at the far end. "Come on." And she was gone.

Alan slowly exhaled. "Mr. S., if she's one of your Aubrey phantoms, don't clue me in, okay?"

Singleton waggled a finger. "Mr. H., pray recollect that you are a married man."

A fact I'm hardly likely to forget. Alan began to follow Barbara, but Charles stopped him.

"Not that way. Not the servants' stairs."

Though he hated to admit his energy was flagging, Charles reluctantly allowed Alan to assist him down to the first floor. They found Olivia and Barbara chattering away in the kitchen like long-lost sisters. A stout grey-haired woman sitting in the breakfast nook began to get up when she saw the men, but Olivia patted her shoulder and told her to stay put. She introduced her as the housekeeper.

"Hattie just got out of the hospital," Olivia explained.

"I trust it was nothing serious?" Singleton politely inquired.

Alan saw Olivia was surprised because Charles didn't know about the latest Aubrey incident. He gestured for her not to mention anything. With an almost imperceptible nod, she said instead. "Hattie had an accident. At the moment, she can't talk much above a whisper, but the doctor doesn't think there'll be any permanent damage."

"Well, that's encouraging," Charles replied. "And now might I play the demanding guest and beg a tot of tea?"

Hattie started to rise, but Olivia wouldn't permit it. "Mrs. Lambert," she said with mock severity, "I already told you you're here as my guest, *not* my employee. The doctor said you ought to be in bed, but if you want to sit up with the big folks, you have to stay put and let us wait on you."

Hattie smiled uncertainly. Charles, seeing she was uncomfortable, sat down opposite her and affably patted her hand. "I've a tyrant of a physician, too, Mrs. Lambert. What say we convalesce together?" Hattie responded gratefully to his amiability and the two chatted in tones too low for Alan to hear. Not that he was especially interested. His attention was divided between Barbara and Olivia, he wasn't sure in which order.

While the blonde filled the teakettle, Alan murmured to Olivia, "Thanks for catching my signal. Charles isn't one for watching the Six O'Clock News. His doctor said if I could keep the news about Hattie's attack from him, it'd be just that much less stress he'd have to deal with."

"Yes, that's what I thought. He's lucky to have a friend like you." Olivia impulsively placed her fingertips on Alan's wrist.

"Nice of you to think so." He was about to cover her hand with his when he noticed Barbara watching. Sudden ambivalence. Alan drew away from Olivia. "Maybe later on, the two of us can talk?"

"About my poems?"

"Uh-huh."

"You name the time and place."

The teakettle whistled. Barbara turned off the heat, fetched cups and poured for Charles, Hattie and Olivia. As she leaned over to do so, Alan studied the way her cool yellow blouse silhouetted and cupped her large breasts. Barbara glanced up, saw him staring and smiled. Her eyes held his for a moment—and then Alan realized Olivia was also watching him. He stared intently at a spot somewhere in the vicinity of his shoes, thoroughly nonplussed.

"Sugar?" Barbara set a cup in front of Charles. He shook his head. "What about you," she asked Hattie, "do you still take milk?"

Mrs. Lambert turned away and totally ignored Barbara, much to Olivia's surprise and embarrassment. Alan guessed that Barbara must unintentionally be threatening the old woman's territorial instincts. *Serving tea is one of Hattie's duties. She obviously resents anyone usurping her place.*

Singleton smoothed over the awkward moment. "This tea is just the thing for outpatients and weary travelers. I confess, though, that I am growing ravenous. I know you haven't had time to shop, Olivia, but if you have eggs and butter and cheese, I can whip up a palatable fondue."

"Tomorrow maybe," she demurred. "You're my guest, Charles. As soon as I help Hattie to her room, I want to take you all out to lunch. No arguments." She squeezed her friend Barbara's hand. "You live around here, you pick the place."

Alan looked from one to the other woman, unable to decide which one appealed to him the most. Barbara was arrestingly lovely, yet she lacked the intense, *vulnerable* sensuality that Olivia possessed. The blonde indeed stirred his passion, but he had a keener need for that lost pulse of feeling that he associated with Ava. He felt, instinctively, that Olivia also longed for something more than just physical intimacy, *but still . . . Barbara . . .*

"Hello, Mr. Hunter, hello!" Charles called. "Is anyone at home in there?"

"Excuse me," said Alan. "I didn't realize you were speaking to me."

"Doubtless," Singleton said, "your mind tosseth on the seas with your argosies, Antonio."

"Doubtless. What's up?"

"We are about to escort these fair damosels to lunch. I cheekily suggested that Porlock Press might be prompted to spring for the tab. Now don't start hemming and hawing, lad. Barbara only chose a diner."

Barbara said that since they were underprivileged New Yorkers, they probably never experienced "that great Philadelphia culinary institution, the cheesesteak," consisting of several paper-thin layers of grilled beef smothered in onions and fiery red sauce in an Italian roll. She and Olivia and Alan each consumed sandwiches washed down with beer.

"Andeker?" Alan asked suspiciously. "Never heard of it."

"It uses Czechoslovakian hops, like European beers," Barbara said. "Trust me. You'll enjoy it."

He took a sip. "You're right. It's good."

"Have I ever led you astray? Yet?"

Alan glanced at Olivia and decided to pass up making a flirtatious comeback.

Charles restricted himself to clear broth, a green salad without dressing and a small quantity of skinless chicken breast. "I need to keep my system clear for later."

"Later?" Alan echoed. "What *are* you planning?"

Singleton waved away the question. "I've been meaning to adopt a more sensible food regimen. No time like now." He turned to Barbara. "Ms. Lincoln, is there anything valuable alleged to be hidden on the Aubrey estate?"

She finished her stein of Andeker before replying. "Are you referring to Josiah Lambert's legendary câche of gold?"

"Am I? How does the story go?"

The librarian steepled her fingers and thoughtfully tapped them to her chin. "Let's see—I can look up the particulars at the library, our clipping file is quite complete. I read it a time or two, so I can fill you in on the general outline of the story."

"I'm all ears," said Charles, resettling himself like a little boy who knows he is about to hear a tale of adventure.

"The land Liv's house was built on was ceded to Col. Ezekiel Lambert, but it originally belonged to his uncle Josiah, a very colorful rascal. He sold weapons to both sides during the Revolution, which made him distinctly unpopular with his neighbors. He was friends with Benedict Arnold. That stood Josiah in begrudging good stead, at least as long as Arnold's name was unbesmirched. Josiah eventually was arrested and accused of stealing a small fortune in gold. Funds intended to finance the needs of a regiment, as I recall. He swore his enemies fabricated the charge to discredit him. He maintained it to the bitter end."

"And what was that?" Singleton asked. "The bitter end of a rope?"

"No, it was wartime—he faced a firing squad."

"And the money?"

"There's a story," she told Charles, "that Josiah buried it under the cellar of his farm and meant to retrieve it after the war. The building burned down—allegedly torched by a Lambert—and every square inch of the foundations has been dug up by the Lamberts and for all I know, maybe even an Aubrey or two but nobody ever found a single farthing."

Charles said, "One of the tidbits of information that I recall running across when I was first investigating Aubrey is that the ruins of the original Lambert farmhouse still may be seen somewhere on the property. Do you have any idea where, Olivia?"

"Not in the slightest. One day, maybe, I'll check into it, but till I can manage to find a gardener willing to brave that overgrown lawn in broad daylight, I think I'll try to contain my curiosity."

"Why are you so interested in the Lamberts, Charlie?" Barbara asked. "Thought you came here to investigate your so-called cold blue light."

"Everything about Aubrey interests me," he replied, daintily nibbling at his chicken. "While Hattie and I had tea earlier, I managed to draw her out a bit. I got the impression there is something of value that the Lamberts knew about concerning the Aubrey estate. Perhaps she was referring to Uncle Josiah's gold."

"Could be," Barbara said, highsigning the waiter for more beer.

"That would explain her remark to me that she knew what her son was looking for. I wonder whether Hattie means the son that's missing or the one who was slaughtered last—"

"Please, Charles," Barbara shuddered. "Not now."

Alan was surprised at her squeamishness. He saw a covert look pass between the two women and wondered what it meant.

Five-thirty P.M. Sunlight slanting through the open door spotlighted dustmotes. Alan sat behind a cherrywood desk in the Aubrey library sipping Dubonnet and reading Olivia's latest poems. He liked them.

Olivia paced, nervously awaiting his Olympian decision.

Well, shall we appear inscrutable?

Why?

Because she needs to develop her own critical eye. What she thinks is more important than my—anyone's—opinion.

"Come on, sit down, Olivia. Let's discuss these." Careful to keep any tincture of emotion out of his voice.

She dutifully took a seat. She looked as if she had a relative in surgery.

Alan tapped his pencil against his teeth but said nothing.

After a long silence, Olivia gloomily said, "I can tell you're disappointed."

"Am I? What about you? Be honest now—are these poems truly representative of your best efforts?" *Say yes, Olivia . . . don't you know they are?*

Olivia stared down at her lap and bit her lip, revealing a jagged incisor that Alan found perversely appealing. She raised in-curved fingers to her cheeks and raked away uninvited tears.

Uh-oh, she can't handle this. Better say something encouraging PDQ . . .

The doorbell rang. Olivia hastily rose, murmured something and hurried out. Alan's first reaction was to curse himself for an inept bungler, but after a moment he decided he really hadn't committed any irreparable damage. Once he explained to Olivia that he'd merely been trying to instill self-confidence in her, she'd be relieved and probably grateful. *But I've got to pick the absolute right time to explain.*

Barbara strode in and planted herself in front of him, hands on hips. "What did you say to upset Liv?"

"Nothing. Why are you in such a huff?"

"You made her cry."

"No. She did that herself."

"I don't know what you mean. You must've said *something*."

"Not necessarily. The two of you are obviously bothered by I-don't-know-what."

"What makes you say that?"

"At lunch, I noticed you and Olivia exchanging mysterious glances. Mysterious worried glances."

"I don't know what you think you saw, but I *do* know she came out of here very upset and I don't like it. Hasn't Liv got enough troubles already? You know about her father, don't you?"

Alan answered yes, though he wasn't sure which father Barbara was referring to: Olivia's real parent Jason, who drank himself to death, or her ostensible father Benjamin Aubrey, the old man who slashed his own throat. *Some choice. No wonder Olivia's so vulnerable. Practically an open wound.*

"So what went on in here that got her so worked up?"

"It was an unfortunate misunderstanding, Barb, but it'll all iron out fine. We were discussing her poetry and she got the erroneous impression that I was disappointed with it. Look, let me find her and clear this up. Where is she now? In her room?"

"In the kitchen, but she's talking to someone."

"Who?"

"The sheriff."

Charles was also in the kitchen sitting at the breakfast bar when Alan came in with Barbara. The sheriff turned out to be an extremely tall young man with a mustache and a quick boyish grin. Olivia introduced him to Alan, but he could see her heart was not in it.

Maybe I made her cry . . . but he must've done something worse.

Josh Pelham fidgeted with a brown paper shopping bag he was carrying. "Look, Olivia," he said, "I know there are probably waterbugs you'd be happier to see than me, but I came over here on the slim chance that I might still be able to redeem myself." He rattled the paper sack. "Besides, I've got some stuff here that I had to bring by."

"Beware geeks bearing gifts," Barbara murmured.

Josh glared at her. "It isn't a peace-offering. I'm not that tacky, Barbara."

"*Do* set us straight on the true nature of your tackiness, sir."

Ignoring Barbara, Josh withdrew a white business-size envelope from the paper bag and handed it to Olivia. "This letter belongs to you."

"Then what are you doing with it? Why wasn't it in my mailbox?"

"I saw it in there yesterday and took it to forward to you in New York. I didn't know you were about to return to Aubrey House."

"Sorry for the inconvenience. You certainly found out fast enough that I'd arrived."

"I keep an eye on this place. It's my job."

"Well," Barbara said, "I hope, for Liv's sake, there was nothing to see while she was away."

Josh shook his head. "Nope. No more mysterious attic lights. Nothing out of the ordinary."

Olivia glanced at Singleton, but he did not appear to be paying attention. "Well, thanks for the postal delivery. Did you enjoy reading my mail?"

"Nobody opened it. Word of honor." Barbara made a rude sound. Reaching back into the bag, Josh took out two thick brown envelopes and placed them in front of Singleton. "Olivia persuaded me to let you look these over."

The color drained from Charles' cheeks.

"What's wrong?" Alan asked, alarmed. "You looked like you've—"

"Seen a ghost?" Singleton smiled wanly. "Yes, Alan, in a way I have." He drummed his fingers on one of the envelopes. "Odd how the house hasn't affected me nearly so deeply as what I know is inside this package. But it makes sense. Aubrey is just a matter of bricks and wood and stone, but these—well, quite another matter." With unexpected briskness, Charles stood up, took the two envelopes and said, "I'll be in my room, Olivia. Please dine without me. I'll forage for supper later."

He was gone before anyone could protest.

"Well," Alan said, "It's obvious what you brought him."

Josh nodded. "All the notes and tapes he and his friends made the last time he was here." He turned to Olivia. "Will that buy me a begrudging thank-you?"

"A small one, maybe." Then she grinned. "What can I tell you, Josh? I don't do 'mad' well. Let's start over, shall we?" With a casual glance at Alan, she asked the sheriff to stay to dinner.

Instant enmity, Alan decided.

Aubrey House was one thing in sunlight, quite another in shadow. Alan felt its brooding hulk when the light failed. Old timbers crackled and muttered.

Barbara helped Olivia set the table for four. They sat down to dinner, two men and two women. Alan recollected there were five people at table the first time Singleton came to Aubrey. *What was the phrase he used in his manuscript? 'Each of us seeking something intensely personal. Five separate houses, if you will. All of them haunted.'*

Alan glanced at the portrait of Charlotte Aubrey on the dining room wall. No trace of that unsettling expression Drew Beltane once saw in her eyes, *but that was in the photo Charles destroyed, not this.* Alan turned and studied Olivia's face, could not see any family resemblance. If anything, Barbara looked more like Charlotte. At least they were both blondes.

Nudging Alan, Josh jerked a thumb at the portrait and muttered, "That lady must've been one fine piece of ass."

Charming chap.

The meal was excellent. Barbara found a dusty bottle of '61 bordeaux in the wine cellar. It was the perfect complement to the ragoût that Olivia prepared. "It'll taste even better reheated," she said, "so if Charles gets hungry later, he won't starve. By the way, Barb, did you take a platter up to Hattie?"

"I tried," Barbara said, reaching for the bowl of garlic bread, "but she wouldn't let me in."

"What does she have against you?"

"She resents me, Liv, because once I dated her sons but haven't devoted my life to mourning them."

"Mourning Matt, anyway," Josh said.

"Since you bring it up," Barbara said sarcastically, "what's the latest in your impressive efforts to find Cam Lambert?"

"Please, not now," Olivia begged.

But Josh propped his elbows on the table and expounded. "The big question mark is whether Cam really murdered Matt. Not that I'm ruling out fratricide, but it's hard to imagine it with brothers who allegedly got along fairly well."

"That's news. According to whom?" Barbara asked.

"According to their mother."

"Every time I saw them, they were fighting."

Josh pretended ignorance. "What about, Barbara?"

"You know damn well what. Cam had a horrible temper, you know that, too. He was insane. Look what he did to his own mother."

"Hold on," said Alan, "are you talking about the way Hattie was injured?"

Barbara turned to Olivia. "I'm sorry, love. I'm afraid I've got a big mouth."

"Never mind, Barb, Alan already knows some of it."

"And I'd like to know the rest. First off, I thought the other Lambert brother was missing."

"Well," Josh said, "we think he may have run away at first, but then came back and hid out in the woods near here."

"Why?"

The sheriff explained. "So he could sneak into the house, probably at night."

"I don't believe what I'm hearing," Alan said, staring at Olivia. She kept her eyes riveted on her plate. *Why in hell would she invite us here, then?*

Maybe for the same reason you came?

"Don't get upset," Josh said. "After the incident with Hattie, I had this place checked out floor to ceiling. If Cam was hiding here, he's gone now, and if he tries to get back in, I'll know."

"How can you guarantee that?" Barbara challenged.

"I want to station a man in the vicinity of the garage to watch the house. I hope you don't object, Olivia?"

She shook her head no.

For an awkward moment no one spoke, then Josh made an effort to lighten the mood. "Hey, folks, too grim. How about capping off dinner by taking a ride somewhere? All four of us."

The idea did not particularly appeal to Alan, and Barbara didn't sound very enthusiastic, either, but Olivia said she wouldn't mind getting out of Aubrey House for a while. She urged her friend to come with her.

"I don't know," the blonde murmured, "I've got a busy day tomorrow. Where'd you have in mind to go, Josh?"

Josh shrugged. "Wherever."

"Well, how about New Hope?" Barbara suggested. "It's not far and it's a nice night to amble around and observe the quaintness. I know a hangout there that, believe it or not, serves beer for a quarter a draft."

"You're kidding," Alan scoffed. "What label?"

"Malted horse-piss. What do you want for twenty-five cents?"

Before they left, Alan checked in on Charles Singleton. He found him curled up on the bedspread of a mammoth canopied four-poster, a sheaf of loose papers in his lap, a pair of reading glasses perched on his nose. Charles was listening to a man's voice that came from a portable cassette recorder.

> "—strange day. Small wars and crises. Merlyn has been less than glamorous. Mistress of the manor warning the peasants to shape up—"

"Dick Creighton," Singleton said. "It's so strange hearing him again after all this time. Sam would call it restimulation, I suppose. I call it . . . what? Painful."

> "—suggested I take a walk with her around the grounds, but I declined. At this stage, my feelings about Merlyn are rather mixed up. True, I still want her, but I don't think I like her much. She's capable of—"

"Charles," Alan said, "me and Olivia and Barbara are going out for a drive. Would you like to come along?"

Singleton shook his head. "I've put off this business long enough. Now that I've embarked upon the stream at last, I fully intend to shoot the rapids. Or drown in the attempt."

"Oh? Well, that's the sort of thing I'm supposed to prevent. Maybe I'd better not go out, after all."

"Now don't go treating me like an invalid or a five-year-old. I'm not going to subject myself to any undue stress. Besides—" He paused.

"Besides what?"

"Hush a moment . . . I want to hear this." Singleton pressed the tape machine's STOP button, pushed REWIND and then PLAY.

"—welter of theorizing and fact gathering about Aubrey House, no significant psychic facts have as yet emerged. Not to my mind, anyway. *If* there is a constant, and *if* Drew ran into it today, all it would seem to suggest is that there is a kind of stored energy that we have not definitely charted as yet. No reason to assume it's in any way connected to the survival of the human spirit . . . other than the possibility that it's emitted by the body during moments of great emotional stress, turning the walls of certain houses into sponges of electric power of a type unlike other familiar forms. A sensitive person might well resonate with certain frequencies of this *psi* force, and his brain could perhaps interpret the experience as supernatural. Thus the whole complex mythic structure of four thousand years—ghosts, demons, heavenly visitants—might be reducible to this one bleak physiopsychological fact—"

Singleton put the tape on PAUSE and shook his head. "Dear, dear, all the time that I was wrangling with Drew, I just assumed he and Richard were on identical sides of the philosophical fence. But the elf never went quite *this* far. Still . . . what if Richard had indeed snagged some fragment of the truth?" Suddenly remembering that he was not alone, Charles snapped out of his reverie and asked Alan what they'd been talking about.

"I was arguing with you about taking it easy tonight, and you said, 'Besides . . .' "

It puzzled the other for a few seconds, then it came back to him. "Ah, yes, what I was going to say, Alan, is that the first time I came to Aubrey, the power took several days to energize."

"And what does that mean?"

"That whatever potential for destruction the Aubrey Effect possesses, it probably does not build to a peak till quite a while after it is catalyzed."

"And how do you think it becomes catalyzed?"

"When people come to investigate. But since neither you nor Olivia nor our blonde Venus intend to probe the cold blue light, I should think you'd all be perfectly safe. As for me, I have no intention of staying here long enough to let it get another crack at me. Now why don't you stop keeping the ladies waiting? Go out and enjoy yourself."

Alan still hesitated. "I can't help but feel funny about this, Charles. Lichinsky told me that under no circumstances was I to leave you here alone."

"But I'm not alone. Hattie's also here. I intend to visit her for a while and chat."

"Well, knowing that makes me feel a little better. In that case, I'll join the others."

They took Barbara's car and rode with the windows open to let the cool air circulate. Alan wanted to sit next to Olivia and clear up the misunderstanding about her poetry, but Josh reached the rear door first, held it open for her and got in beside her, much to Alan's chagrin. Not that it was a form of penance to ride up front with Barbara, but she was a careful driver who kept her eyes on the road and avoided conversation. She did have a tendency to speed, which amused Alan, considering that one of the passengers was a law enforcement officer. But Josh was oblivious to anything other than his backseat companion. Because the windows were down, Alan couldn't hear much of what the other man was saying, and that was a mercy because Josh seemed to be boring Olivia with a long, pointless story about some of his relatives who went to California during the Gold Rush. When he finally exhausted the tale *and my patience,* the sheriff launched into the declamation of ostensibly amusing doggerel verse, presumably of his own authorship. Alan pitied Olivia. *At least I can't hear him all that well.*

As if reading Alan's mind, Barbara muttered, "Poor Liv. Trapped."

"You mean I'm not the only one who would've preferred a threesome?"

"A threesome? Or a menage à trois?"

"What?"

Barbara bit her lip. "Sorry. Sometimes my fresh mouth runs ahead of my common sense. I don't know what made me say that."

"It's all right." *How did Nietzsche put it? 'The degree and kind of a person's sexuality reach up into the very pinnacle of the spirit.'* "So you're not enamored of Mr. Pelham, either, eh?" Alan kept his voice low, *not that he's paying attention to anyone but himself.*

"Can't tell you why," the blonde whispered, "but I don't like him and I certainly don't trust him."

"Join the club."

"Think we can persuade Liv to become a member?"

Alan loathed the tavern. No place to sit down. They stood crowded flank to flank at the bar. True, the beer was cheap and almost drinkable, but the decibel level was ear-shattering; no one could hear themselves think, much less talk. The place was jammed—*tight like the IRT at rush hour*—with college students. Alan found this triply disconcerting—first, because of the accidental press and play of empty-eyed young girls with trim bluejeaned figures that tormented him like Tantalus; second, because they *were* girls and Alan felt ashamed of himself for lusting after every single one of them, even though he realized (at least intellectually) that if his wish were granted, he would fulfill the old Chinese curse: "You should live long enough to attain all you *think* you want in life"; third—

But what if you could *have them all? What about afterwards? Listening to their adolescent prattle, pretending interest in ideas I've already thought and trashed twenty years ago . . . would it be worth it?*

[Well, Mr. Benny? Your money or your life?]

[I'm thinking . . .]

—third, the average age of the clientele isn't much above twenty-one or -two. *Even the bartender's a kid. And I'm an antediluvian frotteur.*

"This place makes me feel like Methusaleh's drill sergeant," he shouted at Barbara standing next to him.

"Cheer up, Pops," she said, her lips close to his ear so he could hear her. "Will it help if I buy the next round?" She turned her head to let Alan talk to her in similar fashion.

"It couldn't hurt," he replied, heroically resisting the urge to lick her earlobe. "You *really* enjoy coming here?"

"Once in a while. Why?"

"It doesn't impress me as your style of establishment."

"Oh?" She cocked an eyebrow. "And what *is* my style?"

"More sophisticated."

"Such as this nectar?" She tilted back her head and drained her glass. Alan watched the pulsing muscles in her throat and wondered what her perspiration tasted like. She set down the empty tumbler and turned to order a refill; as she did, she brushed into Alan with her hips. When she leaned across the bar to signal the tapster, the intimacy increased. *Deliberately?*

The bartender refilled her glass. Barbara kept her back turned to Alan. The loudspeaker began blasting the frenetic rhythms of the Emerson Lake & Palmer arrangement of Aaron Copland's *Fanfare for the Common Man*. Olivia—whom Alan was sure was ignoring him—pulled Josh over to a far corner of the room to join those couples dancing in a style that Alan equated with epileptic seizure. Barbara's hips undulated to the music. Alan's pulse began to match the surge and flow of Carl Palmer's driving percussion. Everywhere young people jounced and jiggled in a feverish animism that crushed him against Barbara *and she knows*—

Positive?

No.

The music peaked, climaxed and died.

"Hi, we're back," Josh shouted in Alan's ear.

Instant guilt. Alan swiveled away from Barbara and saw Olivia staring at him. But he could not interpret the expression on her face.

Did she see? She must have. But why does she look like that? Disapproval? I don't think so.

What, then?

?

Making sure that Alan was watching, Olivia slowly and deliberately put her arm around Josh. Yet Alan still could not fathom her curiously ambivalent look.

It was shortly before eleven o'clock when the foursome returned to Aubrey House. Josh and Olivia got out of the car and walked toward the front door, but when Alan opened his latch, Barbara lightly rested a hand on his leg and asked him to stay. He looked at the other couple, at Barbara, agreed to wait.

"I know you want to be with Liv, but give her a little space."

"What makes you assume I prefer her company to yours?"

Barbara smiled. "I know you've noticed me, Alan. But when you and Liv look at each other, there's a whole different message."

"See what you want to see. But what about Josh?"

"What about him? He's his own worst opponent. Liv's got better taste, you can bet. Her only trouble is she's confused. How can she not be? Before her father died—I mean Benjamin Aubrey—she didn't have many options.

Now, suddenly, she's surrounded by them."

"Meaning me and Josh?"

"More than just men. She's a kid who's just been told she can rope off Macy's toy department and play with anything she likes before bedtime. Sounds terrific at first, but where do you start? Whatever you pick, you know you're going to miss something."

You're absolutely right, Ms. Lincoln. No matter what you think you want, you have to give something up to get it. And then maybe you didn't want it at all. And you can't get back what you sacrificed.

Through the windshield, Alan saw Olivia and Josh enter Aubrey House hand in hand. Outside, crickets shrilled and bullfrogs thrummed in the distant lake. Barbara clutched the steering wheel. After a long silence, she spoke.

"Come home with me, Alan."

When they entered her apartment, Barbara locked the door, took Alan's hand, led him to the bedroom and, turning off the light, pulled him down onto the coverlet. Her directness dizzied him; almost before he knew what was happening, her arms circled him so tight that he could scarcely breathe. She overwhelmed him with a cornucopia of sensations . . . the musk scent of her skin, the stab of her nipples, the strawberry tang of her lips as she explored his mouth with her tongue.

She used him with desperate abandon. Straddling him and smothering his face between her breasts. Barbara reached down and held him in place while she climaxed again and again. Alan found himself stranded on a plateau of passion from which he could neither rise nor descend. He felt curiously irrelevant, a convenient theatrical prop. *Or a dildo.*

When she was finished, she rolled onto her side and immediately fell into a light doze. Alan's lust raged unappeased, but he was afraid to move while she slept. Yet as her breathing grew deep and regular, he found it impossible to resist the recumbent invitation of her body. Slowly, ever so slowly, he molded himself to her contours until the two of them fitted like a nestled pair of spoons. Her flesh felt cool, but his smoldered. When he hardened, Barbara opened her eyes and stared over her left shoulder into his eyes. Alan began to stammer an apology and pull away, but she caught his hand in hers and said, "First wet me."

"How?"

"Like this." She licked the crotch of his thumb.

Afterwards, Alan tried to apologize.

She lay back languidly, arms behind her head. "What on earth are you sorry for?"

"For not being able to come the first time."

"Don't be foolish. I understand better than you think. It's not me you really want, it's Liv."

"Perceptive of you, but that's only part of it."

"What's the other part?"

"I'm afraid to say."

"Let me guess. You're married."

He nodded, unable to pronounce the fatal *yes*.

Barbara guided one of his hands to her bosom. "Don't look so tragic. Even if I'd known, it wouldn't've mattered. I needed to get laid tonight. As simple as that."

"Nothing's that simple. I used you."

Barbara laughed heartily. "I thought it was the other way around. I deliberately kept you from being with Olivia."

"Maybe. But I needed you, too."

"What you needed was a woman. What's wrong? Your wife doesn't understand you?"

"Oh, we understand each other. All too well, I'm afraid."

"I gather you're not making it with her."

"No."

"So what's your method? Going on the prowl for spinster librarians?"

"Mostly what I do is masturbate. And feel guilty."

"You and millions, my friend."

Alan fondled her nipples; the tips tensed. He said, "I think the worst part of it is the way something shrivels up inside. You turn into an actor. You say your lines, pull the strings so your arms and legs and mouth do what they're supposed to, but all the while nothing really matters any more. You're not in the scene—*any* scene—you're just observing. Know what I mean?"

"Yes. Perfectly." She watched the balls of his thumbs trace tiny circles on her bosom. "Keep it up, chum, and I'm going to use you again."

"Let's use each other."

"No. You had your fantasy. Now it's my turn."

"What do you want me to do?"

"You'll find out."

Later, while Barbara was in the bathroom, Alan sat on the edge of the bed and tried to sort out his feelings. That he had willingly submitted to her curiously ritualistic act of degradation did not upset him . . . and that was precisely what disturbed him.

What kind of man am *I?*

What you mean is, what kind have you become?

Yes. Turned into.

You can't blame Miranda.

No?

Not exclusively.

"Storms begin far back."

Yes.

He got up, turned on a table lamp, paced. Barbara's bedchamber was decorated along spartan lines. Unadorned hardwood floor. Single bed, firm mattress. A mirror and small dressing table with minimal cosmetics on top. Only

Barbara's bookcase showed signs of self-indulgence, double-stacked as it was with hardcovers and paperbacks. Alan inspected her books; they included a great deal of Americana: Bruce Catton, Carl Sandburg, Philip Van Doren Stern; Francis Parkman's *The Oregon Trail*; Stanton A. Coblentz's obscure study of pioneer justice in California, *Villains and Vigilantes*; Rufus Nearing's dusty old history of *General Butler in New Orleans*. The latter volume especially interested Alan; he took it out of the case. The book fell open to a spot near the middle.

> When the War of 1812 broke out, Ezekiel Lambert, Sr., was forty-eight years old. As a retired colonel, he was at first consulted out of courtesy, but his strategic genius made him invaluable to the Madison administration. On one occasion, Lambert had reason to meet John Butler, a flamboyant privateer who captured the fancy of seven-year-old Ezekiel Lambert, Jr., who grew up to be a bit of a scoundrel. But John Butler's son was an even more colorful rogue: Benjamin Franklin Butler, the Civil War general whose military governorship of New Orleans was so cordially detested by the southern aristocracy that he was nicknamed Ben the Beast.
>
> Ezekiel Lambert, Jr. was the despair of his father, the colonel. Physically, the lad bore a striking resemblance to the family black sheep, his late uncle Josiah, whose extreme height, bristling mustachios and hatchet face discomfited all his honest neighbors.
>
> When Ezekiel Jr. was twelve, his parents apprenticed him to a law firm, but he ran off and became cabin boy to John Butler in one of his West Indies ventures. When Butler lay dying of yellow fever in 1819, the privateer, fearing young Zeke might catch the dread disease, sent the Lambert boy away to deliver various documents to Mrs. Butler in Deerfield,

Massachusetts. She welcomed the teenager into her home. It is believed that Ezekiel Jr. was present at the birth of "Ben the Beast."

Alan was startled to see the name Lambert so prominently featured in the text. As he mused over what he'd just read, he leaned against the bookcase, which was a mistake. Suddenly, books, leaflets and miscellaneous rolls of paper cascaded onto the floor. David Porter's massive *The Naval History of the Civil War* landed on Alan's foot. With a yowl, he loosed a stream of invective that brought Barbara running out of the bathroom. Despite the warm weather, she wore a silk robe that completely concealed her body.

"What in holy fuck are you doing, Alan?"

"Breaking my goddam toes," he yelped, "what does it look like?" Relinquishing his hold on the book, Alan grabbed his injured foot and hopped about on the other.

Sweeping past, Barbara scooped up a long roll of paper and glared at him. "Why were you messing around in my bookcase, anyhow?"

"You're a librarian, you figure it out!" Alan plopped down on the bed and massaged his bruised toes. "I was browsing. Think I was going to steal something?"

"Sorry I snapped. I'm territorial about my bedroom. I don't invite men over all that often. I'm used to my privacy."

"Okay, I understand." *Better than you think, lady. Someone else taught me the lyrics to the Women's Lib National Anthem. By heart.*

Barbara drove Alan back to Aubrey House. En route, she asked him when Jonathan Brant was due to arrive.

"Why?"

"He's practically Liv's favorite poet. She idolizes him. You know she can't wait to meet him."

"Unfortunately, he can't come."

"What a shame. She'll be very disappointed."

"Can you keep a secret, Barb?"

"Try me."

"There's no such person as Jonathan Brant. It's a pen name."

"Oh? Well, but *somebody* wrote his poems."

"Yes. I did."

Braking the car for a red light, Barbara turned and fixed him with a stern stare. "Do you mean to tell me you based your whole expedition here on a lie?"

"No. Charles insisted on returning to Aubrey House. I agreed to chaperone him."

"And what about Liv's poems? Didn't you promise they'd be published?"

"They *will* be. There really is a new literary magazine called *Incisions*. 'Jonathan Brant' is going to edit the next issue at Aubrey House. I brought all the necessary tools and manuscripts with me."

The light changed. Barbara removed her foot from the brake and turned the car left onto Route 611. "So, when were you planning to tell Liv the truth?"

"I've been debating. Not sure I should."

"*I* would, if I were you."

"You would? Why?"

"Alan, come *on*. Don't be so naive. She practically loves Jonathan Brant, sight unseen."

"I know. But that's precisely the reason why I haven't told her already. Afraid it'd be taking unfair advantage."

"Yes, I see your point. Especially since there's something else she doesn't know."

"That I'm a married man. Yes."

"Look, chum, as far as I'm concerned, your marital status makes no difference, but I'm not Olivia Aubrey. Don't you know you already figure in her fantasies almost as much as the mythical Jonathan Brant? She's going to be plenty upset when she learns you've been lying to her. When did you plan to tell her? After you got her in the sack?"

"I swear not."

"Maybe I believe you. Maybe."

"All right, Barb, I admit I'm frustrated and lonely. And weak. Flattered by the way Olivia looks at me."

"You mean, as a man?"

"More. As if I still matter as a human being."

"Yes. I understand."

He nodded. "I think you do."

Barbara let Alan off at the entrance to the driveway and drove back toward Doylestown. When the headlights faded, the night engulfed him. There was no moon. The evening was chilly with the first tinge of autumn. The forest held its breath. Alan hurried toward the house, his feet crunching gravel. He didn't like the noise he was making, tried the grass at the edge of the path, but it was dew-wet. He looked up and saw a light flicker on the third floor.

Earlier, he'd begun to excuse Olivia for inviting him to Pennsylvania, but that was because the chance that Cameron Lambert still lurked in the woods seemed remote . . . a disquieting yet delicious tidbit of coffee-table grand guignol. But now the threat of his presence hung over Aubrey House like a shroud.

Alan ran to the front door. *Locked*. Olivia must have decided he was going to spend the night with Barbara. He circled the mansion. Most of the windows were set too high off the ground; the ones that weren't were secured. The back door was also fastened.

Alan was momentarily reassured. *At least, no one's in danger*. Then he remembered that Cameron Lambert had disappeared from Aubrey House. *Is there a secret entrance?*

He completed a circuit of the house and looked up again at the third floor. The mysterious light still guttered. He remembered the sheriff promised to station an officer in the garage. *Maybe he'll know how I can get in without waking everybody up. Come to think of it, I'd better check in with him, anyway. He may be watching and thinking I'm Cam Lambert. I'm liable to get shot in the back.*

Alan stumbled along the flagstones. When he was twenty feet away from the garage, he called out to the policeman. No answer. Cautiously approaching the long two-story building, he stopped and nervously peered inside. Darkness.

Footsteps overhead.

Alan balanced on the balls of his feet wondering what to do. The gleam of a flashlight spilled from the open door in the center of the building. Whoever he'd just heard walking on the second floor was coming downstairs.

Alan swiftly enumerated options: *run?*

Too risky in the dark.

Sneak up behind and deck him?

What with?

How about hiding?

He hid.

The shadows danced in the light beam like black flame. A man emerged, was silhouetted in bas-relief. Alan recognized him at once.

"Charles! What are you doing here this time of night?"

Singleton reeled backward, hand clutching his chest. "Dear God, man, you're supposed to protect me, not frighten me to death—that's the house's job!"

Alan hurried to his side. "Christ, that was dumb of me! Sorry, Charles . . . you're all right, aren't you?"

"Yes, yes, I'll recover." He hiccuped. "Oh, dear, I'm afraid I—" He hiccuped again, then tittered. "I feel like you just jump-started my heart." Another hiccup. Singleton inhaled deeply, held it, exhaled raggedly, paused for a brief, experimental moment, nodded. "There. Back to normal."

Alan apologized a second time. "But, what ARE you doing out here at this time of night?"

"Serendipitous research." Charles patted the black leather book he was carrying under his arm. "Earlier this evening, I had a long talk with Hattie. I found out that her sons moved a deal of Aubrey memorabilia out to the storage room overhead."

"I see. So what goody did you discover? Looks like a diary."

"It is. None other than Emily Shipperton's."

Alan emitted an appreciative whistle. "That's quite a find."

"Yes . . . and do you know what the terrible part is?" Charles grinned like the proverbial canary-stuffed feline. "It's small of me, I know—yet I can't help feeling pleased that my late friend Drew never even suspected this book existed."

"Human, all too human. What else have you got there?"

"Things," Singleton said with a trace of his old smugness.

Remembering the light in the third story window, Alan hurried upstairs and found Hattie Lambert sitting on the floor of one of the attic rooms fast asleep. A glass of milk and a plate of cookies rested untouched beside her. He decided not to wake her up.

In his bedroom, Alan delved into the large cardboard box he'd brought and unpacked reams of manuscript paper, a two-foot steel rule, pens and pencils, paste, scissors, paper clips, form sheets and other editing paraphernalia. He opened a bulging manila folder stuffed with poems he meant to use in *Incisions* and took out Olivia's submissions. *Okay, "Mr. Brant" . . . be objective. Is she* really *good enough?* He read for a few moments and was relieved to see that the answer was still yes.

Got to talk to her, clear up this afternoon's misunderstanding.

He checked his watch. Too late.

And yet . . .

?

She might still be awake. Maybe she wouldn't mind my knocking.

Unlikely.

Alan walked to the interconnecting door between their rooms and pressed his ear to the wood; he thought he heard a soft hiss from the other side. The door swung inward.

Deliberately left unlocked?

Come off it. Delusions of adequacy.

But how many nights have I been unable to sleep, yearning?

Every night.

Alan peeked into her room. Olivia's bed was empty.

ssssss

Running water.

He stopped on the threshold, afraid to cross over, unable to retreat.

What if she walks in now—what will she think?

The truth.

He took one tentative step into her bedroom, saw a sheet of paper and an uncapped pen on a writing table. *Poem in progress?* He walked to the table. Overpowering lavender scent. In the gentle lampglow, Alan scanned the work sheet of a piece Olivia had been trying to write in the style of Jonathan Brant.

TO A KINDRED SPIRIT

(Composed in a lonely house on a stormy night)

How can I want a man I do not know?
But in this haunted house, beset by storm,
The power of your craft has kept me warm—
Although the darkness waits for me, I know,
And I may weep before this wish is cold:
To want to want to solve your mystery
In spite of dangers that are history.
The thorns and barbs of hope are cruel and cold—
I've run them through my flesh, and so have you.
I swore I would not bleed for love again,
Or seek a joy that ends in endless pain—
Yet can I shun the wonder that is you?
O, if you cast dispelling spells on me,
I fear I would not strive to struggle free.

Is this meant for Jonathan Brant? Or me?

Maybe neither. She might have written it for Josh.

Impossible!

ssssss

"*I* know you're out there," Olivia calls. Splashing. The giggling of a playful child. "Come in, come in, whoever you are." The yellow oblong of her bathroom door lures him closer. Through the gapped portal Alan sees clouds of steam that partly obscure the pink-white mosaic of tiled walls. The glint of polished fixtures. Closer now: washstand, toilet, bidet, stall shower. In the middle of the room, sunken into the floor, an immense whirlpool filled with soap bubbles. Olivia languishes in the tub, eyes closed, nakedness masked by creamy froth.

"Come to me . . . I know you want me, Alan . . . take me. . . ." Her voice thick with passion.

What's wrong with this picture?

Look at her.

ssssss

* * *

"What's the matter, Alan?"

"Glad you're still awake, Charles. Though you shouldn't be. Sam said you should catch plenty of rest."

"I'll get plenty after I'm dead. What's wrong?"

"It's Olivia."

"Oh, God, it can't be starting already?"

"No, no, calm down, she's okay. Only. . ."

"Only what?"

"A few minutes ago, I was in her room—"

"Tch. Ought you be telling me this?"

"Charles, listen—she called me. I walked in without thinking. I mean, I was drawn to her like a magnet."

"So I've noticed."

"Not that way. It was almost a physical compulsion, going to her."

"Exactly what I implied."

"You're on the wrong wave-length, Charles. The point is, when I saw her, she was . . . well, frankly, she was naked. And asleep."

"But she called you?"

"Yes, but her eyes were closed. It's like she was in some kind of trance."

"Hm. Well, I'd best go check on her. You stay here and wait."

"But—"

"But me no buts, Mr. H. If she wakes up and you're there, she could be very embarrassed. Possibly worse. Don't fret, lad. I can handle the situation."

"Do you know what's wrong with her?"

"I have a hunch."

"The cold blue light?"

"Bite your tongue! No, no, I imagine you simply witnessed an example of hypnagogia. The near shore of slumber. The body sleeps, the metabolic rate slows, the mind teeters on the edge of consciousness, or thinks it does. But this isn't the time to tutor you in the psychophysiology of sleep. Wait, Horatio. I shall be faithful."

Charles left. Alan thought over what he'd just heard. *If he's on the mark, I just saw deeper into Olivia's mind than I have any right to.*

True. Unfair to trade on it.

Definitely.

But what *will* you do with the information?

Shut up.

Alan needed a distraction. Emily Shipperton's diary lay open on the bed. He picked it up and idly flipped through it.

> "—cannot tolerate that a child of her flesh is not comely; and yet there is no deviousness in my mistress, for so long as she does not set her eyes upon poor Olivia, she rests perfectly content. Then why am I haunted by Madame's assurances that were I free to accept new and other duties, she should train me that I become her personal companion and she would install me in a second floor bed chamber, and that with a salary reflective of my advanced station—"

Alan considered the implication, rejected it. That cosseted nonentity, Charlotte, might lack all motherly affection for her baby *named Olivia!* but she hadn't the intelligence to play Bolingbroke, hinting that the crown would be well rid of royal Richard. Suddenly, Alan missed his own daughter, Bess; longed to catch her up in his arms and hug her tight.

Charles returned. He appeared troubled.

"What's wrong?" Alan asked. "Was she hypnagogic?"

The older man waved away the question. "Olivia is

fine. She was wide awake when I went in. Awake *and* clothed. It's been a long day, Alan. We'd better go to bed."

"You look worried."

"Lack of sleep. Good night, lad."

Alan's eyes are open. He hears running water.

ssssss

The others are asleep but he wanders the dark halls and cannot find her room. *Or mine.*

oliviarandavarbara

On. On. In and out of doors. A big closet with boxes piled high. He reads one of the end labels.

M. L. STRASSER
Toymaker
Philadelphia

Lower. Deeper.

In and out. In and out.

Rain angling on roof and eaves. Cobwebs, slants and shafts.

Darkness pivots in
Soft as jelly in a rubber rag
Milk flows within a hole
The wind wets me
Battered on a springy wall
I fall

Suspiration in the dark
I die

Rooms and stairs. Round about. In and out.

Sunset jagged glint on snowspore tint
Golden teardrops etched in endless fall
Spumewhite salt shall flick the fragile claw
Slender skin descends in spittle-fall
Aslant the wrinkled Arctic sheet,
a spectre glides
And spreads the bones and bares
the teeth in which we fall

NoNO*no!*

The black iron bars. Six upright, one horizontal cross-piece.

The railing!

Too late.

A-a-a-laaaannnnn . . .

Hurt a woman?

Down. Down. Falling *dead if i land* but no pain standing cold cement floor concrete walls door gaping faint green glow

In.

Spiderweb of options?

No. Pinpointed. Fixed.

But go in.

No, go round about, Peer.

Straight through.

Stop. You've reached it.

She rises from the centerpit of green fire.

who are you

"The Lass of Rags and Beauties. Fuck me."

She has no face. He leaps on her, thrusts up with the blade of his death gushing over fingers thighs shuddering as she screams and tears at him with spike-long nails, her arms outflung like dying Jesus in the last convulsive ecstasy of death. And now he wrenches out her heart and flings it on the smoldering coals, but its veins and capillaries twine into tough supportive vines scuttling towards him like some monstrous daddylonglegs.

Out.

Mirror-imaged rooms.

The thing crablike close behind.

Faster.

The stairs.

Up.

The landing. Off to one side, a flight of seven steps. He takes them in double bounds but stops at the door *too tight can't push through,* tries to throttle the knobs—

IF YOU GO THROUGH,
THERE WILL BE A SHOWDOWN

Stops.

Her heart leaps at his face.

Down the seven steps, away. Other stairs.

Up.

The Boardwalk.

Empty.

Where are the people?

ssssss

?

over here

Josh?

Then he sees her leaning on the sea-rail: his wife Miranda, her chest torn open. No blood. Charade of death. The old familiar accusation in her eyes: *look what you've done.*

Not guilty!

oh yes daddy oh yes you are

Bess?

No. Not his daughter. Across the Boardwalk, shambling toward him with outstretched palms. Strings of pale, matted hair hanging over eyes that only hold the dullest hint of expression. Delicate brow and nose and chin framing a malformed mouth. With each step she takes, she hunches forward and sideways from the rachitic curving of her spine. Nestled in her open palms—bearing it to him like a prize to treasure—the gross pulsing thing that was a heart.

Leaps at his face.

Away.

Another doorway.

Go round about, Peer.

No. Straight through.

Black iron bars. Six upright. One horizontal crosspiece. *The railing!* Too late. Tries to stop

but the boards are slippery

with semen and blood

plunges over and plummets down and down and

Sudden euphor—

OW!

He cracked his jaw against a hardwood floor. The pain yanked him out of sleep. Alan sat up groggily, squinting his eyes against the glare of early morning sun. *Cold.* A light rain tapped at roof and window.

Must've fallen out of bed.

He cautiously opened his eyes, was surprised how grimy his hands and feet were. Then he saw the red smears on them. He scrambled to stand up and nearly fell. The floor was slippery.

Where am I?

A small chamber that still retained its original gas jets. No electric lights. Near a half-circular window, a heavy antique jug and wash basin stood by the slant wall that formed the inner line of the roof. The window was broader than high and set low in the wall. Shipperton's old attic room.

What am I doing here? What's going on?

Alan looked down and saw Hattie Lambert on the floor.

Or parts of her.

SOMETIME LATE AND WHO CARES? Olivia is to men as tissues are to snot. Mistress of the Manor . . . il faut que rire! Night deposit box for trolls.

Thirty years old and where's the confidence that's supposed to come with maturity? No fucking self-definition. (Les mots justes!) And honor? Whatever that is. (Hochhuth: "Where does a man keep his honor? We know where women do. Half an inch above her asshole.")

So. My first day as official head of Aubrey House. Began well. The ride here was exquisite. Pennsylvania just starting to succumb to autumn. Riot of natural colors. Another time the poet manquess would lasciviate with her thesaurus for adequate diction to describe the colors and the clean bare smell of the air, but for the nonce, the Muse can go take a flying leap. Childish of me, but then I acted like an absolute baby in front of Alan. Asked him what he thought of my new poems. Less than reverential response on his part, and I flew out of the room in tears. Nice going, Li'l Miss Immaturity. At least, Barbara was very consolatory afterwards. With her, I lucked out. A true friend. Admired her from the first time I saw her hefting a movie projector as easily as if she were a man. Why can't I be more like her? No lack of self-esteem, ditto -awareness. Her sleek, splendid blonde hair . . . the good-natured irony in her blue eyes . . . that glorious body! If the government ever figures a way to put a tariff on beauty, Barb'll be tax-poor overnight.

Back to my day: got to the house fairly early. Had an errand of mercy to do, so I dropped off the men at the front door. Poor Charles looked wan and haggard, though he tried his damnedest not to show it. (Or admit it to himself?) I felt ambivalent about returning, but Charles has a lot more reason to dread Aubrey House.

I went to the hospital, got Hattie Lambert and brought her back with me to convalesce. As we rode together, Hattie showed me a photo she always carries of her two sons. Cam looked familiar, can't imagine how since I never met him. Hattie's worried that they'll catch Cam and punish him "for things he never did." Then she more or less contradicts herself by moaning that it's her fault how he turned out. When "my Cameron" was a little boy, Hattie says, she never had the time or patience to show how much she loved him, "running myself ragged for Missy Merlyn or Mistress Charlotte." (Hard for me any more to think of Charlotte as "that bitch" now that I know she was as much my grandmother as Merlyn's).

Hattie said she got so many complaints from school about Cam deliberately bumping into people in the halls—thus the start of his reputation for belligerence—that she scraped up enough money to take him to a child psychologist. Latter said her son was starved for affection. Bumping into other children was a desperate method of obtaining contact comfort. How terrible.

And how achingly comprehensible.

"Y' know, Miss Aubrey," Hattie whispered (all she can manage with her throat injuries), "I went to school, but they never taught me you gotta tell a boy y' love 'im. I was thinkin' about that while I was lyin' in the county hospital. Then all of a sudden, it come to me how I can show Cam he's still my little boy. I just hope I get th' chance. Oh, Miss Olivia, I'd give my heart t' help 'im now."

"Well, if he ever reappears, Hattie, maybe you can do just that."

Continuing the rest of my wonderful day.

Lunchtime was reasonably pleasant. Thanks to Alan and Charles, Barbara was waiting for me when I got back with Hattie. So Barb and I and the men all went out to lunch as guests of Porlock Press. (Charles—who suggested it in the first place!: "If publishers gave up authorial luncheons and put half of what they saved into royalty advances, I suspect both parties would come out ahead.")

Barbara told us some fascinating Lambert lore. Charles asked to borrow a clipping file she mentioned, so on the way back to the house, we stopped at the library and she got it for him.

Josh showed up just before dinner, the last person I expected to see. At first I was cool to him, but I was actually glad he'd come because:

1. I was nursing a bruised ego from Alan's failure to wax worshipful over my new poems. Thus (admits the clay-footed lass) I was gratified to see that Josh obviously irritates my Person from Porlock. (Fantasy status report: Jonathan Brant definitely ahead on points).

2. Josh fascinates me. Beneath his on-off li'l boy smile, there are levels I can't plumb, which makes me want to pluck out the heart of his mystery. (One thing for certain: the man is NOT a poet. Can't even write decent doggerel).

3. Also glad he came because he brought Charles the materials (tapes, notes) he needs to finish revising his MS.

Olivia stopped writing. She suddenly remembered that Josh had also brought her something, an envelope that came in the mail while she was in New York. She had to think for a moment before she remembered that she'd stuck it in the pocket of her traveling dress. *That's why I forgot. Changed for dinner.*

Before retrieving the letter, Olivia finished her diary entry, setting down the dregs of her day: dinner beneath Charlotte's portrait—wondering how often her real father sat there mourning the woman he secretly loved, the daughter he could never openly acknowledge; dancing with Josh while Alan and Barbara found each other *but who can blame them?* and finally asking Josh into her house and her bedroom and her body only to be taught yet again the same degrading, painful lesson: that most men make love in anger.

Putting away her diary, Olivia went to the clothes closet and fished the letter from the pocket of her dress. She examined but did not recognize the block typing. She checked the postmark *New York City,* inserted her forefinger under the flap, tore it across the top, withdrew a folded sheet of white paper and began to read. After the first few lines, her face flushed. She looked at the opposite side to see who wrote it, but there was no signature. She turned back to the top of the letter and started again from the beginning.

Dearest Olivia,

Last night I dreamed I was with you in your bedroom at Aubrey House. You were fast asleep and did not know I lay beside you inhaling the sweet incense of your perspiration. Strange how vividly I saw the quality of your womanliness implicit in each curving line of your body. I felt more alive than in waking life and was wild to know everything about you.

On your vanity table, a silver oval clock ticked away the seconds. I moved my face close to the places where your arms and torso meet. Stealthily I tasted the fold of your left armpit; salt with an acrid tang of deodorant. When I moved away, I left a single pearl of saliva beaded on your skin.

Your breathing quickened as you rolled onto your back. Your legs parted. I averted my gaze, afraid the excitement I felt would suddenly end the dream. I spied your brush on your dresser. A frizz of brown hairs caught in the meshes. Starlight glowing on a mahogany chair revealed the clothing that lay against you all day: a smooth cool silk blouse accordioned over slacks whose twinned hemispheres still cupped the memory of your derriere.

I dared to look at you again. Your hair splayed on the pillow. Pendant lobes beneath the perfect shell of each ear. Your mouth parted, a promise of another pair of lips. I could not help it . . . I ran my tongue over and around and in between your teeth. One of them felt jagged—I wanted it to pierce me and draw blood.

Oh, lady, you are a continent of delights I tremble to explore. I want to map you with my eyes and fingers and mouth. Not in a dream, but really discovering your hidden geography: teasing your nipples; burying my face in the secret openings of your precious body.

I want you so much! I am throbbing with passion. For now I must be distant. But someday we will be together and then I'll know you with my heart and soul and body.

The letter slipped out of Olivia's hand. She was hot with shame and anger and fear and

And?

—and desire.

She thought she remembered Cameron Lambert spying on her while she was asleep, but if he did, why would he describe a silver oval clock that did not exist? Besides, the letter was postmarked New York. And the language of the letter was—

What?

Too professional.

That's right, Li'l Miss Sherlock.

She went to the dresser, rummaged through her purse, found the letter Alan sent her earlier that summer. She'd already read it many times, but now she studied it in a different light.

Phrases remembered from your poetry reecho . . . the quality of the woman implicit in every line.

And the anonymous letter: "Strange how vividly I saw the quality of your womanliness implicit in each curving line . . ."

Hardly happenstance.

And then another phrase in the letter leapt out at her: "Pendant lobes beneath the perfect shell of each ear."

'A Perfect Shell.'

The title of her favorite Jonathan Brant sonnet.

So, uncle, there you are.

It can't be coincidence, Olivia thought. The startled pleasure Alan expressed when he found out she'd purchased a copy of Jonathan Brant's *Love Sonnets*. The way he used Brant's name to wangle an invitation to Aubrey House. The fact that her "kindred spirit" did not show up, after all, *but Alan certainly did.*

This is silly. You're angry at him, so you're trying to turn him into a straw monster.

Yes, but . . .

?

A normal man doesn't write a letter like this to a woman he hardly knows.

Olivia wanted to show the letter to Barbara, but her friend had driven off with Alan.

Jealous?

Damn it, yes!

She fished through her purse, found the key to the door between her room and Alan's. *It's my house. I'll go anywhere I want. He's here on my sufferance.*

Through the connecting door, into his bedroom. Not much to see. Jackets, shirts, pants, socks, handkerchiefs, underwear. A typewriter on the table.

A sealed cardboard box. She pried off the tape, opened the lid. Office supplies. Sudden shame; Alan told the truth

—"While I'm at Aubrey, I've still got to work"—and then she sees a file folder with neat block letters penciled on the front.

INCISIONS

On the stairs, the footsteps of a kindred spirit and *it*he actually wants her.

Hu-rrr-y . . . hu-rrr-y.

Leaving the door open behind her, she bounds into her room, lights one small lamp at the dressing table, and quickly draws a brush through her hair with langorous strokes.

A trick of light. I can't be that beautiful, can I?

She studies herself in Charlotte's mirror. Her hair? Acceptable. Good color. Complexion? Fine skin. Hardly a furrow on her forehead, and those are the hardest lines to control. Her temples? Absolutely perfect . . . not a single wrinkle. A long time ago, someone showed her how to isolate those muscles and hold them immobile while just her lips smiled. The trick kept her from developing crow's-feet, one of the first signs of aging.

The footsteps reach the second floor landing.

Hu-rrr-y . . . hu-rrr-y.

Now! A touch of powder, a soupçon of blusher to accentuate those creamy cheeks. The merest whisper of highlight brings up those excellent facial planes. Lipstick should be blotted gently, and there must never be too much applied when one has a delicate complexion. A quick whisk of her old pearl-handled hairbrush; she sets it down and all is in readiness—

Blood pounding. Feverish. Olivia's pulse accelerates as the old man comes up behind her and tries to fondle her breasts.

—come to me

and I'll pry open your weak flabby mouth

and stuff

your fucking false teeth down your throat

and you can choke and

vite, vite, mes petits poissons—

His footsteps coming down the hall.

Hu-rrr-y . . . hu-rrr-y.

No. Slow. Not fast and harsh and brutal like—

Like?

Someone.

Who?

Someone.

Who?

Can't remember. Not now.

Try.

Michael?

noNoNO!

. . . Josh . . .?

YES!

(. . . a little water clears us of this deed . . .)

ssssss

Someone knocking.

Olivia opened her eyes. She lay on her bed, clad only in a light cotton robe. Her skin felt cool, her hair damp. She had no recollection whatsoever of bathing.

Charles knocked again. "Ms. Aubrey, are you awake?"

"Yes. Just a minute." She got up, cinched her nightgown, let him in. He looked concerned.

"I know it's late, Olivia, but Alan was a bit wrought up, so I promised I'd check on how you are."

"I haven't seen Alan for hours."

"Well, he saw you. He says you called him, so he came in here and found you in some kind of trance. He thought about the Aubrey Effect and got worried."

"Nice of him to care. *How dare he come in here under any circumstances?*

"It appears," said Charles, "that Alan's fears were baseless. You look perfectly all right."

"*Am* I?"

"Well—*are* you?"

"I'm not sure." Olivia sat on the edge of her bed and patted it for Charles to join her. "I was feeling kind of peculiar just now. I mean, when you knocked and woke me up."

"Kind of peculiar?" he echoed. "In what way?"

"Mixed up. Split up. I'm not making sense, am I?"

"Keep on talking till you find the words. How do you mean 'split up'?"

"As if I were—how can I put it?—as if I were someone else. Or even a whole bunch of somebodies."

"You'd best elucidate."

"I'm trying to. I heard someone coming up the stairs, and suddenly I began to put on makeup and brush my hair as if I were getting ready for . . . for a date." She waved her hand impatiently. "That's not it. As if I were expecting a lover. And then it all got confused and I must've gone to sleep."

"Olivia, you say you were expecting someone. Who?"

"I don't know."

"Are you sure? Think hard."

"What *are* you getting at, Charles?"

"Did any unfamiliar face or name come into your mind?"

"Such as?"

"I don't want to prompt the witness."

"I think you have to."

"Well . . . Richard, for instance?"

"No." She thought for a moment, then snapped her fingers. "I *did* think of a name."

"What was it?"

"Michael." Olivia frowned. "What's wrong, Charles?"

LONG AFTER MIDNIGHT. Disquieting talk with Charlie. He thinks the house is beginning to "energize." He wants us to go home first thing tomorrow morning. He forgets that this IS my home.

Something else disturbing: Charles found out from Hattie that her sons stowed Aubrey ephemera on the second floor of the garage. He went out there to rummage—the door was open. I told him the only time I tried that door, it was locked. Charles said I'd better tell Josh. I agreed, but couldn't reach him. Then I remembered he'd stationed a policeman in the vicinity of the garage and that made me feel better. Charles wasn't reassured, though; he insisted on camping out on my bed. He's here now. He also told me that I ought to keep the door to Alan's room cracked, so that we soldiers three will all be within earshot.

Olivia put down her pen and smiled fondly at the bald little man snoring by her bedside like a large watchdog. He tossed and fidgeted in an uncomfortable armchair. *Poor Charles. Looks like he's having a bad dream.*

She glanced at the connecting door to Alan's room. A sliver of darkness along the edge of the portal. She listened. Nothing. The night was humid. Her cotton robe clung to her skin. With a yawn, Olivia put away her diary, switched off the lamp and stretched out on top of the covers.

Aubrey House was oddly quiet. She heard none of the crackle and mutter of old timbers. The only sounds were the whirr of her electric clock—*not a silver oval*—and

Singleton's rasping snore. Still as death. The long day loops through her mind. Faces appear and vanish behind closed eyelids. Colors. Patterns.

L
O O
C R
S
patterns
patterns
and the
sweet sweet
whisperings
of thoughts
the retina
of lust
refracts like
prisms or like
slivers of needle-
pointed light
wet dreams spilling
bloodstains on the plain
plain Vita

NO!

Olivia opened her eyes. The sense of intrusion was very clear this time.

Sure about that?

No.

Why not?

Because I read Charles' manuscript.

Olivia suddenly jackknifed to her feet, took three long strides to her writing table, seized pencil and paper and scribbled a new "dream" to add to her cycle. Only four lines. She wondered whether Alan would think it was any good.

Irrelevant. I *like it.*

Significant?

Yes.

Justify.

Because I'm a writer. I refuse to become one of Aubrey House's pathetic ghosts.

Ghosts? Define.

I don't have to. Now shut up.

Who?

Nobody. A quirk of memory.

Whose memory?

Mine. Twisted into the illusion of objective existence.

Sure about that?

No.

Welcome to the club.

To hell with it. Think up a title, Liv.

She did.

A MADMAN

I have the strangest fractions in my skin:
The whorled tips of sense in intermittent blinks
Fragments of excitated whispers
Neon-winking in a mist of pain

The light in Alan's room went on. She heard him stumble into his bathroom and turn on the shower.

ssssss

She wondered whether he and Barbara enjoyed each other. Thinking of the two of them together in bed was a torment.

Why?

Because.

The shower water stopped. Olivia heard Alan reenter his bedroom and approach the connecting door between their rooms. He pulled it closed with a click. She was annoyed at herself for feeling disappointed.

A few moments later, Alan rapped at her hall door. Olivia opened it and was surprised to see him so pale and distraught.

"Alan, what's the matter?"

"I can't find Charles. He's not in his room."

"He fell asleep in here." Olivia pointed to where Singleton dozed by her bedside like a loyal eunuch guarding a harem of one.

Alan hesitated to wake him up. "Up till now, I never noticed how old and sick Charles looks."

"He wasn't this bad a few weeks ago." *Should've thought about his health, "Mr. Brant," before you dragged him to Pennsylvania.* "The house is affecting him more than he'll admit."

"Yes, I'm sure you're right, Olivia. I've got no choice, though, I have to wake him up." Alan unexpectedly took hold of one of her hands. "I need to speak to him right away. Alone . . . do you mind?"

"No, but what's it about? Or isn't it any of my business?"

"It mostly concerns me."

"What does?"

"The . . . the thing that happened to your housekeeper."

"Hattie?" Olivia started for the door. "What's the matter with her?"

"NO! DON'T GO UP THERE!"

"Shhhh, don't shout . . . you'll disturb Charles!"

"He already has," Singleton groaned. "What's all the fuss?"

"Something's wrong with Hattie Lambert. Alan won't tell me what."

The younger man addressed the elder. "I wanted to break it to Olivia gently."

"My dear Mr. Hunter," Singleton chided, "haven't you

learned better than to try and protect the Modern Woman? I daresay Olivia won't go to pieces on you." Charles frowned. "What on earth are you snickering about? I didn't say anything funny."

But Alan laughed.

And laughed.

SEPTEMBER 4. Two P.M. Hattie Lambert died last night. Murdered. The men wouldn't let us see her, not that I really wanted to. Josh says it's worse than the way her son Matt was killed. And we all slept through it. She had no voice to scream for help.

Why am I sitting here writing about it as if I were Lady Chesterfield recounting polite doings at my country estate? Because that's all I'm good for: glib, drab thing that I am. Using words to stave off a world I've never known how to deal with. Thank God (under the circumstances, an insane atavism) that they let Barbara past the police barricade—as if they could have kept HER out! She's downstairs now making funeral arrangements, calling my attorneys to smooth over the financial juggling necessary to cover costs.

Christ, when I hired Hattie, I practically killed her. And while I'm wallowing in guilt, what about the selfishness that made me invite Alan and Charles here in the first place? But Josh said it was safe, that there was "no way" Cameron Lambert could still be lurking around the premises . . . but when Charles told Josh about his talk yesterday with Hattie and how he went to the garage to rummage for memorabilia and the door was unlocked, I saw the light finally dawn on Mr. Incompetent Bastard Sheriff (and where the fuck was the policeman he supposedly stationed near the garage to watch the house?). Anyway, it's now obvious that Cameron Lambert was hiding upstairs in the garage. A deadly case of mental set on all our parts: after Matthew was massacred, my attorneys had all the house's locks changed, but it never occurred to them to bother with the garage, the top floor of which hasn't been used for years. They didn't know the Lamberts had been carting Aubrey paraphernalia out there. (If they had, they would have stopped them. That wasn't in their agreement with us).

Olivia looked up. A somber Barbara Lincoln stood in the doorway.

"Liv, you had a message . . . and I've got something awful to tell you."

"*More* bad news? Give me the message first."

"Okay. Your attorney rang back."

"And?"

"He said he's on his way with a Mr. Waxman. They'll be here within the hour. I tried to tell him you weren't seeing anyone, but he hung up before I got the chance."

Olivia pursed her lips. "The venerable senior partner, too, huh? Feels funny, rating the VIP treatment." She looked up. "All right, O Bearer of Evil Tidings, what else can you possibly say to rape mine virgin ears?"

Barbara managed a grim smile. "Brace yourself, love. Josh just arrested Alan."

"What?"

"Josh claims he had no choice."

"It's ridiculous! Before yesterday, Alan never met Hattie. And what about the Lamberts?"

"Herr Policeman claimeth that's an entirely different case. Said something about 'periodicity,' implying, I suppose, that this is a copycat crime."

"Bullshit. What can we do to help Alan?"

Barbara took Olivia's hand. "I don't know, love, but we'll do it together. Come on, let's go downstairs."

* * *

"They already left," Charles said. He was sitting on a kitchen stool in the living room by the bar. His collar was open and he was guzzling sherry.

"Ought you to be doing that?" Olivia worried.

"Normally I shouldn't, but sometimes it's better than stress." He tipped more wine into his glass. "Odd how one forms first impressions. The day Drew Beltane died, the former sheriff, a man named Armbruster, arrived here. Joshua Pelham was with him, an anonymous uniformed policeman. For some reason, I did not like that young man. I still don't. Something in his eyes, an expression I've seen someplace else. Where?"

"Never mind," Barbara said. "What kind of case against Alan does Josh think he has?"

"Well," Charles said, "Alan found Hattie in the first place. That's never a plus point with the police. The fact that you and I were together in your room, Olivia, only makes it worse for Alan. The house was locked inside and out. He's the only one without an alibi, who *could* have done it."

"But last year the house was locked up," Olivia argued, "and yet Cam Lambert escaped."

"True. But there's something worse. Do you remember that big cardboard box that Alan brought up here with him?"

"Yes."

"Josh searched and found the murder weapon inside. Hattie was killed with one of your kitchen cleavers."

"Oh, God!"

"No one by that name lives at Aubrey House." He drained the rest of his wine and wobbled to his feet, the half-empty sherry decanter still gripped in his fist. Olivia tried to take the decanter away from him, but he resisted.

"Charles, you're not going to drink any more, are you?"

"Only to excess and not a drop more. If you will excuse

me, I shall do the deed in my room."

"Little man," Barbara said, "you're in no condition to take the stairs alone. Better let me help you."

"No, no, I don't want your assistance." He took a step and stumbled against the bar. "I do seem to be a trifle uncoordinated."

"Don't be stubborn. Barb, you take one arm, I'll get the other."

"There's no need, Liv. I've lugged library books that weigh more than Charlie." She circled his arms around her neck and scooped him up like an infant.

"Come to Mama," he tittered, laying his head upon her breast. Barbara started upstairs, Olivia close behind. Halfway up the flight, Charles gasped. "Dear God, I almost forgot."

"What?" Olivia asked.

"I promised Alan faithfully that I would, but at the moment I appear to be a trifle inca—" Charles sucked air into his lungs. "—pacitated. It would be better, I think, if one of you ladies called her."

"Who?" Barbara asked.

"Alan's wife. Now *do* be careful, Olivia . . . you nearly tripped and fell!"

Barbara deposited Charles on his bed and left the room, but Olivia lingered behind.

"Yes, child?" he asked. "What is it?"

"Do you think there's any chance Alan actually murdered Hattie?"

"Not for a moment. I've known Alan for years. Not intimately, perhaps, but enough to take the measure of the man. He always impressed me as essentially gentle. Whoever slaughtered Mrs. Lambert is a madman."

"Maybe I'd better show you a letter Alan sent me. It's in my room. Be right back."

"Take your time. I'm not going anywhere."

But when Olivia returned, Charles was asleep. She put down the letter and pried his fingers away from the neck of the decanter.

The doorbell rang.

Must be Messrs. Dodson and Fogg.

The sleeper muttered groggily. Casting a pitying glance on him, Olivia hurried downstairs to get the door before it rang a second time and woke Singleton.

The policeman stationed on the porch was not going to allow them to enter. "The sheriff gave orders no one is supposed to go into the house."

"Josh is trying to spare me the press," Olivia explained. "This is my house and these are my attorneys. Now let them in."

The deputy reluctantly stepped aside. Two men followed Olivia into Aubrey House. The first was Mr. Donald P. Barton III, junior member of the Philadelphia law firm of Waxman Sand & Barton; a rotund, florid attorney in his early fifties. He wore a three-piece silk suit, custom-tailored white shirt with wing collar over an imported Italian handpainted necktie, laceless gloss-polished black Mansfields and a twenty-four-karat gold watch on a chain depending from his vest.

His companion and ranking partner, Jim Waxman, was about to say goodbye to his seventh decade. He had salt-and-pepper-grey hair, whisky-red cheeks mottled with blue veins and a bulbous lump of flesh where most folks' noses are. His glasses magnified his eyes; he reminded Olivia of the dog with eyes as big as windmills in an old Grimm fairy tale. Waxman wore golf shoes and a loud Hawaiian shirt that hung loose over his white tennis shorts.

Olivia, amused by the contrast between the two men, decided she preferred Waxman's mode of dress. *Why not? At his age, who does he have to impress?*

She showed them into the library which, though smallish, had sufficient room to provide them all with seats. She asked whether she could bring either of them a drink. Barton was about to decline when the old man demanded to know "whether the Aubreys still stock the best single malt scotch the other side of the Glen." The junior barrister promptly changed his mind and requested a vodka and tonic. Mr. Waxman made a face not meant to be seen by Mr. Barton; Olivia definitely liked the old gent's style.

"This is a dreadful business," Mr. Barton began. "Mr. Waxman and I wish to extend our sympathies, Ms. Aubrey, for all that you have undergone. Mr. Sand had to be in court today, but he asked me to assure you that his sentiments are precisely the same. He is truly sorry he cannot be here."

Olivia raised an eyebrow. "Really? The same Mr. Sand who never used to return my calls?"

Mr. Barton coughed and cleared his throat. Mr. Waxman smiled, swirling his glass of Talisker between sun-leathered hands.

"I am sure," the junior partner continued, "that any such oversight on the part of Mr. Sand was not at all intentional. He is frequently in court. That is why your interests were reassigned to me."

"Oh, is that the reason? I thought it was because he only regarded me as an insignificant temporary executor."

Mr. Barton began to look decidedly uncomfortable. "Certainly that was not Mr. Sand's intention, Ms. Aubrey. However, if that unfortunate impression was made—"

"Oh, knock off the bullshit, Don. The lady knows when she's been diddled up the spout." Mr. Waxman smiled at her. "I hope you don't object to my language, ma'am. I could've said 'bovine effluent', but it doesn't have the right ring."

"It certainly doesn't," Olivia agreed.

"Let's come right to the point," Waxman said. "Until a few months ago, I was the only member of the firm who knew you were the sole remaining heir of Jason Aubrey. So Murray Sand jerked you around. Then there was that business about Lambert stealing stuff from our office. The upshot is, we're damned sorry about it. Our firm has handled the Aubrey interests ever since my father's time. I came to ask what we can do to make things up to you."

"You've done the first thing already. Being up front with me earns points. I've heard that you personally know a lot of Aubrey history. Do you mind answering some questions?"

"Well," Waxman said, holding out his empty glass, "If I'm going to do a lot of talking, I'd better keep my pipes oiled."

After Waxman and Barton finished their business and departed, Olivia tried to think what to do next, but couldn't make up her mind. She wanted to talk things over with Barbara but the blonde was nowhere to be found so, instead, she went up to see if Charles was awake yet.

In less than a minute, Olivia thundered downstairs, flung open the front door and frantically called for help.

Sitting in a modified lotus position on the bedspread, Charles Singleton rearranges the materials brought by the sheriff into three neat piles. He picks up his microphone and presses RECORD.

click

The battery-powered tape recorder on the squat bedside reading table begins to loop and turn as he speaks.

"Singleton, Tape One, Side One." Déjà vu. His pulse quickens. He wills it to slow, succeeds. Charles continues. "Home again, home again, jiggety jig. My first night back at the Aubrey Funhouse. The resident gargoyles are in hiding. Not that they fool me one jot. They're here, all right. I knew it when I stood at the bottom of the servants' staircase this afternoon. A new experience for this grizzled head, or should I say for these tired limbs? I actually read the power, the way Drew claimed he could. It was the strangest sensation—like a cold breath blowing ever so gently along the hair of my arms.

"I conducted a brief tour for Alan. Except for the rear stairway and that loathesome laundry room with its morgue of long-dead comestibles—I still remember that awful pungent stink when the jug exploded and Merlyn fell face-first into the splinters—I felt virtually nothing. Not even when we reached the sight of the infamous cold blue light, where I ripped out Granny Charlotte's eyes. But why should I feel anything? Vita and Merlee and the rest are all buried. So am I. What's left? Mortar and bricks, blood and bone.

"On the third floor, we met no less estimable a personage than the local head librarian, browsing no doubt through Aubrey's accumulated memorabilia. Her name is Barbara Lincoln and she is probably Bucks County's closest thing to an Amazon, though I don't believe those Eternal Feminines normally number blondes amongst their set. Alan took one glance at her and looked as if he'd swallowed a sialagogue. He may be an old married man, but I suspect my-friend-the-editor would gladly be a galley slave—pun intended—to Ms. L. That's their business. She seems capable of handling anyone and anything. Not so our hostess. She and Alan stare at one another in a fashion that I doubt either would be equipped to manage if put to trial.

"Ms. Aubrey indeed concerns me. Once or twice, I saw her hands steal to her face in a manner frighteningly reminiscent of Merlyn's old mannerism. I'm probably overreacting. Still . . . I am determined *not* to be caught unawares this time. In spite of all the philosophic doubts that torment me nowadays, I must keep reminding myself that Aubrey is not only bricks and mortar but a corpse-strewn battlefield."

click

Charles frowns at the microphone in his hand. *Verbal diarrhea, Mr. Singleton. What* are *you about?*

Digression as a means of delaying the moment of immersion in the past. The tapes. Drew's final memorandum. Now do stop jabbering.

But there's no guarantee I'll weather Aubrey a second time. I must *record my impressions . . . who knows who may need to hear them a year from now?*

There's a cheery thought.

Better than being sole survivor two times in a row.

Point conceded. Now *do* get on with it.

click

"Earlier today, I met Olivia's unfortunate housekeeper, Hattie Lambert, fresh from the hospital after a murderous attack committed upon her person. I pretended ignorance of the circumstances. Alan thinks I never catch news reports . . . an impression I encourage. We *are* such a nation of page-turners—'feuilletons,' as Hesse called us. But after what happened to Hattie a few months ago, I was, as usual, plagued by pestiferous reporters. Thus I learned the facts of the most recent Aubrey atrocity.

"Hattie and I hit it off, a circumstance I deliberately cultivated. Deep sympathy expressed over tea anent her will-o'-wisp son Cameron. Knowing wink and my hushed reassurance that *I* would never reveal any great Lambert secret shared by mother and child. My crude ruse worked, but I expected no less. Hattie is a *naif*. Fierce whispered pride on her part. 'The land rightfully belongs to the Lamberts. Addison Aubrey cheated them out of it.' Her sons had no intention of becoming lowly innkeepers. All Cam wants is what's rightfully his. That, of course, gave me something to think upon. Asked Milady Librarian about it at lunch and she told us the tale of Uncle Josiah's hidden treasure. Afterward, I borrowed me a fascinating library file full of Lambertiana reproduced from antique newspapers and local historical publications. I perused it before dinner. What a brood the Lamberts are! Villains and lack-wits, scoundrels and black sheep.

"The last new face I encountered today is one I'd seen before, if ever so briefly. On that melancholy afternoon when I found Drew Beltane dead, Joshua Pelham was deputy to Harry Armbruster—that egregious ass who actually suggested that a man as severely crippled as Drew had the stamina, let alone the coordination, to beat poor Vita with his own cane and rape her.

"Mr. Pelham is now sheriff. A tall, sinewy hulk whose boyish charm struck me as somewhat calculated. His eyes are anything but innocent, especially when he looks at Olivia. I suspect she does not know how to deal with the Joshua Pelhams of this world. She appears unable to take the true measure of her own femininity. At the risk of sounding chauvinistic, I do think Ms. Aubrey is in dire need of protection. Well, at least Milady Librarian appears to be looking out for her. Said Amazon does not emit friendly vibes towards the sheriff, nor does he in return. The silent cross-talk I observed between them is elaborately hieroglyphic.

"At any rate, Mr. P. was good enough to bring me the cassettes and notes I wrote to him about earlier this summer. I've done some preliminary culling. Vita's tape doesn't tell me much, and Merlyn never made one, so there are now three piles resting before me on the bed, one apiece for Drew and Richard and yours truly. I'll begin with our Scottish friend's final handwritten message to Dick Creighton."

click

> RICH: Out-of-body travel is the only way to get near the thing, so I've gone OB to track it down. It is definitely Charlotte.

"The deuce it is," Charles grumbles, skimming the laborious penciled scrawl. The next part concerns Phyllis and

Harold Burton, the mediums who lost their minds during a séance at Aubrey House.

> Remember Phyllis' diary: "We were so wrong. It's lower. Deeper." Deeper in the mind, Rich . . . One must descend to a primitive level of mind. The Burtons could not have figured this out without going under themselves, but they stopped in time, and even had enough wit to analyze what had occurred . . . The question is, once they knew the risk, why the hell did they try it again? Perhaps liquor—they were heavy drinkers, remember? Might've thought booze would sufficiently alter state to bring them into contact without actually resorting to OB travel. Idiotic. They must've been blind drunk when it got them. The danger—the pain in one's skull—remember I mentioned it to Charlie—that's the first symptom of birth memory. I've been through it, Rich, and believe me, there can't be much of anything harmful rattling round my little Ayrshire id. Except for the animal wish, sometimes, to be free of pain for good and all, but that's one of those irrelevant urges that I've had to ignore through the years. . . .

Singleton's eyes widen. He puts down the loose sheets and reaches for the microphone.

click

"Insight. What if Drew's death resulted from a repressed death-wish? On the surface, he seemed to relish life enormously, even though he was so crippled that he could not function without taking an endless stream of pain-killers. I was the one who found his body. I vividly remember that for the very first time, there was peace in his eyes instead of anguish. That may well have constituted something akin to Heaven for Drew. Isn't it possible, perhaps even likely, that when he went OB, the sensation seduced him? I have had no personal experience of out-of-body travel, but from what I've read on the subject, the condition is often reported as feeling rather euphoric."

click

> You'll also find some observations on Vita on another sheaf of papers beneath this pile. Things she told me the night before she succumbed to Aubrey may explain why her experience was so very different from all the others recorded here.

Startlingly different. Vita said something that none of us paid any attention to at the time—that we all might be experiencing totally different things at Aubrey.

Charles quickly scans Drew Beltane's notes on Vita, but finds nothing he did not already know about his old friend: how she and her bland minister husband Walter rarely made love. Walter Henry had difficulty maintaining an erection. *Probably couldn't reconcile a life devoted to God with his basic animal needs.* The only "true love" in Vita's otherwise sexless life was her high school sweetheart, Michael, *but her mean-spirited mother and cold-fish minister father prevented Vee from going away with Michael to Australia.*

Charles cannot see how Vita's past has anything to do with her hideous death. According to Drew's memo, she hallucinated hearing the Aubrey phone ring at midnight and imagined it was Michael calling to give her one more chance to run off with him—alive or dead.

Very farfetched, Mr. Beltane.

> Now I'm on my way down to meet Charlotte on her own ground, the id level. I have the advantage this time. I've run her energy very low and she won't be able to siphon mine because we'll be on the same plane. By now, she must be scared out of her vacant

little mind, probably thinks it's Judgment Day, and she has good reason to fear that event, I'm afraid.

Now there, if I catch Drew's drift, is another extreme unlikelihood. Exiling one's own daughter to the attic is certainly dreadful, but not even Charlotte Aubrey was unnatural enough to think of disposing of her own flesh and blood.

—Sure about that, Charlie?

click

"Odd. Dick Creighton just popped into my mind with remarkable clarity. In some ways, he, of all our hapless party, was the saddest. Vita went down ignorant of what hit her. Merlee, I'm afraid, was primed from the start to immolate herself. Drew? For him, death may have been equivalent to transfiguration. But Richard, for all his stainless steel logic, could not deal with the loss of his wife and daughter. Both were killed in one of those meaningless auto accidents that we're supposed to accept as a natural offshoot of God's devious game-plan.

"At any rate," Charles says as he sets aside Beltane's notes, "Drew's message is a disappointment—a surprising lack of help from the self-proclaimed authority on Aubrey House. Well, let's see what Richard has to say."

He removes his cassette from the machine and replaces it with a tape labelled "Creighton". As it begins to play, Alan Hunter enters Charles' bedroom, listens a moment, then asks Singleton if he'd like to take a drive with him and Olivia and Barbara.

Singleton shakes his head. "I've put off this business long enough. Now that I've embarked upon the stream at last, I fully intend to shoot the rapids. Or drown in the attempt."

"Oh? Well, that's the sort of thing I'm supposed to prevent. Maybe I'd better not go out, after all."

Nonsense, you're dying to join the ladies. "Now don't

go treating me like an invalid or a five-year-old. I'm not going to subject myself to any undue stress. Besides—"

"Besides what?"

"Hush a moment . . . I want to hear this." Singleton presses STOP, REWIND and then PLAY. They listen to Richard Creighton. After a moment, Charles puts the machine on PAUSE and shakes his head. "Dear, dear, all the time that I was wrangling with Drew, I just assumed he and Richard were on identical sides of the philosophical fence. But the elf never went quite *this* far. . . ."

After Alan Hunter leaves, Singleton stares at the last tape on the bed. His own, recorded *four years ago tomorrow night* just before he went to the attic and subsequently had his stroke.

One final fragment.

Suddenly afraid, Charles decides it is time to take a break. *I've waited four years for this moment. Another half-hour's delay won't hurt.*

In search of diversion, Charles considers foraging in the kitchen, but then remembers that he needs to keep his system clear. *One more séance before I'm through with Aubrey House.*

Perhaps I'll drop in for another little chat with my friend, Mrs. Lambert.

"I never liked her," Hattie whispers.

"Why not?"

"She played off Matt against Cam, Cam against Matt. Never seen neither o' them wastin' time around a lib'ry, not till that blonde bitch took over."

"Well, if that's so, how did they meet Barbara in the first place?"

"They hadda look some'n up."

"Yes, I've heard that libraries are not altogether inutile in that pursuit."

"Huh? Was that English?"

"Never mind, Mrs. L. Have some more sherry."

"Thanks."

"You know, I've always been fascinated by the Lambert family."

"Y' have? Why?"

Positively feral suspicion. "Because they are a significant part of Pennsylvania history. I've been reading some wonderful stories about Colonel Zeke, for instance. Quite the dashing figure. Entered the Continental Army at thirteen, but he was so tall and wiry, he looked older. Besides, he grew a mustache. By eighteen, he actually had his colonel's commission. After the war, they sent him to France as a diplomatic attaché. His exploits during the French Revolution could be turned into a Regency romance."

"That true? I'd like to hear."

So Charles regales her with exploits of her illustrious ancestor, facts he gleaned from the Lambert library file (and somewhat embellishes for Hattie's benefit). Even though he has an ulterior motive for softening her up, he still cannot resist playing to an enthusiastic audience . . . and she is certainly that: drinking glass after glass of sherry but swallowing even more greedily Singleton's narrative, consisting as it does of heroic Lambert deeds. Perhaps Hattie has heard the story before, but the fierce pride in her eyes suggests that the latest retelling is always the best.

"And now we come to the part about Uncle Josiah's gold," Charles says with a conspiratorial wink. "When Ezekiel Lambert left Europe during the French Revolution, he brought with him a beautiful aristocrat, Katherine Deauville. Not only did he rescue her from the terrorists, but he even managed to smuggle out a fortune in gold louis belonging to her parents, who did not survive Robespierre's bloodbath. Colonel Lambert married Katherine within the year, which made him a very wealthy man. He built a new home not far from Uncle Josiah's farm—on *this* very tract of land—but if he knew where Josiah hid his stolen gold, Zeke never let on about it."

"Oh, he knew where it was, all right."

"Indeed? How can you be so sure, Mrs. L?" Pouring the last of the wine into her glass.

" 'cause I'm a Lambert. Hard t' talk . . . but you go get some more wine, Charlie, then it'll be my turn t' entertain you."

"Thought you'd never offer," Singleton mutters under his breath.

"Charles! What are you doing here this time of night?"

"Dear God, man, you're supposed to protect me, not frighten me to death—that's the house's job!"

Alan fusses over him. An attack of hiccups. Breathe deep. One, two, three, four. Hold one heartbeat, two. Exhale, two, three, four. Again. Again. "There. Back to normal."

"Sorry and all that," Alan says. "But what ARE you doing out here this time of night?"

"Serendipitous research. Earlier this evening, I had a long talk with Hattie. I found out that her sons moved a deal of Aubrey memorabilia out to the storage room overhead."

"I see. So what goody did you discover? Looks like a diary."

"It is. None other than Emily Shipperton's."

"That's quite a find."

"Yes . . . and do you know what the terrible part is? It's small of me, I know—yet I can't help feeling pleased that my late friend Drew never even suspected this book existed."

"Human, all too human. What else have you got there?"

"Things."

Back in his bedroom, Charles secrets one of his finds into his suitcase. He puts Shipperton's diary on the bed next to his final unplayed cassette. Singleton glances back and forth between the two. . . .

No. I'm not quite ready for Ye Final Fragment. Read first, listen afterwards.

A long time later, Charles puts down the old book and utters a melancholy sigh.

click

"I've just been reading Emily Shipperton's diary. Her childhood was dreadful. Born out of wedlock to an ignorant Irish farm girl who emigrated to Liverpool and married a brutish cobbler, Thomas Shipperton, who raped Emily when she was thirteen. She stole whatever money she could find in the house and crossed the Atlantic in a rat-infested merchant vessel. She had the Hobsonian choice of being used by the crew or bargaining her favors with one of the officers. At least this chap appears to have been fairly decent. On arrival, he conveyed her to a reputable boardinghouse and made sure she had respectable employment before taking his leave. For these minimal courtesies, Emily enshrined him in her heart, a White Prince who someday would return to claim her hand. Of course, she never set eyes on him again.

"Eventually Emily scrimped sufficient capital to train as a nurse. She became affiliated with Garfield Hospital in Washington, D.C. The Garfield administration highly recommended Emily to Derek Aubrey for her special skills in problems of child-rearing. Derek totally entrusted his infant daughter Olivia—yes, Olivia—to Emily's care. Shipperton writes that the child's spine was malformed and there was also brain damage. Taking care of Olivia was an exhausting round-the-clock business complicated by the injunction to do so chiefly in the confines of that ugly attic prison. Shipperton did not mind overmuch. She had her own room, no matter how small and slanting; she had enough food—and when Mistress Charlotte was not at home, she dared take her small charge exploring in and out of those grand second-floor bedrooms that apparently dazzled young Emily. She never risked bringing Olivia to the main floor, but once when the child was six years old, she got into one of the second-floor closets and found the assortment of fashion dolls that her father bought her before he realized that such fragile playthings could not be entrusted to his daughter. The Aubreys were out that day and Emily was doing her laundry. Olivia wandered off, came upon the dolls and with an inexplicable clarity of purpose took them all downstairs and lined them up neatly on the living room sofa. When Charlotte saw them later, she became hysterical with rage. Emily was very nearly sacked.

"This unpleasant incident sheds new light on something dreadful that happened to Merlyn Aubrey when she was a little girl. She discovered the same fashion dolls, brought one of them downstairs and was literally attacked by her grandmother, who repeatedly struck the poor terrified child. Merlyn didn't learn the reason for her grandmother's seemingly unmotivated viciousness until just before Merlee died here, four years ago almost to the day.

"Returning to Emily Shipperton's journal . . . it reveals that little Olivia died when she was seven years old. She fell down the servants' staircase and broke her neck—the same death her niece Merlyn suffered more than fifty years later. Emily blamed herself for the accident all her life, and who is to say what really went through her mind at that teetering instant when her hand shot out a scant second too late to catch hold of the seven-year-old's arm?

"One thing seems certain—though it is improbable that Charlotte actually would have plotted to get rid of her unwanted child, one cannot for an instant imagine her regretting Olivia's loss. But what, I wonder, did she feel later on when the Aubrey Effect first began to manifest itself? If me and my friends experienced such vastly differing phenomena—"

A rap at his bedroom door. Charles is surprised to be

disturbed at so late an hour. He opens, sees Alan obviously looking worried, asks him what the trouble is.

"It's Olivia."

"Oh, God, it can't be starting already?"

"No, no, calm down, she's okay. Only . . ."

"Only what?"

"A few minutes ago, I was in her room—"

Charles knocks, but Olivia does not answer. He tries the door, but it is locked, so he enters Alan's bedroom and finds the connecting portal ajar.

ssssss

The water in the whirlpool tub is still running, but she is lying naked on her bed, legs wide as if expecting a lover. Her attitude so powerfully recalls the way he found Vita that for a few seconds, Charles stands rooted with terror. But there are no bloody cuts on Olivia's body. Her face is bland with slumber, not mindlessness.

Charles finds a robe, gently struggles her into it, hopes she will stay asleep till he's done. *She would be terminally embarrassed.* Olivia does not wake. He has to shake her repeatedly before her eyelids flutter. He swiftly tiptoes to her bathroom, shuts off the water, hurries into the hall, drums his knuckles on her door.

Olivia lets him in. They talk. Charles finds out that the second floor of the garage should have been locked. He is disturbed. Then Olivia describes her recent schizoid trance and he is downright alarmed.

He goes back to his room, dismisses Alan with feeble assurances that their host is all right, then grabs his pillow and returns to take up the post of guardian angel by Olivia's bedside. She tries to argue him out of camping there all night, but Singleton will not be gainsaid.

"Olivia, you must indulge me in this. I've been here before and believe me, the worst danger facing us is surnamed Aubrey, not Lambert. Nighty-night."

Charles dreams lucidly of Shipperton's attic room.

Waiting. Every line, corner and texture etched with tri-dimensional clarity: stuffed, overflowing boxes of Aubreyiana; dustweb filaments in the angles of the ceiling's inverted V.

Footsteps.

In here, son.

The tall man with the hatchet face and savage smile shimmers in the doorway in a nimbus of cold blue light.

My bad little boy?

Mama

Hattie

The colors of the dream ran into one another as if an invisible artist swirled them together on his palette.

"—too know where. Think what Mama—"

DON' PLAY

the railin

GAMES

falling dead if

B

I

TCH

ELL

and

ever had ti

ME

for

A-a-a-laaaa-nnnnn

who are you

The g s

L a a beau—

a r n

ss o f d

—OW!

Hardwood floor. Glare of early sun. Cold. Light rain.

Jesus God . . . what have I done?!

Afternoon of the following day.

Singleton sits in the Aubrey living room on a stool borrowed from the kitchen. Olivia and Barbara come downstairs and catch him guzzling sherry.

"Ought you to be doing that?"

"Normally I shouldn't, but sometimes it's better than stress."

They discuss Josh's arrest of Alan Hunter. At length, Charles rises unsteadily and tries to wobble his way upstairs, wine bottle in hand. The feat proves too difficult. Impressions blur like swirled colors on a painter's palette. Barbara totes him up the front stairs.

Mama's bosom, The Fulness Thereof. Nice for a change.

A murmur in his ear. Charles says something. Olivia nearly trips and falls. *Occupational hazard of distaff Aubreys?*

Barbara dumps him on top of the bedspread and walks out. Charles stares up into Olivia's concerned eyes.

"Yes, child? What is it?"

"Do you think there's any chance Alan actually murdered Hattie?"

"Not for a moment," he replies with a certainty he is far from feeling. Charles remembers a hideous story he read once: a mild-mannered scientist meets a woman in the woods and takes her with only token resistance. Then he strangles her so he can observe with detached curiosity the final intense play of emotions on her face . . . pain, pleading, hatred, resignation. Afterwards, the scientist is stunned by his own ferocious behavior and reflects that all mankind potentially teeters on the brink of bestiality. *Then what is Alan capable of under stress?*

"Maybe," Olivia says, "I'd better show you a letter Alan sent me. It's in my room. Be right back."

Charles' eyelids close. A sudden alcoholic rush. First he plummets into a spiraling vortex at light-speed, then the flow reverses and he shoots upward with a giddy elation wholly new to him. Giggles silently. *Free among the pillows and the billows*. The sunlight alters, backtracks into morning.

"Here it is, I want you to read—" Olivia hesitates.

Looking down, Charles sees her standing by the bed trying not to disturb his sleep. The doorbell rings. An envelope in her hand slips onto the coverlet. *But where am* I?

Must be Messrs. Dodson and Fogg. Charles reads Olivia's thought as clearly as if it were a neon sign blinking on and off in his mind.

Olivia goes downstairs. Singleton hovers somewhere near the ceiling, pondering his predicament.

Why can't I look down and see myself?

He suddenly hears a voice in his head: "Charles, I'm surprised at you! Didn't you once tell me that out-of-body travel is dangerous?"

Vita! Is that really you?

"If you like, boyo."

Drew? Are you still here, too?

"What do *you* think, Charlie?"

By now, you and Vee should have crossed over to the other side.

The ghost of Vita's laughter. "Charles, we are NOT chickens!"

—Go easy on Charlie. He's afraid to cut loose.

Et tu, Richard?

—At your service.

Where's Merlee?

—Upstairs with Charlotte.

Well. So what shall I do now?

"That, boyo, is your decision."

But I've never been out of body before. What are my choices?

"Think it over."

Am I . . . dead?

"That's one possibility."

But how did this happen? I had no intention of traveling OB.

—Then you should have been more careful.

In what way?

—Drugs + alcohol = hypnagogia.

"Remember when you drank too much at your last séance, Charles? You had a stroke."

Never mind that, Vee. Is my present condition irrevocable?

?

I mean, can I return to my body?

Nothing.

Vita?

A pale twisting haze at the foot of the bed, a phantom glimpsed in the skyward-curling smoke of an opium pipe.

Drew?

Sunlight gone.

Merlee?

Blackness pinpointed by millions of cold blue stars.

dea$^{r}_{d}$ friends, why hast thou forsaken me?

Fingers of mist that shape nothing but themselves swirl over an irrelevant body far below, hiding it.

No pain. No fear. Ennui. Resignation.

Better this way.

—Sure about that?

RICHARD!

—But a touch of my hand, Charlie, and ye shall be upheld in more than this.

A bracing torrent of skepticism tugs Singleton towards life.

Stay with me, Richard!

—I never left you.

Oh, yes, you did. You all did.

—No, Charlie. I'm right here. You're the one who's been doing the running. Why?

Because.

—?

Because I'm frightened.

—Of what?

Finding out the truth.

—They say it liberates.

There's such a thing as too much freedom.

—But now you can become an authority figure, like you've always wanted.

And drink the energy of others, as Drew did mine? or Aubrey itself?

—Then what *do* you want? Anything? Are you ready to end?

I have always craved Meaning.

—Old habits die hard.

Life without belief is too lonely.

—No. Just lonely enough.

Tell me what to do! How to live!

Nothing.

Richard?

A whisper fading down the corridors of thought:

Play your tape, Charlie.

```
CHARLES!
W     W
A     A
K     K
E U P E
```

"WAKE UP!"

Vita?

"WAKE UP!"

"WAKE UP!"

Merlee?

"WAKE UP?"

"OH, GOD, PLEASE DON'T DIE!" *I V I A!!!*

As he opens his eyes, the first sight Charles sees is Olivia's tear-streaked face.

"A thousand pardons, Ms. Aubrey," he says feebly. "I've ruined your mascara."

"Charlie! Oh, thank God!"

The next few minutes are taken up with medical pokes and queries, which Charles endures with weary grace. At length he and Olivia are allowed to talk.

"No, you didn't have a stroke," she tells him. "In fact, for a man whose heart decided to play possum you seem to be in pretty good health. They said they're going to keep you here overnight for observation, but you'll probably be able to leave tomorrow."

"Where am I? This place looks all too familiar."

"You're in Bucks County General."

"Thought so." Singleton sighs. "My home away from home."

"Well, later on, you're going to have a visitor from your other home."

"Hm?"

"Dr. Lichinsky. I called him earlier."

"Oh, dear, that's going to be an expensive house call, I'm afraid."

"It won't cost you a cent. You got sick in my house, so I'm taking care of your medical bills. No arguments."

A grateful smile. "That should be my cue to say I cannot unbend my fierce Gasçon pride to accept your offer, but I no longer want to play Cyrano. Peer Gynt is more my speed."

Olivia presses his hand between hers. "Mr. Singleton, do you know how very fond I've grown of you? Try to stick around, love, I need all the father figures I can get."

"I doubt that, Ms. A., but if you think an aging Tinker Bell will fit the job description, you will receive my application on the morrow."

"I really thought I'd lost you. I came into your room and you weren't breathing. What happened?"

"I behaved very foolishly. I was already distressed about Alan's arrest, but I complicated it with sherry. But those are merely the symptoms. The real culprit once more is the Aubrey Effect."

"In what way?"

"That's what I mean to find out. First I have to listen to something."

"That couldn't be one of those tapes that Josh brought you, could it?"

"Yes. How do you know?"

"In the ambulance you kept muttering about it over and over. 'Play your tape, Charlie, play your tape, Charlie.' I assume you meant this one." She hands him a cassette.

Charles peers at the label. "The very one, O Miracle Lady. How did you think to bring it?"

"We had no choice. No one could pry it from your fingers."

"I don't suppose you had the fortuitous foresight to bring the player as well, did you?"

Olivia laughs. "It's not enough I saved your life, I should also serve you a fingerbowl?"

Charles kisses the back of her hand. "Lass, I know I'm an awful nuisance, but perhaps you might be able to scrounge up a cassette player somewhere in the hospital?"

The door opens. A man pokes his head through. "Is another visitor allowed?"

"Gadfry Daniel!" Singleton exclaims. "Is that actually you, lad?"

"One and the same," Alan Hunter says, walking in. "See how you take care of yourself when I'm not around?"

"But . . . I don't mean this pejoratively . . . what are you doing here? I thought you were under arrest."

"I was. Josh locked me up for a few hours, then said I was free to go. No explanations, not that I hung around for one. Hello, Olivia."

She nods antarctically, withdraws a folded sheet of plain white paper from the pocket of her skirt and hands it to the editor. "I'm returning this to you. Don't ever send me another." Ignoring Alan's confusion, Olivia tells Charles she will try to find a tape player and leaves the room.

Alan stares after her, mystified, then glances down at the letter. "What is this thing, anyway?"

Charles recognizes it. "Something Olivia claims you wrote to her. Earlier she asked me to read it, but fate intervened. What does it say?"

Alan begins to read aloud, but by the second paragraph is too choked to continue.

"Oh, my," Singleton murmurs, "that *is* vivid. You may have a new career ahead of you, Alan."

"I didn't write this."

"Ms. Aubrey seems to think so."

"She's wrong."

"Your word is bond with me. But *do* go on reading."

Alan does so with difficulty. Just before the end of the letter, Olivia reenters with a portable tape player and earphones.

"Don't stop on my account," she says dryly, "you're almost at the best part."

"Damn it," Alan snaps, "what makes you think I sent this?"

"The style."

"I didn't write it."

"Then who did?"

"Maybe your boyfriend, Wyatt Earp."

"Children, don't bicker," Charles chides. "Olivia, may I peruse that document?"

"It's no longer mine. Ask the author."

With a futile gesture, Alan hands it over and watches Charles read. When he is finished, Singleton ponders the letter with a puzzled frown on his face. Alan loses patience.

"Well? What's the decision from on high? Do you really think I could have written that thing?"

"Uno momento," Charles says, scanning it once more before turning to Olivia. "For what it's worth, missy, I think Alan is telling the truth."

"Oh? What did you see that I missed?"

"It's what I don't see." He hands it back to Olivia. "Look for yourself. . . ."

"I don't feel the need to hang around till I'm exonerated," Alan says sarcastically. "I'm going back to Aubrey House and pack. Maybe I can hitch a ride with Barbara."

"She isn't here," Olivia says. "I rode over in the ambulance with Charles. You'll have to take a cab." She removes a ring of keys from her purse and hands it to Alan. "If you're gone before I return, put these in the mailbox." Her tone makes it clear that she would prefer him to do just that.

Alan takes the keys and leaves. Olivia gives Charles the tape recorder she borrowed from one of the other patients. He thanks her and snaps his final tape into the slot just as a nurse enters and asks Charles whether he feels up to seeing another visitor.

"Oh, I feel remarkably lively for a revenant," Singleton replies.

"Wha-aat?"

"Never mind, madame. Who is it?"

"The sheriff."

"Show him in."

As the nurse leaves, Olivia puts the anonymous letter back in her purse, snaps the catch and says, "Charles, since you seem to be doing all right now, would you mind if I go home? I'll come back tonight."

"Precious lady, that's not necessary. I will survive even unto daybreak. Go home. You look worse than I feel."

Olivia blows him a kiss. "Thanks, Tinker Bell. You do wonders for a girl's ego."

Josh Pelham enters. Charles notes the coolness that passes between him and Olivia. She leaves.

"Hope you don't mind answering a few questions?"

"I thought this was purely social. I didn't realize you were paying me a professional call."

"You took things out of the garage storage room. I need an inventory."

"Why on earth?"

"Because Cameron Lambert evidently was hiding up there. It's unlikely he left a clue to his whereabouts, but I have to check it all out, anyway. I heard you found a diary."

"That's correct."

"Where'd you put it? In your room at Aubrey House?"

"Yes, it's in the top drawer of the nightstand on the left of the bed." Singleton sighs wistfully. "I suppose it will become part of police archives for quite some time to come?"

"Probably."

"I see." Charles yawns. "I beg your pardon. My little ordeal today *has* sapped my strength. Have you any further questions?"

"Only one more. Besides the diary, did you take anything else out of there?"

Charles shakes his head innocently. "No, not a blessed thing."

Josh leaves.

Singleton's final visitor of the day, Sam Lichinsky, takes a seat opposite the patient's bed and nods to show he is listening.

Charles punches PAUSE. "All right, Sam, I've found the place. I originally recorded this as a message to Dick Creighton—this is me the night of my stroke." He presses PLAY.

click

> "—I've had a terrible new insight into Aubrey House and I feel I must share it with you. I . . . I simply haven't the stamina to write it all out on paper. Nor the time. Right now, it's shortly before six, not even an hour since I called and told you that Drew died. I don't suppose you'll be getting back here for a while yet, but just to be sure, as soon as I'm finished taping, I intend to run an experiment upstairs in Shipperton's old room. In order for it to be valid, I must be alone in the house—"

"That," Charles explains to the psychiatrist, "was so that no one else's thoughts could muddy up the experiment."

> "Frankly, Dick, I hope it fails. Had Drew proposed the theory to me a few days ago, I'm sure I should have swiftly rejected it. But in this dreadful place, the most godless things begin to seem possible to me.
>
> "I've left Drew's memoranda for you on the top of your dresser . . . what chiefly triggered me was the sheaf of notes I read concerning Vita—"

click

"I read the identical set of notes this afternoon, Sam, but got nothing out of them at first. Isn't that strange?"

"Not at all, Charles. You understood all too well and rejected your train of thought. You weren't quite ready to confront your final fragment."

"Indeed not. Instead, I nearly died."

"What do you mean?"

"I mean, Sam, that for the first time in my life I experienced an out-of-body experience—and had great difficulty getting back inside myself again." A crooked smile. "Remove that Doubting Thomas expression, Dr. L. Whether or not one interprets it as objective experience or hallucination, the fact remains that I *did* undergo a unique event."

"Can you decribe it?"

"Yes. I was lying on my bed, feeling lightheaded and dizzy from drink. Suddenly I felt myself floating up near the ceiling—yet at the same time, I was aware of still being in bed. The latter awareness quickly faded, though. I began to feel stranded. Disembodied. Then I actually saw the cold blue light materializing beneath me, hiding my body from view. That's when I knew I was dying."

"Except you didn't die."

"No . . . an old friend led me through the crisis."

The psychiatrist glances suspiciously at Charles. "What old friend are you talking about?"

"Dick Creighton."

"You're not claiming that Creighton's ghost came to your rescue? Your spiritual mentor, guiding you back to life?"

He shakes his head sadly. "No, Sam, that's what the old Charles Singleton wanted to—*needed to*—believe. And almost died before letting go of."

"Then you're saying—"

"Patience, Horatio, I shall be faithful. For now, pay heed."

"—Drew speculated that whatever psychic energies Vita sensed at Aubrey House were distorted by the memories, wishes and fears of her psyche.

"I find this enormously suggestive, Richard. The thing which has puzzled me the most about Aubrey is the disparity of experiences the five of us have undergone. Vita's catastrophe, Drew's struggle on the rear stairs, the two sides of Merlyn's personality flickering in and out of focus . . . and hardly anything for you or me.

"However, Richard, if one expands on Drew's thesis concerning Vita, this problem begins to sort itself out. Look at it this way: a nine-volt battery may—"

Charles' voice merges into the tape's background hiss and disappears. He shuts off the machine.

"What happened?" Sam asks. "Did your battery run down?"

"In a manner of speaking. Aubrey drained it. Haunted houses replenish *psi* power by tapping energy sources at hand: portable radios, flashlights, human beings. This siphoning of vitality accounts for the unmistakable coldness one feels in the presence of a ghost. Anyway, while my tape machine was happily attaining nirvana, I propounded the theory that Aubrey is particularly adept in complex electrical interaction with the human mind."

"Translation, Charles?"

"Consider this: a battery is capable of running a calculator or a radio or a flashlight. The application means nothing to the battery, it just provides power. What if Aubrey is a perfectly amoral battery that is also a ditto ditto transmitter?"

"All right, say it is. What then?"

"Picture our beloved white-frame horror vampirizing thoughts, then beaming them back as concrete images to the very minds they just emerged from. Remember Orwell's Room 101?"

Lichinsky nods. "A torture chamber that holds whatever one dreads the most."

"Exactly. I believe Aubrey House is its psychic counterpart. Are you afraid of the night? *Here There Be Darkness*. Perhaps you're frightened of the Headless Horseman? Stay away from Aubrey, then, or you might encounter whole regiments of decapitated Hessians. Does Charlotte Aubrey upset you? *Come home and give Grandma a kiss*." Charles shudders. "All my poor dear, dead friends. Richard and Merlyn and Vita and Drew, all of them tormented by pain or grief, riddled with depression or guilt or the longing for death. Aubrey's harmonics."

"You're saying that the house feeds on the mind's worst terrors and renders them back in the form of hallucinations?"

"That's it in a nutshell."

"But why? What makes it work that way?"

"Must there be a reason? The cosmos contains sharks and black holes and door-to-door bible salesmen. There are plenty of irrelevant horrors. Why not Aubrey?" Charles yawns. "Sorry, Sam. No impeachment of present company intended."

Lichinsky gets to his feet. "Well, rest is definitely what this doctor orders. Get some sleep and you'll be fine tomorrow. When you get back to New York, call me."

"To schedule an appointment?"

A warm smile crosses Sam's capuchin-monkey face. "Maybe just for lunch. So long."

Charles stares out at the early evening sky. He wonders when he lost the capacity to cry.

Gone. All gone. Nothing but remembered voices.

—And what about you, Mr. S.?

Me? To paraphrase Dottie Parker, I might as well live.

—Sure about that? Life without Meaning?

A priori meaning implicit in decision to endure moment to moment.

—Bravo, Charlie. And your reasons?

Olivia needs a father figure.

—A good start.

Yes. Now kindly let me go to sleep.

—Who, Charlie?

Hush.

But where's my cane?

Olivia didn't bring it.

Not your cane, boyo . . . mine.

Hush.

For the first time in four years, Charles Singleton is not afraid to shut his eyes. He falls fast asleep—

"Human, all too human"
? ?
? ?
??
?
? ?
? ?
? ?
"Things"

—and sits bolt upright in bed, terrified. He switches on his bedside lamp, snatches up the telephone and dials Aubrey House.

"We're sorry. The number you have dialed is not in service at this time."

Singleton hangs up, now twice as frightened. His mind races through options, but he already knows there is only one thing he can do.

Face the cold blue light alone.

Olivia left Charles at the hospital and got back to the house shortly after four. There were three policemen on duty: one in a patrol car at the head of the driveway; a second standing guard at the garage; the third one on the front porch was the callow young man who almost turned away her attorneys.

Olivia paid her cab fare and got out. She smiled perversely at the sound of stripped gears as the taxi driver hurried to get away from Aubrey House. As she crossed the porch, the young policeman hailed her.

"Ma'am, we've got orders not to let anyone upstairs of your garage."

"No problem. I have no reason to go there."

"We'd appreciate it if you'd ask your guests to stay out of there, too, ma'am."

"It's hardly necessary. Mr. Singleton is in the hospital and as for Mr. Hunter—"

He interrupted her. "Excuse me, ma'am, I was particularly talking about Miss Lincoln."

"Barbara? Why?"

"We caught her out there a while ago."

"Probably going to her car."

"Yes'm. She claimed she just wanted something from the glove compartment, but when she didn't come out right away, Officer O'Haire investigated and found her rooting through stuff up on the second floor. We're gonna have to report it to the sheriff."

"I understand," Olivia said, trying not to show how much the news took her aback. "I'll talk to Barbara about it."

She went to the front door and searched her purse for her keys, then remembered she'd loaned them to Alan. She rang the bell and waited. Alan let her in.

"Where's Barbara?"

"Sulking in your bedroom," Alan answered. "Why?"

She ignored his question and went upstairs.

"Yes, of course I'll explain, but please don't stare at me that way, Liv."

"How am I supposed to? I thought you were my friend."

"I still am."

"I thought I knew you, Barbara, but you're a stranger."

"No, I'm not. Give me a chance to explain."

The blonde sat hunched on the bed hugging her knees. She projected an uncharacteristic vulnerability that touched Olivia and made her regret her initial harshness. She took a seat in the armchair Singleton slept in and said, "All right, Barb, go ahead. I'm listening."

"Earlier today, Liv, I became restless. It was after Josh took Alan into custody and Charlie Singleton got drunk. I forget what he said or you said, it's not important, but all of a sudden, I had this need to go outside and clear my head. I took a walk down by the lake, rowed out to the island and back. Then I hiked to the north line of your property. Are you familiar with that part of the grounds?"

"Only schematically. But I know it's where the foundations of the old Lambert farmhouse are supposed to be."

"Uh-huh. You have to really look hard to see any trace of where it once stood. I walked around, thinking about Uncle Josiah's gold . . . and suddenly, Liv, I *knew.*"

"Knew what?"

"The reason Cam's been skulking around here all this time."

"Why?"

"He must be looking for General Butler's letter."

"What are you talking about?"

"Bear with me, love. First, I have to teach you some Lambert history. . . ."

> Ezekiel Lambert, Jr. returned to Pennsylvania in 1820 because his father was on his deathbed. The dying colonel ceded the deed to the property to his son with a solemn injunction to take care of his mother and his sister Norah.
>
> Norah got nothing but a sealed envelope and instructions not to open it unless her brother proved remiss in providing for his family, and then only in case of extreme privation.
>
> While the contents of this letter are unknown, Lambert family tradition maintains that it held the location of Josiah's stolen gold. If so, it sheds a curious new light on the colonel's character, generally regarded as sterling. Perhaps he could not bring himself to touch ill-got gains, yet he did not return Josiah's loot to the government, either, reserving it instead in case of family misfortune.
>
> After the colonel died, Ezekiel Lambert, Jr. settled down to run the farm, though it is said he immediately dug up the cellar in a vain effort to find Uncle Josiah's treasure. In 1849, evidently still obsessed

with gold, Ezekiel Jr. went to California. There he married a Spaniard of modest means, ran through her money and left her with a son, Ezekiel III, and the deed to his heavily mortgaged property in Pennsylvania. (Ezekiel III eventually sold the deed to a Chicago businessman, Addison Aubrey).

If the colonel's letter really contained the secret of Josiah's hoard, it is ironic that near the end of his life, Ezekiel Lambert, Jr. very nearly found it.

The year was 1862. Back east, the Civil War was raging. Zeke's sister Norah had recently wed a wealthy Louisiana planter. That in itself was a tempting lure to Ezekiel Jr., but when he also learned that New Orleans was under the martial governorship of his old friend, General Ben Butler, Zeke said goodbye to wife, son and California, wrote his sister that he was coming and signed on as a sailor on a packet ship that left San Diego for New York. Zeke deserted in the Bahamas and went to New Orleans. General Butler was delighted to see Lambert, even though Zeke's sister Norah had recently fled the city with her husband, who had been secretly supplying weapons to the Confederate Army.

The day after Ezekiel Jr. got to New Orleans, a sealed envelope was delivered to Butler with a personal note from Norah Lambert entreating the general to give it to her brother Zeke when he came to town. Butler promptly sent for Ezekiel, but Fate had already intervened. The same night he arrived, Zeke was killed in a tavern brawl.

"And nothing is ever heard again of Norah Lambert's letter," Barbara told Olivia. "But let's just suppose that it remained in Butler's files until after the war. Maybe one day he came on the sealed envelope, remembered it belonged to the Lambert clan and tried to deliver it, but by some accident or error it ended up, instead, in the hands of the Aubreys."

"That's a mighty big supposition, Barb."

"But it explains something that's puzzled me for over a year now, Liv."

"What?"

"The first time I met Cam Lambert was when he showed up at the library and came to my desk for assistance. He looked like your average jock. I expected he'd ask me to help him find the National League batting averages for 1965, or something like that, but he surprised me. What he was looking for was incredibly obscure."

"What was it?"

"The history of rural mail delivery in Bucks County since the Civil War. Day by day, if possible."

Olivia shook her head. "That sure doesn't fit the mental picture I've conjured up of Cam Lambert."

"It was totally out of character. Believe me, I found that out."

The door connecting Olivia's room to Alan's suddenly opened. "I'm sorry to disturb you," Alan said through the open portal, "but I've got a favor to ask."

"Knock first next time," Olivia told him. "What do you want?"

"I'm all packed to leave, but I can't call a cab."

"Why not? Won't they come out here?"

"No, Olivia, that's not the problem. I can't get a dial tone. The phone's dead."

Olivia sighed. "The pleasures of country life. Maybe you can persuade the police to call in on their car radio."

"I already asked, but they said no. I thought maybe Barbara might give me a lift to the train station."

The two women looked at one another. Barbara shrugged.

"We're involved in an important discussion," Olivia said. "You'll have to wait, Alan."

"Okay." A resigned shrug. He made no move to quit the doorway.

"This is a private conversation," Olivia added.

"Look, Alan, if you're anxious to get going," Barbara suggested, "you can borrow my car, drive into town and have a taxi follow you back here."

"Thanks." He sounded anything but thankful. "Where are your keys?"

Barbara rose, rummaged in her purse, found them. Alan took the keys and left the room.

"I have to start locking that door," Olivia murmured. She patted the bed. "All right, Barbara, sit down and go on with your story." The blonde hesitated. "Come on, I'm not going to bite. Continue."

"Okay. Lambert tradition has it that when Norah married into wealth, she no longer saw any reason to conceal the whereabouts of Josiah's gold from her brother, and so she revealed all in the letter Zeke never received. If my theory is correct, General Butler eventually tried to deliver it to the Lamberts, but the Aubreys got it, instead."

"How could that happen?"

"Liv, what's the use in speculating? Doesn't Cam's peculiar interest in old-time rural postal delivery point in that very direction?"

"Maybe."

"*Maybe?* Then why is Cam hanging around here so long? He *has* to be searching the house. It'd take one man more than a year to go through all the papers in your attic."

"So you think that if Norah's letter exists it's somewhere in the garage? Is that why you were rooting around out there, Barb?"

"Yes. It was only a hunch, but after I thought of it, I got excited and wanted to check it out right away. I *was* going to tell you, Liv, honest." Barbara impulsively grasped her friend's hand. "Please don't be mad at me."

"I'm not. But you were wasting your time."

"Why do you say that?"

"Because. If Cam's really been looking for Norah Lambert's letter all this time, wouldn't he already have checked out the stuff that he and his brother Matt lugged out to the garage?"

Barbara's lips tightened. "I never thought of that."

"Well, anyway, your letter theory does provide a motive for Cam sneaking in and out of the house. And now I know how he managed to do it."

"Managed to do what?"

"Come and go secretly."

A dead pause. Barbara let go of Olivia's hand.

"What are you talking about, Liv?"

"How Cam disappeared from the house after his brother was killed. How he's been getting in again. Aubrey House's architectural plans have been missing since just before Matthew was murdered, but my lawyer, Mr. Waxman, is old enough to remember that there used to be a tunnel connecting Aubrey House with the stable."

"That's silly, Liv. What possible reason could there be for building a tunnel? So the Master could make secret assignations with loose women?"

"A possible side benefit, I suppose, but it's more mundane than that. Charlotte Aubrey didn't want the staff tracking mud into the house, so my grandfather had a passage dug between house and stable so the servants could go back and forth during bad weather and still stay dry."

"Where's this primitive subway supposed to be? Did your attorney remember that, too?"

"Yep. The house end of it opens into the wine cellar. That's why my father—still seems strange to call Jason that—that's why he had the tunnel sealed off back in the thirties. Apparently he got fed up with the staff filching his best bottles."

A brief silence, then Barbara asked, "Well, now that you know, Liv, what are you going to do with the information? Have you told Josh yet?"

"No, but I will. I thought I'd check it out myself first."

"Don't do that!"

Olivia's eyebrows rose. "And why not?"

"Well, you said it was sealed off."

"Cam must have reopened it."

"But wouldn't Josh have found it, then?"

"Maybe not. Señor Sheriff is only minimally competent."

Barbara seized Olivia's hands and squeezed them tight. "Liv, please, I ask you as a friend . . . *don't go down there*."

Her intense earnestness impressed Olivia. She looked at the two strong hands holding hers, then up into Barbara's wide blue eyes, and almost forgot to breathe. It was a moment before Olivia trusted herself to speak. "All right, love, tell me why you don't want me to go into the wine cellar."

"Because—don't you see, Liv?—if your tunnel is real, that's where Cam must be hiding."

A rap at the hall door. *Now what?* "Who's there?"

"Me again," Alan called. "May I come in?"

Olivia gave Barbara a long-suffering look. "If you must."

Alan opened the door and saw the women, hand in hand, obviously involved in something deep and important. He hesitated to enter.

"Well?" Olivia prompted. "What is it?"

"The car won't start."

"What's the matter with it?" Barbara asked.

"Beats me. I'm not mechanical."

Barbara gestured impatiently. "Put the keys on the dresser. I'll check it out later."

"I want to leave before it gets dark."

"Later, Alan!"

He slammed the door. The women were alone again.

"All right, Barb, it's time to stop avoiding the issue. I want you to tell me about Cam Lambert."

"I already have."

"You know what I mean. What did he do to you?"

"I can't talk about it."

"Why not?"

The blonde lowered her eyes. "Too ashamed."

"Hey, this is *me*, kid. Liv. I won't be shocked—I promise."

"I'm no good at opening up, Liv. I never had a sister."

"Well, I did. I still do. Two halfsies—does that add up to one whole sister? I don't like Des. I hardly knew Merlyn. I'm not much of a sister, either, but *we* could be closer, Barb. Kindred spirits. You were here for me when my father—when Ben died. I'm here for you now. Okay?"

Barbara nodded yes, unable to speak.

Olivia pressed her companion's hand to her lips. "All right, now, Li'l Miss Gibraltar, I've seen you strong, there's nothing wrong with a little vulnerability, too. Drop the macho bit and talk to me. . . ."

Barbara began to cry. Olivia felt each sob like a spasm in her own body.

****

". . . tried dating his brother Matt to keep Cam away from me, but that didn't help. All it accomplished was to turn them against each other. Hattie blamed me for the way they began to fight, and I'm afraid she was right." Barbara stopped speaking. Her words had come in one continuous flow, but now she stared mutely at the floor.

"Well? Is that all, Barb?"

"Isn't it enough? What do you think of your 'kindred spirit' now?"

"I think Cameron Lambert treated you horribly, Barb, but you're not to blame for his actions."

"No? Then why didn't I do something to stop him?"

"Obviously, you didn't know how to handle the situation."

"No, Liv, it's just not that simple. Or innocent. On some level, I must have wanted it. That's the hideous but undeniable truth. I loathe myself for it . . . maybe even more than Cam. And I had no right to encourage Matt. If Cam killed his brother, I'm probably the reason."

"Now listen to me, lady," Olivia said, taking Barbara's chin in her fist and turning her face toward her, "I know a thing or two about levels and degrees of guilt. Remember that cathedral dream I told you I had the night Ben committed suicide? Where I dreamed I crucified him?"

"It's not the sort of thing one forgets, Liv."

"Well, I have. Or at least stopped agonizing over it. I told myself—you told me—how useless it is to tear myself apart over something that's not my fault. My nightmare didn't make Ben slit his throat. He did that all by himself."

"But what does this have to do with what I just told you?"

"Everything. The nails I drove into my father are the same ones you're driving into yourself."

She shook her head. "No, Liv, you're wrong. You committed murder in a dream. What I did with Cam really happened. I don't know how you can still stand to look at me."

God help me . . . I've never been able to stop.

Barbara misinterpreted Olivia's silence. "So it's finally starting to sink in, what I told you? I can just imagine what you think of me now."

"I . . . I don't think you can."

"Liv, why are you looking at me like that?"

"I don't think I ought to say."

"Why? Is it that bad? Why are you smiling?"

"Because this is ironic. You're afraid of what I might say—and so am I."

"Liv, please don't shut me out. I want to know what you really think of me."

"All right." Her words tumbled out in a torrent. "Barbara, you're the most glorious woman I've ever known. Not just physically. Totally." Olivia heard the sudden intake of breath, dared not look at her. *Keep going. Say it all while you've still got the nerve.* "Ever since the first time we met at the library, I've admired your strength and confidence. You seem so at home with your femininity. A luminous heavenly body in the midst of so much neon. Except, no, that's poetic hyperbole. Poetry lies. You can't condense wonder into discrete packets. I look at you and feel joy and fear and excitement and I want—" Her courage suddenly fled. She faltered to silence.

"Yes? Don't be afraid to say it."

"I . . . want . . . to touch you."

Silence. Barbara stroked her friend's cheek. Olivia interpreted it as a pitying gesture. *Oh, God!* Suddenly suffused with shame and embarrassment, she wished the setting sun would go down and darkness hide her disgrace . . . but then Barbara took Olivia's hand and gently guided them to her breasts.

"Please, Liv . . . turn out the light."

****

Fingertips brush down all the long line to the whirlpool. The hot insistent press of soft lips on naked breasts.

Lower. Deeper.

Vortex.

The wheels spin.

Crossbeams end in wide gaping mouths. Into the open archway *down all?* the long sloping corridors where the serpent slips in *and I am free behind the jamb—*

quantus tremor est furturus
—prisoned in the prism of corrosion—
Quando Euphoria Est Venturus!
Olivia
Hush
OliViaViaVia
HUsh HUsh
VIaVIaVIaVIaVIaVIaVIa
HUSh A HUSh HUSh
V
VIAVIAVIAVIAVIAVIAVIAVIAVIA
HUSH HUSH

****

Grey light spills down from stained glass windows. The candles gutter. The lid of the coffin is open, but the box is empty.

My name is Olivia.

Nothing.

Daddy?

Nothing.

Mama?

Nothing.

Ben?

Nothing.

Alan? Josh?

Nothing.

Barbara?

Gone.

The candles go out but the air shimmers. Alone . . . yet pleasure washes her in plangent waves. Olivia feels herself building toward another peak—

No! Pull back!

An intrusion.

Why?

—beware the sensation of well-being . . . guard against sudden euphoria. It might well be a danger signal warning one that the "cold blue light" is setting one up for attack . . .

Charles!

Grateful that she does not have to face the empty cathedral alone, Olivia opens her eyes.

On darkness.

Memory flooded back. Barbara. Alan. Ecstasy and slumber. Strange, empty dreams. She remembered that Aubrey House could be dangerous to fall asleep in.

Olivia tried to stay calm and assess the situation. She was naked and alone and it was pitch-black. *The servants' staircase again?* She stretched out her arms to see if she could touch the walls, but could not. She took a careful step in one direction, then the other. Nothing. She knelt down, felt the floor. Smooth and cold to the touch. She followed it along on hands and knees till she finally came to a barrier of some sort. She stood up and ran her hands along the obstruction. A wooden framework, something like a large, wide bookshelf but with sloping compartment floors. She reached farther in and touched something round and gritty. A bottle.

She was in the wine cellar.

The thrill of fear. She remembered the night she heard footsteps. *Cameron Lambert coming out of the tunnel. And I told myself it was only mice. I could have been killed.* Now that Olivia knew Barbara's degrading secret, she had no doubts of Cameron's madness.

A stealthy shuffling sound.

Someone coming.

She clapped a hand over her mouth to muffle the sound of her too-rapid breath. She walked on tiptoes, following the border of the wine rack around to a right turn that must be one corner of the cellar. *Quick!* Another long row of shelves. A second angle. A third.

The shuffling was closer now, more distinct.

An unbidden whimper rose in her throat. Olivia ran along the fourth side of the dark room, was stopped by another wine rack perpendicular to her route. *Four angles. Back where I started? Hard to tell.* The wooden steps she sought were somewhere in the middle of the cellar. She moved away from the wall, both arms outstretched, felt more wine piled above her head on transverse shelves. She rounded the edge of one high unit, entered an aisle, quick-stepped through the narrow passage, palms brushing racks on either side.

Ow!

Olivia gasped at the sudden stab of pain in her thumb. She pulled out a splinter, sucked her finger, tasted blood.

The footsteps were directly above her now.

Panic. She ran swiftly to the end of the aisle and headed back up another. A third. She gasped for air. Another long, narrow passage and then—

Open space. Nothing to guide her. Lost in the middle of the room. Turning, turning, unable to tell which direction she'd come from. Wide aimless circles. Her hand flicked something overhead.

The light!

Olivia raised both arms and fumbled till she touched the wonderfully reassuring roundness of a dangling lightbulb. She ran her fingers up the neck of the socket but could not feel a turn-switch. She circled her hand around the bulb and groped for a cord, found it. Pulled.

It clicked but did not light up.

Bitterly disappointed, Olivia let go of the bulb, backed away and immediately banged her foot against something hard. She knelt and felt cautiously for the thing she'd bumped into.

Stairs going up. At first she felt enormous relief. Then she realized she couldn't risk climbing them. The footsteps were overhead. *What if it's Lambert?*

Suddenly she was afraid for Barbara.

Olivia sat on the steps and tried to will her racing heart to steady itself. Her ragged breathing was too loud, she forced herself to hold her breath.

The door above her opened. A filament of light spilled down the steps. She jumped to her feet.

"Who in hell—?"

Before Olivia could hide, a flashbeam caught and temporarily blinded her.

"What are you doing down there in the dark?" Alan asked. "For God's sake, you're naked!"

The hysteria of relief. Alan ran downstairs and put his arms around her while she wept like a frightened child. When Olivia was calm again, he sat her down on the cellar steps, took off his shirt and draped it over her shoulders and asked what was wrong.

"This isn't the first time I've walked in my sleep," she explained. "I only seem to do it at Aubrey House. Last time, I almost fell down the back stairs."

Alan glanced around him. "Where are we? The wine cellar?"

"Yes."

"Didn't Charles tell me something about the light bulb down here once being on a timer?"

Olivia smiled, was surprised she was able to so soon after her fright. "As far as I know, it still is. Cousin Merlyn was a differential tightwad. She'd spend oodles of money on herself, then scrimp pennies. She got mad at a summer tenant who left the bulb burning down here, so she installed a timer that'd turn it off automatically after five or ten minutes."

"Well," Alan said, "you sound like you're back to normal."

"Yes. Thanks for finding me, Sir Galahad. It must be late. You wanted to leave before dark. I'm sorry."

"Never mind. But it is dark out. And in, for that matter."

"What?"

"I mean there's been a power failure. A few minutes ago, all the lights went out. I was trying to find the fusebox when I heard you down here."

"*All* the lights? That's not possible."

"I'd say see for yourself, but that's ridiculous. Why is it impossible?"

"Because the house in on circuit breakers. When there's an overload, the only system that's supposed to shut off is the one it happened to. There'd have to be a major power failure to lose everything at once."

"Well, that's not the case because I just went out to the garage and the cop on duty has the lights on there."

A flicker of suspicion. "What were you doing in the garage?"

"Looking for a flashlight. I brought my own, but it's not working, either. Funny. I could've sworn I bought new bat—" He suddenly stopped.

"Alan, are you thinking what I'm thinking?"

" 'fraid so. The cold blue light?"

"Yes." Olivia pointed to the flashlight he was holding. "But there's nothing wrong with this one."

"It wasn't in the house when the power failed. Maybe by now the place has all the energy it needs."

As if in answer, the 150-watt overhead bulb lit. They stared up at it, then at one another. Olivia suddenly remembered she was wearing nothing.

"Oh, Christ! Don't look at me, Alan."

"You ask a lot of a man, Ms. Aubrey."

"I must be a mess."

"The loveliest mess I've ever set eyes on."

She couldn't help laughing. "Is that what the French call savoir faire?"

"What else do you say to a naked lady?"

Olivia's mirth suddenly vanished. In the stark cellar light, she got her first good look at the all-white plastic flashlight in Alan's hand.

"Alan, where did you get that? In the garage?"

"It was in the glove compartment of Barbara's car. Why?"

"Yoohoo! The lights are back on. Where IS everybody?"

Barbara peeked through the open cellar door and saw them sitting on the steps. At sight of Alan, she cinched her robe tight. "What is this? Hide and seek?" She started down the stairs. Olivia jumped up and backed away. Alan's shirt slid to the floor, but she did not bother to retrieve it.

"Liv, what on earth are you doing down here with him? Where are your clothes?"

Olivia seized a wine bottle. "Alan, move away from her."

"Liv, what's wrong?"

"My God, it was you! The first night I came to Aubrey House. You!" Olivia pointed at Alan's flashlight. "That was in the garage next to the horse stall."

"So?"

"So . . . did you put in that horrible hay?"

"*What* hay?" Barbara turned to Alan. "Do you have any idea what she's raving about?"

"You know what hay," Olivia shrilled. "You put it in to deliberately disguise the other end of the tunnel."

"Before today, I never even heard of your tunnel."

"I'll just bet you didn't."

"What tunnel are you talking about, Olivia?" Alan asked.

"It runs between this room and the garage."

"Look, Liv," Barbara protested, "you own this place and you only just found out about it. How do you figure I could possibly be aware of its existence?"

"You're head librarian. You've got a complete file on the Lamberts, you must have one on the Aubreys, too. You certainly know all about Josiah's hidden gold. God, I thought you were my best friend. You're a total stranger." Olivia's eyes widened; her indrawn breath was like the hiss of a serpent. "No, you're worse . . . you're my enemy!"

"Is that what you really think, Olivia? Upstairs when you told me what you wanted, did I treat you like an enemy?"

"Hush." Olivia glanced nervously at Alan.

"Oh . . . I *see*. You're ashamed. You can't deal with Alan finding out we just slept together."

"Shut UP, Barbara!"

"No! I don't regret what happened—I love you!"

"Did you say that to Cam, too? And Matt?"

"No-o. I told you about them, Liv."

"Lies. Hattie hated you. Why? Because you deliberately played her sons off against each other?"

"Why would I do that?"

"To keep them off balance so you could search the house for Norah Lambert's letter."

"How? By slipping in and out through your mysterious tunnel? Come on, Liv, you yourself said it was sealed off and forgotten. Even if I *had* heard about it, how in hell could I find it?"

"By stealing the blueprints of Aubrey House from my attorney's office."

"You can't prove that!"

"*I* can," Alan said. "You've got them hidden at your apartment."

Barbara rounded on him. "God damn you! I *knew* you saw them!"

Alan ignored her. "Last night," he told Olivia, "I accidentally knocked some of Barbara's stuff out of her bookcase. She charged into the room like a tigress and snatched up a long roll that could have been your blueprints."

"*Could* have been?" Barbara's voice climbed. "You didn't actually *see* them?"

"Only a glimpse. I was testing you just now to see how you'd react."

"You miserable fucking bastard!"

"Tch, tch . . . your opinion of me seems to have slumped since last night."

"There's nothing funny about this, Alan," said Olivia. "Don't you see?"

"See what?"

"That Barbara must have murdered Hattie."

"Liv!" The blonde went white. She took a step towards Olivia, who still clutched a wine bottle in her fist. She brandished it threateningly.

"Don't come any closer."

"Put that down!" Barbara tried to snatch the bottle, but Olivia smashed it against the wall. Wine bloodied both women. "Stop it, Liv. If you give me a chance, I'll tell you the truth!"

"Why don't I believe you?"

"Just listen, okay?"

"You've got my attention," Olivia said. She did not relinquish her hold on the broken bottle.

"All right," Barbara admitted, "I *was* looking for Norah Lambert's letter to her brother. For years, I researched General Ben Butler's life to find out what happened to it."

Butler could not return the letter because Norah, while hiding in the swamp with her rebel husband, contracted and succumbed to yellow fever. For years after the war, her undelivered note languished in the general's files. Then, in 1870, one of Butler's political supporters, a Chicago tycoon named Addison Aubrey bought the mortgaged Pennsylvania property that once belonged to Colonel Ezekiel Lambert. Hearing of the transaction, Ben Butler ascertained that the deed was sold to Aubrey by a nineteen-year-old Californian, Ezekiel Lambert III—none other than the long-missing son of Butler's old friend. At the general's request, Aubrey forwarded the letter to the youth, but it came back undelivered. Apparently, Ezekiel and his mother moved shortly after he disposed of the land. Neither were ever heard of again. Eventually Addison Aubrey ceded the Pennsylvania property to his son, Derek, a Philadelphia lawyer who built a home there. Derek was ultimately entrusted with Norah's letter on the theory that since members of the Lambert clan were his neighbors, he might one day discover news of Ezekiel III.

"So," the librarian said, "I figured that the letter is still somewhere in this house. I shared all this with Cam and Matt."

Olivia's lips tightened. "So the three of you *were* working together."

"No. I had no intention of splitting with Matt and Cam, not after I'd spent all those years doing the research. But Cam worried me . . . he was headed in the same direction. I had to keep tabs on him. At least he didn't know anything about the tunnel." Barbara took a deep breath. "I hope you realize I didn't *have* to tell you any of this."

Olivia eyed her suspiciously. "How come you're being so candid?"

"To firm up my credibility. So maybe you'll believe me, Liv, when I swear I did *not* murder Hattie."

"Barbara, I really want to believe you—"

"You should. She's telling the truth."

The voice came from above. They all looked up. Josh stopped halfway down the cellar steps. "Well, well, the cast assembled. Considerate of all of you. Aren't you afraid you'll catch cold, Olivia?"

"Hey," Alan protested, "why are you aiming that gun at me?"

"Because, Mr. Hunter, you broke out of jail."

"Wha—aat?! You let me go."

"That's the unofficial version. Officially, you killed Hattie Lambert, escaped, came back here and committed two more murders. I shot you for resisting arrest." He paused to observe their individual reactions. No one spoke or moved. Josh descended to the bottom of the steps. "They say confession purifieth the soul. Mea culpa. I killed Hattie. Next up? Aubrey, Olivia, caucasian, female, age thirty. Lincoln, Barbara, caucasian, more or less female, age classified. I would've killed Matt and Cam, too, but Cain rose up and slew Abel and disappeared east of Aubrey. Now I finally know how Cam escaped." He noticed Barbara edging along one wall, swung the gun muzzle towards her. "You stay still. Is that where the tunnel is?"

"Yes. What's this all about? Josiah's gold?"

"Damn straight it is. By rights it belongs to me. Or will once I find that fucking letter."

"Who *are* you?"

He grinned at Barbara. "You might call me a kissin' cousin."

Her eyes widened. "Jesus God! The West Coast Lamberts?"

"Very astute, blondie. I'm the last. Didn't even know it myself till six years ago when—when my daddy died. I sorted through his papers, got a crash course in family history." Josh tittered. "Ever see a picture of Uncle Josiah? One handsome dude. I look like him." His titter became a giggle.

Olivia glanced at Alan. He rolled his eyes upward, stared at her, repeated the action. *What's he trying to tell me?* Suddenly, she knew. The lightbulb! *How long has it been burning?* She realized that they had to keep Josh talking for a few more minutes till the automatic timer turned off the bulb. *Cousin Merlyn's pennypinching might actually save us.*

"Josh," Olivia asked, "why did you kill Hattie? What did that poor old woman ever do to you?"

"She wouldn't tell me where to find the letter."

"What makes you think she knew?"

"Oh, come on, add up two and two. I didn't make up those lights in the attic. Cam Lambert *is* still hanging around, sneaking into the house at night through the tunnel. Hattie figures out what he's doing, finagles a job with you. She starts sitting up late in the attic where most of the Aubrey shit is stored. She knows what Cam's trying to find, decides to help him out, get some for herself."

"Has it ever occurred to you that Hattie may have just been worried about her missing son?"

"I gave it a passing thought, Olivia. But the first time I caught her in the attic, she was telling Cam about Josiah's gold."

Barbara was horrified. "You *saw* Cam?"

"Hattie was batty. Batty Hattie." He laughed at his 'witticism.' "Cam wasn't actually there, but Batty Hattie was talking to him as if he were. Telling him where he ought to be looking for Norah Lambert's letter."

"Would you mind satisfying my curiosity?" Barbara asked. "Where did Hattie say it was?"

"In one of the boxes that Cam moved out to the garage. Without you pests around to interfere, it won't take me long to find it."

Keep him talking. "Josh, you can't shoot us. Your men will hear."

He gave Olivia a pitying glance. "What men?"

"The . . . the ones outside."

"You mean the men I sent home?"

"It's going to look pretty fishy," Alan said, "when they dig your bullets out of our bodies."

Josh guffawed. "Man, you people have no imagination! Hey, don't you know what tonight is? The anniversary of the cold blue light . . . the deaths of Merlyn Aubrey and Richard Creighton, the massacre of Matthew Lambert . . . the mad slasher strikes again—only this time the noble sheriff guns him down. Ain't it a shame he arrived too late to rescue the ladies that got carved up? Does the scenario piss you off? I mean, I'm going to come out of this a goddam hero!" He laughed uproariously.

He's becoming progressively high, Olivia thought.

—guard against sudden euphoria—

"All right, who's first? Not you, Alan . . . I've still got one man out at the garage. The bullet has to come last, or this will no longer be a private party." Josh opened his shirt, reached in and pulled out one of the Aubrey carving knives. "All right, any volunteers? No crowding, ladies. Just raise your hands."

With a brief glance at Olivia, Barbara said, "Take me."

"I did once," he snickered. "Weren't you paying attention?"

The blonde smiled sweetly at him. "I've never had a head for small details."

For a second his laughs stopped, then Josh smiled back at Barbara. "Just for that, Babs, the mistress of the house goes first. Won't that be fun to watch?" He turned to Olivia. "I saw the look she just gave you. Drop that bottle."

"Don't do it, Liv! He's going to kill us all, anyway. Don't make it easy for him."

"Shut up!"

"Hey, Mr. Policeman," Barbara taunted, "what if we rush you? How are you going to take on all three of us at once? Or do you shoot as fast as you fuck?"

"SHUT YOUR MOUTH, BITCH!" For the first time, a flicker of doubt. He glanced from one to the other, calculating distances . . .

The light went out.

Josh roared in anger and surprise. Frantic scuffling. A sound of something heavy scraping along the floor . . . a hand shot out of the darkness and grabbed Olivia. She shrieked.

"Shhh!" Barbara whispered in her ear. "Hold on. The tunnel's open." A sudden rush of relief. *We're going to get away!* Olivia's heart beat faster. She felt like laughing.

—guard against sudden euph—

The ghost of a cloying sour-sweet smell emerged from the deeper blackness. Her companion squeezed Olivia's hand tight. *Josh or no Josh, Barb's afraid of the tunnel . . . and so am I.*

A thud. A groan. The flashlight clicked on. Josh aimed the light at the women. "All right, hold it. Don't go in there." He pulled the light-cord. The bulb lit. Olivia gasped. Alan lay slumped against the steps. The carving knife was buried in his ribs. Gun still pointed at the women, Josh snatched up Alan's shirt and wiped bloody fingers on it. "Why'd that fucking lightbulb go out?"

"It's a haunted house," Barbara reminded him.

"Bullshit. Don't try to scare me with your cold blue light. I'm not afraid of ghosts."

"Sure about that?"

Josh whirled. Charles Singleton stood framed in the doorway at the top of the steps, a slight figure leaning upon an aluminum cane. *But he looks different.*

Josh stared at Singleton with weary pity. "Christ, you, too? Why didn't you stay in the hospital where you were nice and cozy and safe?"

"It was your fault, lad," Charles said. "When you visited me earlier, you shouldn't have mentioned the diary I found in the garage."

"Why not? You told me about it when I questioned you and Hunter after Hattie's death."

"No. Precisely not. I said I found memorabilia. I never mentioned the word 'diary.' Alan is the sole person I confided in and that was late last night at the garage. Conclusion: you must have been close by, eavesdropping on us. Furthermore, the door to the second floor of the garage was mysteriously unlocked. You were up there rummaging. Heaven knows what stratagem you employed to steal the key from Olivia."

Olivia flushed with anger and shame.

"Okay," Josh shrugged, "so you have to be disposed of, too. Looks like I've got my work cut out for me." He laughed. "I've come too far to balk at one more murder. Nothing's going to stop me."

"I will," Singleton said.

"*You,* you old fruit? You and who else?"

Charles pointed to the mouth of the tunnel. "Them."

Olivia felt a sudden thrill of fear.

The lightbulb flickered. Josh glanced up apprehensively. He reached for the pull-string. The bulb went out. Josh yanked the cord. Nothing happened. Josh flicked the button of the flashlight. It flared briefly, dimmed and died. Charles pulled the cellar door shut, plunging them all into darkness.

"Christ Almighty," Josh swore, "what IS this?"

"This," said Singleton, *"is Aubrey House. . . ."*

---

chkk

Josh pulls the string of the lightbulb, but the cellar stays pitch-black.

chkk chkk

Darkness.

Distant noises from the tunnel. The dry skittering of things that dart across deserted beaches at night. Josh thinks he sees a faint flickering far off in the shaft.

chkk-chkk CHKK

The rustling and the pale glow draw steadily nearer.

CHK—

The cord pulls off in Josh's hand.

Whispers.

"Who's there?"

The whispering suddenly leaps to the opposite corner of the cellar.

"Stand still!" Josh shouts. "Shut UP!"

Whispers. Behind him. In front. Everywhere.

"SHUT UP!"

A cold blue light flares at the mouth of the tunnel.

Screams.

daddy?

The shattering of glass.

Josh fires wildly.

A-a-laaaann A-a-laaaaannn

. . . hurt . . . ?

semen and blood

the wind wets me

go round about

and spreads the bones and bares the teeth

and blood

in which we

NoNO*no!* Straight through!

IF YOU GO THROUGH,

THERE WILL BE A SHOWDOWN

. . . of rags and beauties . . .

Darkness. Distant noises.

A-a-laaaaaannnn A-a-laaaaaaannnnn

A-A-LAAAAAAAANNNNNN

Her voice and the cold blue light grow louder and closer.

A-A-LAAAAA—

"Who's there?"

"SHUT UP!"

A woman cries. The shattering of glass. Explosion. Screams.

The sphinx totters. Falls.

blood

---

sscrrrp-sscrrrp SSCRRRRP

Darkness. Distant noises from the tunnel. Footsteps. The painful crippled gait of someone dragging one leg behind the other. Barbara thinks she sees a faint glow far down the shaft. The footsteps and the flickering light come steadily nearer.

quis est iste qui uenit

"Who's there?"

SSCRRR—

Barbara backs away from the tunnel.

"Stand still! Shut UP!"

Knuckles against her mouth, choking off all but a whimper of fear—

"SHUT UP!"

—in the sudden glare of cold blue light, she cringes as she sees a tall hatchet-faced man emerge from the tunnel; his right leg, bleeding from a deep cut, drags behind him. His head lolls at an unnatural angle.

Hi, Babs. I hear you've all been looking for me.

Recoiling from Cameron Lambert, she stumbles against Olivia and gasps in shock and pain as the jagged wine bottle slashes Barbara's cheek.

The shattering of glass. A shot.

Barbara reels towards Olivia.

Screams.

---

in one two three four hold one two out one two three four

Charles collects filaments of thought, channels them into the great mindless Aubrey battery, shapes, amplifies, beams back.

A cry. The shattering of glass. A shot.

Singleton's concentration wavers. He observes Barbara reeling against Olivia and suddenly realizes the danger.

Oh, dear, what do they see?

Olivia screams.

In the cold blue light, she gapes at the dead woman shambling out of the tunnel. Hattie Lambert's torso is a mass of severed tendon, lacerated muscle and bone. Her left wrist ends in a chopped stump. Blood and mucus dribble from two ragged holes where Josh sliced off her nipples. Stench of intestines dangling from a great V-gash apexed at her crotch. Punctured eyes oozing down the flayed remains of her face.

The housekeeper totters towards her. Her hacked wrist invades Olivia's nakedness, burning like dry ice. Olivia jabs at the nightmare with the broken wine bottle . . . and suddenly the corpse shimmers and changes and the—

Vortex.

dies irae, dies illa

"Black. You lose."

—crossbeams spin *and I am trapped* in the darkening cathedral as the old man plunges into her with erect penis and arms outflung like crucified Jesus so—

daddy?

ME, BASTARD!

—she drives the jagged glass into Ben's flesh.

The bottle slips from her fingers, shatters on the floor.

An explosion.

The thing that was Ben rears up on hind legs like a lion and shrieks as it reels into Olivia with huge stone breasts stabbing at her face. She screams. Staggering out of its grasp, she finds the cellar stairs, clambers up them on hands and knees. Someone stands in her way . . .

"No, child, stop, it's not real!"

. . . wrestles him aside and bursts through the door into the mudroom.

Vite, vite, enfant! Montez!

Yes, grandma.

A vaguely familiar voice calls a name she ought to recognize, but she cannot remember where she heard it before. She lurches into the kitchen, into the hall, each step a painful effort as her spine contracts into a crooked curve.

Dining room. In.

Mm . . . muh?

Picture. Stretch hand. Face.

Muh-muh.

Not down. Not see.

Vite, enfant!

Not see.

Howling with rage, the rachitic little girl slashes at the empty portrait-face with one great lateral slash of her nails and rips out Charlotte Aubrey's eyes.

Montez. Vite!

Out again. Up front staircase past fingers of trailing mist. Giddily hauling herself up two steps, two more. Face flushed, temples throbbing. Forcing her legs the final distance—*Gramma's waitin', Li'l Miss Dollytop*—but the cold blue light thickened and the sad little child O! without a *daddy pick me up carry me home i don't like it here*

This way. Through this door.

No! Fight it!

Who?
Don't go through there!
Gramma wants me.
No. Merlyn.
I'm Merlyn.
No!
Then who *AM* I?

. . . the lass of rags and beauties . . . .

I remember!
Good . . . who are you?

DREAMS OF POWER AND LOSS
by
Olivia Aubrey

Silence. Olivia's mind and vision start to clear. She pushes open the second-floor door, enters the unlighted servants' staircase, calmly and carefully descends to the first floor and passes down a dark aisle between high shelves crammed with jugs and glass containers of mouldering foodstuff. She steps into the laundry half of the chamber and hears unintelligible gibbering close by. In the dim spill of light coming through the kitchen door, Olivia sees Josh sitting naked on the floor. His hair is completely white, his eyes bulge grotesquely. Spittle dribbles from his lips stretched wide in an imbecilic grin. He sees her *oh no please keep away keep away* but the words stick in her throat as the thing that was Josh comes erect and lurches after her as she retreats between racks of decaying preserves and *it*he catches hold of her hand and shoves her legs apart with one knee and Barbara presses her mouth against her crotch and Alan tongues her breasts and Ben spreads her buttocks and Mama and *daddy* lick my ears eyes nose tits ass cunt fuck my earseyesnosetitsasscunt coming now coming*now* COMING *lowerdeeperpainsin-baseofskul—*

"NO! OLIVIA, WAKE UP!"

Explosions. Crashes. Cracking glass. Tight-sealed bottles and jars splinter outward, potbellied crockery jugs blow up. Splinters fly through the air, driving themselves deep into Josh's cheeks and eyes and privates. He shrieks like some idiot god finally feeling the mindless pain of existence and she, too, screams and screams and—

"OLIVIA, WAKE UP!"

Dreams of Power and Loss.
The lass of rags and beauties.
Li'l Miss Dollytop.
Mm-muh?
Montez!
Breasts stabbing at her face.
ME, BASTARD!

"WAKE UP!"

and I am trapped
—crossbeams spin—
"Black. You lose."
dies irae, dies illa
Vortex.
Hattie.
Olivia screams.

"WAKE—!"

Olivia slumped into Charles' arms.

". . . Li— . . . *Liv* . . ."

Below on the cellar floor, Barbara lay laboring for breath, her cheek sliced open where Olivia lashed out with the broken bottle. The blonde clutched at her chest. Blood streamed from the hole where Josh's bullet entered.

"Liv!"

"Hush, Barbara," Charles cautioned. "Save your strength. The parameds will be here directly."

But the wounded woman struggled to sit up. Easing Olivia into a sitting position on the cellar steps, Singleton hurried downstairs, knelt beside the blonde and put his ear close to her whispering lips.

"Yes, Barbara," Singleton said. "I thought so."

****

3 A.M. The nightmare is over, or one of them, anyway. Josh murdered Hattie Lambert and very nearly killed the rest of us. Charles came to the rescue, never mind how, I don't want to remember, I don't need to remember, I NEVER want to remember. When I came to, I was halfway up the steps of the wine cellar. Charles was shaking me. He says if he hadn't yanked me back from the brink, I would have probably gone the Vita Henry route—the way Josh did. So, status report: we are all in Bucks County General Hospital, me and Charles for overnight observation. Josh is in the psychiatric wing. Alan is in surgery, condition critical. Lucky L'il Miss Aubrey got to telephone his wife, which was not much worse than almost being hit by a bullet Josh fired in the wine cellar. My friend Barbara got in the way and was shot, instead. She's in the hospital, too.

Oh, God . . . in the morgue.

On the morning Alan Hunter was to be released from the hospital, Charles Singleton found the patient sitting up in bed writing. Alan put away pad and pencil and greeted his friend.

"Charles, I understand they found Cam Lambert's body in the tunnel."

"What was left of it. They had to look up dental records to identify him."

"How did he die?"

"Probably a broken neck."

"Sensational ingredients galore," Alan observed. "*Tragedy in Bucks County* just might end up a best seller."

"Merely ending it will be paradise enow."

"Speaking of endings, Charlie . . . what in all good hell actually happened down there in the wine cellar? What drove Josh out of his mind?"

"A combination of factors. But Josh didn't go mad, Alan. Madness implies the existence of a mind. They ran an EEG on him. It was Vita Henry all over again . . . every trace of personality or cognition burned away by the Aubrey Effect."

"Which you controlled and used against him?"

"I only helped it along. Josh carried his own chamber of horrors within him. We all do."

After Singleton went away, Alan finished what he'd been writing, took a fresh piece of paper and made a clean copy from his work sheet. As he transcribed the last line, the door opened and Olivia Aubrey entered. It was the first time he'd seen her since the night he had been stabbed.

An awkward silence.

"You asked to see me, Alan?"

"Yes." He folded the sheet in thirds and held it out to her. "I wrote this for you."

She did not take it. "What is it?"

"A new sonnet."

A lemony lip twist. "Sure it wasn't written by Jonathan Brant?"

"Will you accept it?"

She shook her head no. "Your wife's waiting to take you home, Alan."

Olivia walked out.

While Miranda drove, Alan slept beside her and dreamed.

The spiderweb of chambers looked bleak in the cold gray light of morning. No one waited in the middle of the maze. He climbed the steep stairs, came to the platform that led to the short separate flight, wearily mounted it, put his hand on the knob—

IF YOU GO THROUGH,
THERE WILL BE A SHOWDOWN

Go round about, Peer Gynt.

No. Straight through this time.

He opened the door.

A woman sat at a vanity table, her back turned to him.

Barbara?

Nothing.

Olivia?

Nothing.

Ava?

Nothing.

Who are you?

"You know."

Do I? Let me see your face.

"Why? Are you going to hurt me again?"

I *don't hurt women.*

"NO?"

She turned and showed him her wounds.

Waking, he stares at Miranda in the driver's seat, then reaches over and lightly rests his hand against her right cheek.

"Yes, Alan? What is it?"

"Sweetheart, we have to talk."

GHOSTS OF NIGHT AND MORNING

■

"Punting on the pond," Charles giggles. "I've always wanted to come out here, Olivia. I only wish I were up to helping you row."

"You've exerted yourself enough on my behalf. It's my turn to pamper you." Bending forward from the waist, Olivia pulls on the oars, driving the little wooden rowboat over the surface of the calm lake some forty-five yards northeast of Aubrey House.

Smiling at her affectionately, Singleton says, "I feel like Lewis Carroll grown old. I wonder if my namesake, Mr. Dodgson, ever would have permitted 'Liddell' Alice to row, no matter how big she was."

"Speaking of namesakes, I still shiver when I think that my father—I mean, Jason Aubrey—named me Olivia after a sister he never even knew existed."

"Ah, but *was* he ignorant of the fact? If you read Emily Shipperton's diary, you'll see that she had her suspicions about Jason. Little boys love to snoop around musty attics and play with the past."

"Well, I hope he didn't know. Imagine learning such a terrible thing about one's parents."

"Just imagine," Charles murmurs.

In the middle of the weed-brown islet, they find one patch of dark green grass covered with wildflowers.

"You think this is where, Charles?"

"It's the only spot that fits Shipperton's description."

"But why would my grandfather bury her here? This island doesn't belong to the Aubreys."

He shrugs. "Who knows? Maybe Charlotte didn't want her buried too close. Or perhaps Derek just thought this was a sweet place for his baby to sleep."

The morning sun slowly climbs toward noon. They sit beside the unmarked grave and listen to a songbird caroling in the trees. After a long silent time, Charles says, "Well, shall we read our mail?"

"Yes, let's."

They both take out envelopes from Porlock Press and tear open the flaps.

"Well, well," Charles beams, "talk about a vote of confidence."

"Good news?"

"I should say so. A check for the rest of my royalty advance for *Tragedy in Bucks County,* and I haven't even turned in the rewritten version yet."

"You will."

"What about your letter? Or is it too personal?"

"Yes. No. Here. Go ahead and read it."

Dear Ms. Aubrey,

We haven't met, but Alan Hunter tells me you admire my poetry. He has passed along your own work to me and I believe you have talent well worth developing. It may surprise you to learn that Alan has spoken of your writings with great enthusiasm. He has a bad habit of being rather niggardly in praise, but I've known him all my life and will confide the reason behind this frustrating trait. Alan contends that artists must seek confidence from within. If a critic of any sort makes you feel less than adequate, you must ask yourself this crucial question: "Have I accomplished what I set out to do the best way I can?" If the answer is yes, if you have stretched your technique to the absolute limit, then who gives a damn what anyone else thinks—family, friends, teachers, mentors, editors? To quote Cyrano: "Never make a line you have not heard in your own heart."

And then . . . put your trust in it.

Cordially,
JONATHAN BRANT

P.S.: Enclosed is a sonnet Alan says he has heard in his own heart. In my opinion, it's not bad for a beginner.

"May I read the poem, too?" Singleton asks tentatively.

"In a little while. Would you mind if I asked you a rather personal question?"

"At my age, Olivia, 'personal' is a slightly quaint concept. Go ahead, you won't shock me."

"You . . . you *are* gay, aren't you?"

Singleton laughs. "Remember how all good fairy tales begin? 'Once upon a time.' Ever since my first run-in with Aubrey House, I've been—how shall I put it?—as neutral as Switzerland. Why do you ask, child? Because of Barbara?"

"You *know*?"

"I surmised. The very first time I met her, I suspected she was sexually ambivalent. The more I observed, the certainer I became that she was after you . . . for more than one reason, as it turned out."

"But you've got it backwards, Charles. I seduced her. I mean, I made the actual suggestion . . . you know."

"Don't you realize, lass, how she manipulated you?"

"But she slept with Alan!" Olivia's hand flew to her mouth. "I shouldn't have said that."

"It will go no further. I suspect the only reason Barbara bedded Alan was to keep him away from you. And find out what she could use against him."

"How can you say that?"

"Remember when I drank too much and Barbara carried me upstairs?"

"Yes."

"While she was toting me, she whispered that I must tell you to call Alan's wife. Which I did. Now honestly, Olivia, before that moment had you *any* idea that he's married?"

"I . . . I didn't think about it much."

"Hm." Charles decides not to pursue it. "At any rate, whatever doubts I had concerning Barbara's motives were confirmed once I read that salacious love letter she sent you."

"*She* sent me? It came from Alan!"

"He denied writing it."

"I found phrases in it he'd used elsewhere."

"Then Barbara must have deliberately put them in. But she also left something out, something that made me suspect the letter was written by a woman."

"What could have been left out? The letter wasn't exactly reticent."

"Oh, I grant you it was graphic, but that's precisely what niggled at me. Vivid images of oral lovemaking. Some mention of digital stimulation, too, as I recall. Nowhere, though, was there any reference to penetration by the penis. Now you may take it from this ex-gay . . . that is a rather significant part of masculine sexual fantasy. I'm sure you'd find it in any erotic missive Alan might compose." Singleton suddenly regards Olivia with avuncular concern. "Oh, dear, I'm afraid I've upset you, child."

"No, I'm upset with myself. Li'l Miss Trusting. Thirty years old and still taking candy from strangers."

"Cynicism is no remedy, lass. But I can imagine how you feel."

"Can you? I don't know *what* I'm feeling, Charlie. Anger. Hurt. I want to scream at Barbara, shake her, smack her, but she's dead and I still remember holding her in my arms and I miss her and . . . and I think I loved her."

"I doubt that, Ms. Aubrey. I suspect you were merely infatuated with the kind of woman you'd someday like to be."

"But she loved *me*."

"The way she loved the Lambert brothers?"

"What do you mean?"

"She murdered them, you know."

A long silence.

"Olivia?"

"Yes, I heard you."

"Well?"

"I already suspected she killed Cam. When I told Barbara about the tunnel, she got quite upset. Begged me not to go in there. But . . . Matt?"

"Just before she died, Barbara whispered a confession to me."

"Wh-what did she tell you?"

"Not much, she didn't have time. She claims Cameron tried to do something dreadful to her at the house. She went berserk and broke his neck."

"I don't blame her."

A curious glance. "Why do you say that, Olivia?"

"Never mind. Why did she kill Matt?"

"He walked in as she was dragging Cam's body to the cellar."

"But why did she cut him up so horribly?"

"One can only speculate. The night Hattie and I chatted, I learned Cam was a vicious sadist—expelled from school for tormenting animals, twice arrested for mutilating cattle. I think Barbara butchered Matt to make it look like Cam's handiwork and she succeeded."

Olivia shudders. "I just stopped missing her."

****

TO OLIVIA

Because I can't afford to pay the price
Of love, I pledged an oath to Winter's King,
Who sped me to his realm of frost and ice
And pressed upon my soul his sigil-ring.
Then, yielding to the snow's seductive power,
I begged my liege to set my heart at rest.
He led me to his daughter's crystal bower
And bade me suck December at her breast.
I kissed her flesh and found I could not thaw
Again to joy, except at one remove . . .
Until I glanced into your eyes and saw
Reflected love, that we must still reprove.
And when we part (though we were never one)
I shall be Winter's King, and mourn the sun.

"It's lovely," Charles says, lowering the sheet of paper. "Every day, I learn new things about people I thought I knew."

"I'm flattered," Olivia demurs, "but Alan didn't write it for me."

"He claims he did."

"No. Whoever he thinks he sees in me."

"Aaahh. We grow wise." Singleton's stomach growls. 'And hungry. Shall we assay lunch?"

"I don't think I can eat."

"Nonsense. Of course you can. You need your strength. You have poems to write."

"There doesn't seem to be much point."

"Now, now . . . just because Aubrey House taught a harsh catechism is no excuse for quitting the church."

"But it's all so ugly. And everything hurts."

"Youthful overstatement, Ms. Aubrey. And you're not alone in your despair. We all yearn for something sure and beautiful and lasting, but all we ever find are doubts and endless loss. So write about the way that feels, child, and make us cry. Or show us how it looks, and make us laugh." He helps her to her feet. "Now let's stop being cosmic and consider our bellies."

She attempts a wan smile. "I *am* a little hungry."

"Of course you are. You'll see. The lake will still be as lovely as it was this morning. And a Charles Singleton cheese fondue preceded by vintage Veuve Cliquot and washed down with Black Mountain coffee will restore your spirits wondrous well."

Rowing back, Olivia muses aloud. "I wonder whether anyone will ever find Josiah's gold?"

"Oh, dear!" Charles exclaims. "I meant to tell you. I found Norah Lambert's letter."

"What? Where?"

"Remember the second package that Hattie was about to mail to Drew Beltane in Scotland when Merlyn caught and fired her? Well, it was still in its postal wrappings on the second floor of the garage along with Shipperton's diary. I was a bad boy. I hid the package in my suitcase and didn't tell Josh."

"Why the secrecy? Obviously not to go after the gold

yourself, or you wouldn't be telling me about it now."

Singleton shakes his head. "When Josh interrogated me, I hadn't yet opened it. Hattie's package was originally meant for Drew, which, I must confess, afforded me a positively wicked delight. I wasn't about to give it up till I'd at least had a chance to examine the contents."

"Remind me to sue you, Charles. Now don't keep me in suspense. Did you read Norah's letter? Do you know where the treasure's buried?"

"Yes. We just came from the very place."

"The island? But that isn't part of the estate."

"Maybe that's why Josiah picked it. I don't know the precise spot, but it couldn't be too difficult to discover. If one just started digging here and there I suppose that sooner or later—"

Singleton sees the expression on Olivia's face and breaks off. "Well . . . perhaps that's not such a good idea."

"No, it isn't. Maybe nothing but our bones survive us, Charles, but I am not going to disturb poor little Olivia's."

"I wonder," says Singleton, "who owns that island. Have you any idea?"

"Yes. Yesterday I had my lawyers check it out. They said it's perfectly worthless and I can buy it cheap."

"From whom?"

"The Lamberts."